A Lover's Regret

A Lover's Regret

✦

The Ramseys

Book IV

AlTonya Washington

iUniverse, Inc.
New York Lincoln Shanghai

A Lover's Regret
The Ramseys

Copyright © 2008 by AlTonya Washington

iUniverse books may be ordered through booksellers or by contacting:

iUniverse
2021 Pine Lake Road, Suite 100
Lincoln, NE 68512
www.iuniverse.com
1-800-Authors (1-800-288-4677)

Because of the dynamic nature of the Internet, any Web addresses or links contained in this book may have changed since publication and may no longer be valid.

This is a work of fiction. All of the characters, names, incidents, organizations, and dialogue in this novel are either the products of the author's imagination or are used fictitiously.

ISBN: 978-0-595-48656-4 (pbk)
ISBN: 978-0-595-60752-5 (ebk)

Printed in the United States of America

To the LoveAlTonya web group-my second family. I love you guys. Thanks so much for believing that I could do this. I hope you'll be pleased with the results.

PROLOGUE

Seattle, Washington Spring 2001

You're a coward. A true coward and you know it!

Melina Ramsey shivered and rubbed her hands together. She shook from head to toe: freezing, in spite of the fact that the heat was going full blast in her hotel suite. It was the beginning of spring; or at least it was supposed to be, according to the calendars.

The actual weather system seemed to have other ideas, Mel thought as she stared out over the evening skies. The lovely skyline was just starting to twinkle with lights from the scrapers lining it.

"Coward," Mel hissed at herself for the tenth time that evening.

Sadly, she didn't see what other choice she could take in resolving the matter before her. There was no way she could have this discussion at his office. Even discussing the subject over a restaurant meal wouldn't suffice. Too many people would just have to stop by their table and chat.

Even their beautiful, spacious, secluded home in Woodway was the wrong setting for the conversation. Mel knew the moment she told a quarter of her story, he'd stop her. Hell, she didn't even want to *talk* about the truth. Clearly, it would be just as difficult to hear-perhaps more so.

Besides, Yohan Ramsey knew his father adored him. Though the feeling wasn't reciprocated on his part, Yohan greatly disliked hearing his wife speak about Marcus Ramsey in the negative.

So, Mel resolved, smoothing her hands across the black sweater she wore over an empire wasted floral embroidered top. This was her last resort-a hotel room. It was spacious, but not nearly as much as their home. He'd have to listen, right?

True, he could storm out, Mel reasoned with a weary sigh. Still, she was confident he'd not do that. He'd never leave her there alone. No matter how ugly the conversation turned, Yohan would remain the gentleman. He wouldn't abandon the conversation and leave her in a downtown hotel regardless of how capable she was of handling herself.

"This will work," Mel assured herself and flexed her fingers as she paced the living area. When her unease still pulsed, she drew all ten fingers through her short, glossy bush of jet black hair which framed her exquisite dark face like a hovering cloud.

The conversation had to be successful. It *had* to be-for living a charade; pretending the horror she'd witnessed had been a dream, had become unbearable. Yohan knew she was hiding something and with each passing day he grew more impatient to know what that *something* was.

Mel had to tell him and let the chips fall where they would. She cast a quick glance upon her wristwatch. Any moment he'd be arriving. She left the letter on his keyboard when she went to his office at Ramsey Acquisitions where he worked directly with Marcus. Brenda Weaver, his assistant, told her that he'd only stepped out for a staff meeting. Mel, of course, had no desire to speak with him there and silently celebrated his absence. She left enough in her one page note to pique his curiosity regarding the situation she'd hidden far too many years-a 'situation' that could be silenced no longer.

"Come on, Han," she whispered, using the pet name she'd given her husband shortly after they began dating. Those days seemed like a millennia ago. Mel often wondered if the relationship that began so sweetly during their college years would ever have flourished if she'd known who his father was.

The firm knocking on the room door gave her a start. She closed her eyes and took a deep breath to prepare herself. Then, with an inviting smile on her face she raced to the door. Flinging it open, she expected to greet her husband but her face froze in its expression as she looked into her father-in-law's cold black stare.

Melina backed away instinctively, like a deer that could sense its demise. She detested even being in the same room with Marc let alone face to face with him.

Yohan isn't coming. He doesn't even know that you're here, Mel told herself, grateful she hadn't revealed more in the note to her husband. But then, Marc knew her secret-he knew all too well.

"I expected more from you," he softly, menacingly remarked, closing the door yet remaining just inside the entryway. "Although I did wonder when and how you'd choose to turn my son against me," he added.

Mel smirked, her slanting ebony gaze fiery with hate. "I don't have to *do* anything to make that happen. Yohan will see who you really are sooner or later."

"Why are you here?" Marc demanded, as though he hadn't heard her.

"Clearly you know," Mel retorted, folding her arms beneath her breasts, "either you have the letter with you or you destroyed it after reading what was meant for Yohan only."

Marc strolled forward and Melina maintained her stance. "Before you deliver the threat you came here with, you should know that I'm not afraid of you," she sneered, her eyes narrowing almost to the point of closing. "I'm not going to live in fear like *I'm* the one, who did something so evil," she promised, coolly moving away to put more distance between them. "It was cowardly to leave that note-I admit it. But it's a mistake I intend to correct," she went on, "Yohan will know he has the devil for a father and he'll know tonight."

"Mel," Marc sighed, his sinfully handsome features softening in a phony show of sweetness. "I don't want you afraid of me, love. But it's obvious that my son is the only one on your mind and that's a mistake."

Melina couldn't speak, though her suspicious frown was explanation enough. Marcus was satisfied that he had her full attention and began to stroll the hotel suite like he hadn't a care.

"There've already been tragedies, no need for more," he elaborated finally.

"Are you threatening me?"

"I'm not."

Mel shook her head once. "Surely you're not threatening to hurt Yohan?"

Marc rolled his eyes. "Absurd," he sneered, and turned to face her with both hands hidden in the pockets of his sandalwood trousers. "One young woman's life ended all too soon, Melina. If I were you, I'd think about that before running off to your husband in some foolish attempt to turn him against me."

Mel's frown remained in place. Now, it was one of confusion instead of suspicion as she watched Marc leave as coolly as he'd arrived. "To hell with this," she hissed and waved her hand in the air. She was more frustrated with herself than Marc then. How could she continue to allow him to rile her after all these years? She'd hidden this for so long and it was ruining her marriage anyway. *It's time for that jackass to sweat a little*, she decided, thinking of the smug expression her father in law always paraded.

She went to retrieve her purse from the message desk and almost jumped from her skin when the phone rang.

"Who else knows I'm here?" she muttered, letting the phone on the desk ring once more before she answered. "Melina Ramsey," she greeted.

"Hey girl."

"Jo?" Mel whispered, stunned to hear her cousin's voice come through the line.

"Yes?" Johari Frazier drawled as though she'd expected a more substantial greeting. "Everything alright?" she asked.

"Um … yeah, yes. Everything's-everything," Mel replied, forcing a light quality into her voice. "I'm just dreading a conversation I'm about to have with Yohan," she confessed.

"Well I won't keep you. So what did you need me to remind you of? I hope you remember, 'cause I didn't have a clue what you meant."

Mel was already searching her purse for car keys. "I didn't need you to remind me of anything," she said in an absent tone as her key search produced no results.

Johari chuckled. "Then why was there a message on my service that it was *imperative* that I contact you at this number and that I needed to remind you of something?"

Mel was only confused a second longer. Then, she was freezing more than ever and fell to her knees right there in the middle of the floor.

CHAPTER ONE

Seattle, Washington—Eight years later

Yohan Ramsey muttered a savage curse and took a step closer to the punching bag he'd massacred. Long sleek brows drew close above deepest set dark eyes as he studied the rigid tear in the bag. Third one he'd ruined that month, he noted, shaking his head as his teeth tugged at the laces of the boxing gloves he wore.

He knew it wouldn't be the last bag to suffer such a grizzly fate. Slowly, his need to relieve aggression was mounting. Once a workout at the punching bag had been used solely for exercise purposes, he acknowledged. Now, the bag served as a pathetic substitute for a live body. Bowing his head, Yohan massaged his eyes and urged himself to calm. The advice was rebutted by a barbell being hurled across the floor.

Yohan hissed another curse. This one however was spoken, not out of anger, but fear. He was scared-something he could admit to no one. Besides, it was something no one would ever believe. Laid back and seemingly un-riled by anything, Yohan was the youngest son of Marcus and Josephine Ramsey. Of course, he was no less formidable than his brothers and cousins. Over six and a half feet tall, he was dark as midnight and massively built with fierce looks that could instill fear in a man as easily as they could ignite passionate fire in every woman he met. Once extremely loyal to his father, Yohan had been the man's pride and joy.

Marcus, of course, savored that fact since Moses and Fernando appeared to have little respect and no love for him. The two elder sons had been one headache after another-from school to girls to the law …

Yohan, on the other hand, had excelled in school. Intellect and diligence allowed him to skip two grades and graduate alongside his brothers and cousins. He'd been the first to marry and settle down. Sadly, this did nothing to please Marc who would've been all too supportive had his son married anyone other than Melina Dan.

Yohan grimaced, a furrow marring his brow and bringing a sinister element to his magnificent features. Just hearing her name in his head sent his heart to his stomach. They'd been married little over four years when the problems took too much of a toll.

Standing in the middle of his darkened gym, Yohan smoothed one hand across his chiseled abdomen that glistened with sweat. His steady, intense gaze focused unseeingly at the wall as his memories carried him into the past.

If they'd been anywhere other than Seattle, those problems may never have existed. How many days had he cursed himself for not leaving when she wanted him to? He'd vastly underestimated her aversion to his father. From the day she'd met Marc, something had changed inside her. The light and laughter in her exotic stare had dimmed and mingled with something morose.

Still, Yohan thought, shoving both hands into the pockets of the nylon sweats he wore, he wouldn't succumb to the signs she practically screamed at him. Marcus set everyone on edge and Yohan contented himself thinking his father and wife would find common ground one day. That never happened and then, she simply gave up and out.

Cold pierced his bare chest and back as he recalled the day he came home and saw no trace of her. Everything she owned was gone and the reality of it had almost killed him. He felt himself dying a little every moment since that day.

She'd come to see him. Brenda, his assistant, told him his wife seemed on edge. Unfortunately, Melina seemed unwilling to wait until he'd returned from the staff meeting he'd attended.

Yohan clenched his fist inside his pocket. Soon after she left, the divorce papers arrived. It was then that the anger took root in his soul. He knew without question that Marc was the reason. Not surprising, the man would admit to no wrong doing. Yohan's only hope was that he could somehow force Melina to come clean. He stifled any and all attempts for the divorce, hoping she'd become angry enough to face him. She never grew angry enough. Out of desperation, Yohan finally sent a letter in care of her attorney since he had no idea where she was at first. He literally begged her to tell him whatever it might be. He made things very clear that he'd fight letting her go until she revealed everything.

They were both so stubborn, he recalled, tugging a white T-shirt across his torso. Melina had tried so many times to talk to him about Marcus and he wouldn't hear it. Then, when he wanted her to confide-she wouldn't. Now, eight years had passed. Long ago, he'd discovered she was living in Memphis, Tennessee. According to her uncle who worked for Ramsey's London offices, there was no family in the area.

Yohan figured she was serious about wanting no links to the past. Satisfied with the knowledge of where she was, he'd given her space. Once a month, however, he broke down and went to Memphis to check on her. Of course, no one, not Melina or his family knew of the trips.

Lately, though, those trips were beginning to stir his temper into frenzy. She'd run from something-something gruesome. He could tell she was afraid in spite of the time that had passed. He was supposed to be the one person she could count on and he'd let her down. Worse, he hadn't a clue of how to convince her that he wanted to hear and believe all she had to tell him.

The ring of an old-fashioned rotary phone pierced the air. Yohan recognized the tone of his cellular that lay on the CD system in a far corner of the gym.

"Yohan," he answered, grinning when he heard his brother's voice. "Good to have you back," he said.

"You home?" Fernando asked.

"Yeah, down in the gym. Why?"

"I'm with Mo, we're on our way out. We should be there within the hour."

Yohan braced himself. "This about Marc?"

"You bet," Fernando confirmed, before handing up.

Yohan stopped himself from pitching the delicate phone against the wall. Instead, he slammed a taped fist to his palm and decided the massacred punching bag could stand a bit more punishment.

◆   ◆   ◆

Memphis, Tennessee

Melina Dan kept her slanting black stare focused on her laptop while silently summoning her lunch date to appear. She could feel at least a half dozen pairs of eyes on her from her place at the small round table.

Just don't look up, Mel ordered herself. If she just coolly acknowledged one of the male glances, her lunch partner would have to vie for a place at the table.

Please, you are not all that, Mel chastised herself playfully as a tiny smirk softened her mouth.

All that; or *not,* rarely mattered, she realized. A woman alone in a restaurant beckoned the heavy male customer base of The Stone like water to a thirsty soul.

"Come on Crane," she chanted once more for her boss.

Melina Dan, however, would have drawn attention to herself regardless of her 'single' status at the table for two. Of course, she'd never admit any truth in the fact having never been one to put much stock in her looks. It wasn't necessary when her beauty was so exquisitely blatant.

Mel's heritage of African American and Chinese ancestry, contributed to her exotic loveliness. She was fine-boned; like a China doll, many proclaimed. Her rich, mocha skin tone captured and held a man's attention almost as reverently as her alluring eyes. The jet black cloud of hair that framed her face, was now a bouncy thick afro that could easily rival the outstanding naturals of the seventies era.

Extremely graceful and quick minded Mel possessed an abundance of willpower and courage. Those traits were effectively masked though, behind the solemn aura that followed her like a fine mist. The depth of emotion in her eyes proved that she'd been dealt more than her fair share of heartache. Her heart *still* ached. Men regarded her like crystal-tough and beautiful, hard yet fragile.

She had a lion share of admirers and all were gorgeous, charming and quite suitable. Unfortunately, none of them were Yohan Ramsey. With his flawlessly smooth ebony skin, hair and eyes, he was the only man who could erase her sadness and repair the heartache. More unfortunate still, he was the one man she could never have again.

"I swear I can feel at least a dozen pairs of eyes firing daggers into my back," Crane Cannon teased when he took his seat at the table.

Mel shut down her notebook and tapped her nails against its surface. "Is that why you wanted to meet me here? To have your ego stroked?" she asked again, before turning to secure the device in its leather case.

Crane shrugged, his black gaze crinkling devilishly when he grinned. "Are you gonna hold it against me?" he asked.

Mel closed her eyes and waved as though she were shooing an annoying gnat. "I'm far more interested in knowing why you wanted to meet here at The Stone when your office is so much quieter."

Crane's handsome, deeply tanned face lost a bit of the confident allure it exuded. Mel took quick notice, the natural arch of her brows rose higher.

"So?" she challenged and patiently waited for his response.

Clearing his throat, Crane pulled a hand through his dark hair which was just beginning to silver at the edges. "I thought a public setting might sway you against cursing me to hell when I tell you what this is about."

Mel smiled adoringly and leaned forward to stoke his cheek. "Oh sweetie, you know you can count on me to curse you out in public just as quickly as I would in private," she sang.

Crane erupted in quick laughter. He took Mel's hand and pressed a hard kiss to her palm.

Concern began to fill Mel's eyes as she watched Crane more observantly. She loved him so-almost as much as her own father. That wasn't surprising considering how similar their personalities were. When she'd blindly decided to re-create her life in Memphis, she hadn't given a thought to how long a process finding a job would be.

Crane was there the day she'd given up hope and broke down in tears at the mall. She stood just outside an art store where she'd gone to check on the application she'd put in for a store associate. Crane approached and consoled her. He asked if she was lost, having believed her young enough to require a chaperone.

Mel had taken no offence and told him she was of age and was at last admitting that she couldn't support herself. She went on to tell him that her five week old application was probably being used as packing paper for one of the paintings. Her jaw almost dropped to the floor when Crane told her he owned the place. She was further stunned when he informed her that as her new boss, he expected to see her bright and early the next morning. She'd worked for him ever since.

Smiling a bit more brightly, Melina shook her head over the memory and refocused on the man. Yes, he was so very much like her father. Warmth and security clung to them like moths to flame.

Still, Mel knew there was even more that drew her to Crane. In spite of all he had and all he had accomplished, she sensed loneliness-a sadness that lurked beneath his obsidian stare. It was an emotion she was all too familiar with.

"Why are you so down?" she whispered then, squeezing his hand in both of hers.

Crane turned the tables and took both her hands in one of his. "I need you to handle some business for me."

"Campaign business?" Mel asked with a slow nod.

Crane smiled, knowing how she'd long to really get her feet wet in the campaign. The two of them butted heads regularly since he'd embarked upon capturing a Senate seat for the state of Tennessee.

"It's just regular business, love," he dashed her hopes.

Mel glanced down at the floral print of the chic halter blouse she wore and told herself to remain calm. "Regular business?" she repeated.

"I'd like you to handle some PR for a project for the new gallery out in Washington," he explained and noticed her bristling.

"The Seattle gallery?" she clarified. Her *bristling* now had to do with more than feeling as though she were being bustled off to do 'busy work' in the midst of an important campaign.

"Aren't you pleased?" Crane asked, knowing she was far from it. "You told me Josephine needed you back there. This should work out perfectly."

"My mother-in-law?" Mel scoffed, clenching her fists against her thighs encased beneath her white slacks. "You're sending me to Seattle because of my mother-in-law?"

"With everything going on in that family, it's understandable that she'd want the family to put forth a strong front," Crane reasoned.

Except that's not even close to what she wants, Mel corrected in silence. "You *do* know that I'm not part of that family any more?" she asked.

"You're still married to her son," Crane noted, leaning back in his seat and folding his arms across the front of his black John Phillips suit. "I think that still makes you her daughter-in-law i.e. *family*."

Mel rolled her eyes. "This has nothing to do with that," she muttered.

"Right. It has to do with Yohan," he clarified, smiling when her eyes snapped to his face. "Are you saying you're not in love with him anymore?"

The question sent Mel's heart lurching, but she masked her emotions with a sour look. Setting aside her water glass, she clasped her hands atop the table. "I'm about to say something that's been on the tip of my tongue for weeks, months …"

"Please," Crane urged her to continue with a wave of his hand.

"You're ashamed of me."

"What?!" he hissed. A fierce expression emerged on his darkly handsome face when he heard the words.

Mel was undaunted. "Somehow, having me tied to your campaign is a negative."

Crane leaned forward. "How the hell can you say a thing like that to me?" he asked, failing to keep her voice at a whisper.

"Oh please. Admit it," she ordered her slanting stare just as fierce as his. "You've been progressively keeping me out of the loop as far as your campaign goes. I've handled *every* aspect of your PR until now. Not to mention the fact that your campaign *manager* is a novice-having never handled a major client. Dammit Crane what did you expect me to think?"

At that point, Crane was stunned silent and could only shake his head.

The reaction simply fueled Mel's argument. "That's why you wanted to meet here instead of your office, isn't it?" she demanded to know, her fist pounding the table as she spoke. "Expecting some powerful good 'ol boy constituents and don't want 'em to know you've given this little mixed up black and Asian girl a chance to roll with the big dogs?"

Crane lost his temper at last. He brought his fist down on the table with more force than Melina could ever hope to muster. "You're being a damn fool," he grated.

Melina stood and collected her things. "Well, I guess there are worse things I could be," she said and left him with a pointed stare before she stormed away from the table.

CHAPTER TWO

Yohan Ramsey's stately, secluded home in Seattle's Woodway division was rarely visited by family. Even his brother's visits were infrequent and scheduled far in advance. Everyone from family and friends to employees and business associates knew how Yohan craved his privacy. Though no one voiced it, everyone believed that if he could, he'd have a blinking neon sign constructed high above the property that would read "No visitors. This means you!"

The house was beautiful and situated in a valley amidst towering trees and brush. At dusk, spotlights illuminated and added an even more radiant ambience to the grounds and the red brick mansion.

The home was equipped with every convenience its privacy-driven owner desired. In truth, Yohan rarely needed to travel outside for any recreation he chose to indulge in. In addition, his socializing and visits to family were usually few and far in between.

Moses and Fernando believed their brother's hidden abode; nestled in the depths of such a wooded area, would be the perfect place. It was the perfect place to discuss the latest scandal regarding their father.

Yohan was already there to greet them. He stood in the main entryway and was leaning against the hinges of one of the glass double doors. His arms were folded across his chest and his dark gaze was focused in suspicion. "What's up?" he asked.

Fernando and Moses exchanged knowing looks when their younger brother spoke.

"Damn man, may we come in for a drink first?" Fernando asked, grinning as he placed a playful slap to his brother's cheek.

Moses followed, clapping Yohan's shoulder as he strolled on into the house. With a grimace, Yohan slammed the door shut and informed his big brothers where their drinks of choice were located. Sam Adams in the fridge beneath the bar for Fernando and Killian's red on tap for Moses.

"So, what's up?" he asked again, once the men had taken a few swigs of their drinks.

Moses tipped his frosted mug in Fernando's direction.

"The Wind Rage is a sex ship-a sex slave ship," Fernando reported bluntly and tipped back his beer bottle to allow the brew to wash down the bad taste rising in his throat.

Yohan took a seat on the back of one of the living room sofas. "Sex slaves?" he questions in evident disbelief.

"Young girls," Fernando continued, "eighteen and younger. *Way* younger."

"Jesus," Yohan breathed, running a hand across his face.

"I talked to the man who runs the damned thing. He says Pop supplies him with all his *feisty* Americans."

Having prepared himself for the worst, Yohan was stilled floored by the news. "Are you sure, Fern?" he had to ask.

"Saw it with my own eyes," Fernando confirmed somberly.

Silence settled between the three. Yohan stroked his jaw as though he were assessing the information. Suddenly, he looked back at Fernando. "Mo said Contessa was there-she alright?"

Fernando nodded. "Yeah, yeah she's fine. Back in Chicago."

"With protection," Moses added.

"I'm headed out after I leave here," Fernando said.

"And the rest of the girls? They're alright?" Yohan asked.

Moses and Fernando shared troubled expressions.

"We weren't able to leave with any of the other girls," Fernando explained. "Mo called telling me our cover was blown and we had to hustle out of there."

"We found the ship, but it was completely empty," Moses said.

Yohan's expression darkened. "But how can that be?" he asked.

Moses went to refill his mug. "The ship wasn't supposed to set sail 'til the following morning. We figured they decided to book it once they discovered they'd been found out. They must've vacated during the night while we were busy securing Fernando and County."

"Son of a bitch!" Yohan roared, smashing fist to palm.

"Need a drink?" Fern asked, smirking as he tilted his bottle of Sam Adams toward his brother.

"Won't do a damn bit of good," Yohan muttered, deciding to pay another visit to the punching bag in his gym. "What about Pop?" he asked, remembering Marc then. "He's got to know what's up."

Moses shrugged. "Pop's missing too, Yo," he revealed.

"Ma said he left last week on some business trip," Fernando said. "She hasn't seen or heard from him since."

"I'm sure she's a happy lady," Yohan told Moses and joined in when he and Fernando laughed. "So what are we gonna do?" he asked, once they'd sobered. "We can't just let this go."

"What's this?" Fernando queried in a teasing tone. "You didn't even want me to take this trip in the first place."

Yohan grimaced, unable to voice a quick response. First Melina, and now a ship full of innocent girls. God only knew what else Marcus Ramsey was involved in. But his father had to be stopped, Yohan acknowledged.

"Yo?" Fernando called, settling both hands in his jean pockets as he prompted a response.

Yohan massaged his wrist and shrugged. "I've had a change of heart," he admitted. "So what's next?" he asked.

Moses set aside his mug and took a seat on one of the high backed leather stools at the bar. "My men are on it. I've even got guys out tryin' to track down Marc."

"Bastard could disappear easy and never be heard from again," Yohan grumbled, hearing his brother's words of agreement.

"Nice dream," Moses said, tugging on the hem of his denim shirt, "but we all know Pop's too meddlesome and vindictive to let us think we've won."

"Damn right, he'll find a way to stay on top of things," Fernando predicted.

Moses nodded. "And then we'll get him."

"With what?" Yohan snapped. "Hell, the man's virtually lily white in the eyes of the law."

Moses smoothed a hand across his shaved head. "Marc's got skeletons, Yo," he assured his brother. "He's just got 'em hidden in very good places. But they won't stay hidden forever. Don't worry man, his time's coming."

◆   ◆   ◆

"All rise! Court is now in session. The Honorable Judge Teena J. Webb presiding."

The petite fifty-something woman approached the bench. Her robe swayed around the black pumps in a graceful manner as she took her place. She slammed the gavel once and all conversation silenced.

"Order," she requested, browsing the folders before her and nodding when she located the one she wanted. "We're here this morning to discuss competency to stand trial for the defendant Houston Octavius Ramsey. Mr. Cornelius, your arguments."

Franklin Cornelius, attorney for the prosecution rose and began to state his case. "Your Honor, the people wish to examine Mr. Ramsey with a doctor of the state's choosing. Thus far, Mr. Ramsey's been treated by a psychiatrist appointed by the Ramsey family."

"Your Honor! Dr. White is-"

"*Mr.* McNeil," Judge Webb interjected, her small face carrying a stern expression, "once I've finished hearing Mr. Cornelius's arguments, you'll have your turn. I think that's both fair and satisfactory, don't you?"

David McNeil, Houston's counsel, nodded. "Yes, yes. Of course, Your Honor. My apologies."

"Very well," Judge Webb said and raised her hand towards the prosecutor's table. "Continue Mr. Cornelius."

Flashing a quick smirk towards David McNeil, Frank Cornelius braced his finger atop the pad he held. "Your Honor-the heinous nature of the crime demands the swiftest justice. Mr. Ramsey has successfully eluded prosecution for well over fifteen years. The psychiatrist for the defense tells us he'll be able to stand trial, but they can't say when. The people ask for an impartial psychiatrist to offer a second opinion-at least to give an idea of when he'll be fit to account for his actions, your Honor."

Judge Webb nodded, making notes in her folder. Soon, she looked over the tops of her gold-rimmed spectacles toward Houston Ramsey and his sea of attorneys. "Mr. McNeil," she encouraged.

"Thank you, your Honor. Your Honor, Dr. White is a respected psychiatrist. May I remind you that in the past he's been most cooperative on cases for both the prosecution *and* the defense?"

"How kind of you to bring that to my attention, Mr. McNeil. However, we're here to discuss matters pertaining to *this* case and not Dr. White's previous showings," she said, banging the gavel when a low rumble of chuckles filled the courtroom. "Now I happen to agree with Mr. Cornelius. Using a court appointed psychiatrist to present findings and a timeframe on which, we may expect Mr. Ramsey's cooperation is perfectly reasonable. Furthermore, to allow the doctor ample time to research and observe Mr. Ramsey, I am hereby suspending Dr. White's visitations."

"Your Honor, I must strongly object!" David McNeil stood and proclaimed. "Your Honor I'm concerned about the wisdom of this decision. Mr. Ramsey's condition must be our top priority!"

"And this way, the court may determine that Mr. Ramsey *has* a condition," Judge Webb replied.

"Your Honor-"

"*Mister* McNeil. I will not have a debate with you."

"But Your Honor-"

"Continue down this road, Mr. McNeil, and you may join your client as a guest of our jail." Judge Webb retorted, her meaning clear. "This is my ruling gentlemen. This hearing is adjourned."

The gavel resounded in the silent room.

◆   ◆   ◆

"Thanks for letting me know," Melina told her cousin who has just informed her of the trip she'd be taking to South America.

Johari Frazier chuckled, her silver eyes sparkling wickedly. "I can just see you flying off the deep end if you called and couldn't reach me." She stretched and then whipped her hair into a loose ponytail. "It may be next to impossible to get a signal in the jungle where I'll be spending most of my time."

Mel let her lashes flutter. "Ah, the glamorous life of a photographer."

"Ha! A fashion photographer maybe." Johari corrected. "My art is composed of far more grizzly subjects."

Mel nodded, her solemn demeanor resurfacing just then. "Be careful, alright?"

Johari sighed. "You worry too much. Always have."

Melina grimaced and tugged on the hem of her black halter tank. "Can't a cousin be concerned?"

Johari heard the bite in Mel's voice. "Of course you can, but you know you don't have to call every other week to check in on me."

Melina bristled, stifling her urge to tell Johari she had good reason to check in. She'd die if she lost her the same way she lost Jahzara, Johari's sister.

"Mel?" Johari called, leaning across her cousin's desk as she spoke.

Blinking, Melina slipped out of her reverie. "Have a good trip, then."

"Speaking of trips, why don't *you* take one?"

Mel stood from her swivel chair. "As in vacation?" she prompted.

Johari nodded. "As in vacation," she confirmed. "You sound like you need one."

Mel toyed with a tendril of her natural locks. "That doesn't sound like a bad idea," she said to herself. "So do you have someone to watch your apartment in San Francisco while you're away?" she smoothly changed the subject.

"It's all taken care of," Johari assured her and stepped around the desk to envelope her cousin in a hug. "I love you. I only wanted to come out and say that in person before I left."

"Mmm," Mel gestured, savoring the embrace. "Thanks. I love you too."

"Alright then, I'm out," Johari called in a refreshing tone when she moved back. "I'll give you a ring when we land," she promised, scooping up her luggage and the bag carrying her motorcycle helmet. Then she bounced out of Melina's office.

Mel chuckled and shook her head once before she reclaimed the white leather swivel behind her desk. She turned the chair around to stare out over the picturesque view of downtown Memphis. She was so engrossed by its old world allure that she missed the knocking on her office door. After a moment, the visitor entered. It was Crane.

"Hello?" he called.

Melina hesitated a moment before turning her chair back around. She watched him step inside and shut he door behind himself. She kept her face void of any expression.

"I thought we could both use some time to cool off after lunch."

"Both?" Mel retorted, subtle disbelief clouding her eyes as her brows rose. "I'm the only one who had reason to be upset."

Crane's dark eyes narrowed sharply at her words. "You practically call me a racist and you think *you're* the only one who has reason to be upset?"

Mel looked down at her thumbs twiddling where her hands rested atop the desk.

"I've never and *will* never feel that way," Crane went on to proclaim when Mel offered no response. "For you to even skirt around something like that offends me more than you could know."

Slowly, Melina's rigid demeanor began to melt. She grimaced, just as frustrated with herself as she was with Crane. "What do you expect me to think?" she snapped, standing from her chair. "I've been a valuable employee from the day you hired me at the store. Then as your business began to diversify, you gave me more challenges and I met every one-*beyond* expectations," she ranted, pushing her hands into the side pockets of the pearl white slacks she wore. "Now at *this* point when you're vying for something as astounding as a Senate seat you cast me aside to handle *regular* business? *That* is offensive."

Crane sighed, rubbing his thumb across one of the gold cufflinks adorning his sleeve. "You're right," he noted softly, grinning as her point hit home. "I am sorry, love," he said, moving over to pull her into a hug that lasted several moments.

"I still want you to take this trip," Crane insisted when their hug ended.

Melina rolled her eyes and turned her back on him. Silence refilled the room for a time and then her voice rose soft and somber. "I never want to go back there," she admitted.

"Hey," Crane soothed, his hands settling to her shoulders as he pulled her back against his chest. "Shh ... have you ever thought that perhaps if you just talk to Yohan it might erase all the hurt I'm sure you're both living with?"

Mel closed her eyes and hid her face in her palms. "Crane," she groaned, her voice muffled, "this all has to do with so much more than me and Yohan."

Crane pressed a kiss into the fragrant dark cloud of her hair. "You have to start somewhere, love. The two of you have been living in limbo for *eight* years. Don't you think you both deserve to be free to get on with your lives?"

"He won't allow it!" Mel snapped, wrenching out of Crane's light grasp. "I've tried-he's made it too hard to leave!"

Crane folded his arms over his chest. "Now I think you're over exaggerating," he said.

Mel shook her head and returned to stare out of her office windows. Crane was right, of course. Breaking that last tie with Yohan ... just the thought of it still chilled her inside.

"Sweetheart, clearly you're needed back there," Crane said, moving close again. "Otherwise your mother-in-law wouldn't have called."

Mel frowned then and turned to pin Crane with a suspicious glare. "As you said, Yohan and I have been living this way for eight years. Why, all of a sudden, are you urging me to go back there because of some family drama?"

"*I* need you to do this," he whispered fiercely, taking both her hands in an unbreakable hold. "Please don't argue with me over it anymore."

Mel's suspicion was replaced by concern in her exotic slanting gaze. The uncharacteristic look of fear in Crane's voice and eyes held her captivated. When he turned away, she caught the sleeve of his suit coat and made him look at her. "What is going on?!" she demanded.

Crane massaged his nose and looked as though he were trying to muster courage. "You really have no idea of how dirty a campaign of this magnitude can become."

"I don't care about that!"

"But I do!" he raged, taking her hands again when his outburst caused her to flinch. "Mel, in the coming months, things about my past will be revealed-"

"And this is why you're sending me to Seattle? To protect me?"

Crane's stare wavered. "Partly, but not completely."

Mel set her cheek against her palm and closed her eyes as if she were muttering a prayer for calm. "Okay Crane, now you've just got me worried. I'll go to Seattle and handle whatever business you need me to," she assured him. "But first you've got to come clean. You've got to tell me everything."

Crane's smile was relief personified. He cupped her face in his hands and kissed her forehead. "Don't worry, love. I intend to."

◆   ◆   ◆

Marcus Ramsey founded and headed Ramsey Group Acquisitions. That morning, the three men he'd assigned to the company's highest positions, sat across a wide table. Their eyes were riveted on the young man who they regarded with nervous, uncertain stares.

Yohan's focused, intense midnight gaze was discomforting in its thoroughness. "What the hell is this?" he asked, his baritone voice holding the unmistakable traces of humor at the expression on each man's face.

Ronald Grimes, Morris Tucker and Sean Fellowes all exchanged glances. The three VPs began to clear their throats in unison. Ronald was first to regain use of his verbal abilities and leaned across the long conference table separating he and his colleagues from their boss's youngest son.

"Yohan we're all concerned about Marcus's ability to uh … keep it together."

His glare narrowing, Yohan studied each man more intently. "How concerned?" He inquired lightly, smirking at the surprised expressions that illuminated the VPs faces.

Sean Fellowes cleared his throat. "We have good reason to be *very* concerned, son."

"Has he been in touch?" Yohan asked.

Sean shook his head. "No."

"How was he before he left?"

Morris and Ronald exchanged quick looks.

"Dazed-quite um … out of it."

"Out of it?" Yohan asked, propping his chin against his fist. "Dazed. Could you guys be jumpin' the gun a bit? I mean, maybe the man just needed time away."

"He wouldn't go without leaving us a way to contact him," Ronald certified.

"Your father's not quite on top of his game." Sean added. "Not since your Uncle Houston's troubles and-"

"So what the hell do you three expect me to do about it?"

Morris raised his hands and scooted closer to the table. "If you'd just consider talking with your father-"

"And asking him what?" Yohan challenged, his heavy sleek brows drawn close. "You three still ain't told me what you want. I know it's about a damn bit more than concern for his mental state."

The men nodded as though coming to agreement about what would be said next.

"Yohan there are certain decisions we need someone here for."

"A Ramsey," Sean cut into Ronald's explanation. "A Ramsey in the company will at least help to maintain the illusion that all is steady."

"Good plan," Yohan commended and got more comfortable in the black leather armchair he occupied. "May I ask why you haven't gone to the elders?"

"They have no influence over Marc!" Sean blurted.

"And you think *I* do?" Yohan challenged.

"Fernando and Moses couldn't be found Yohan," Morris explained, tugging at the collar of his blue dress shirt. "We doubt they'd give a damn about this situation anyway," he added.

"Besides," Ronald shrugged, "we'd be wasting our time and theirs by having them here."

"Marc would want no one other than you to take over," Sean confessed, "You know how he feels about you."

Yohan felt sick inside and rubbed his hand across his abdomen where the dark brown Enyce T-shirt fell across. "I guess you three forgot I have my own business now?" he inquired, trying to ignore the persistent rumbling in his stomach.

Ramsey's Architectural Division was created by Yohan after he obtained his degree in Architecture. The division boasted the largest number of award winning architects-who were responsible for the stunning designs Ramsey Group's real estate clients loved them for. Yohan's company in addition to his other, numerous holdings made the thirty year old a powerful mogul independent of his family's successes.

Yohan stood, pulling his keys from the pockets of his sagging deep indigo jeans. "Guys, even if I were unemployed and in dire straits, you couldn't pay me to step in and bail out that jackass."

Silence filled the room for a full minute once the door slammed behind Yohan's back.

"What now, Marc?" Ronald Grimes asked finally.

Listening silently via speaker phone, Marcus Ramsey was silent a few seconds longer. Then, his voice came through the line and sounded uncommonly hollow. "I'll be in touch," he told them and ended the connection.

"Too bad that man doesn't have another son," Ronald mused, massaging his tired eyes.

Sean tugged his tie free. "Yeah, one who doesn't hate him."

◆   ◆   ◆

San Diego, California

Tykira turned to face her husband across the gear console of the rented 4Runner she drove. "Baby are you sure about this?" she asked.

Quay cast a lingering dark glare toward Lena Robinson's house. "Someone has to represent the family and pay respects," he said and sighed worriedly. "Besides, Wake was my best friend next to Q. It's only right it should be me."

"Your phone conversation was just so tense," Ty recalled, smoothing back a loose tendril from the heavy braid she wore. "This visit's gonna be a hundred times more tense than that," she predicted.

"I don't doubt that," Quay admitted, pushing his cell phone into the front pocket of the white denim shirt he wore over a black T-shirt. "I've got no choice but to go in there though. I've waited too long already," he decided.

Ty only nodded, biting her lip on her next question.

Quay glimpsed it and his grip loosened on the door handle. "What?" he asked his wife.

"I was just thinking about what Fernando said at Mick's shower. What if-what if Wake isn't dead? What if this is all …" she couldn't finish.

Quay didn't need her to. "Tyke if this is a hoax then I'm more than willing to play along if it'll get us some answers. We certainly don't have a damn thing else to go on," he said and reached over to shut off the ignition.

"Do you think there's more?" Ty asked. "Do you think Marc's involvement went beyond concealing evidence?"

"I pray there ain't more to it," Quay groaned, rubbing his hands across the silky close cut hair. "Hell that'd give my father two monsters for brothers."

"It might at that," Ty whispered, smoothing the back of her hand across his cheek.

"But everything in my heart tells me Marcus's involvement goes *way* deeper than anything any of us could imagine," he confided, and then forced a smile to his face when he pulled his wife close.

"Gimme some," he urged, requesting a kiss that she very willingly provided. "Let's go," he whispered once they were done.

◆   ◆   ◆

Ketchikan, Alaska

Melina gave her hands a quick shake and flexed them to increase the circulation she felt had grown stagnate. She did manage a smile, however, feeling refreshed already in the midst of the sea-kissed air.

She arrived in Seattle from Memphis the night before. Mel decided to spend the first night in her hotel room at The Montgomery. The next morning, she took the ninety minute flight from Seattle to the port city along Alaska's Inside Passage.

More than once on the previous night, her fingers reached for the phone. She wanted to call Yohan. Of course, she didn't know what in the world she'd say. To hear the sound of his voice … she believed the call would be so worth it.

A second later she reminded herself that she'd be seeing her estranged husband soon enough. She didn't have to be a psychic to know that the reunion wouldn't be all hearts and flowers. The thought roused a wave of anxiety and shivers throughout her tiny frame. She warmed her hands inside the front pocket of the pink zip front hoody she wore with a pair of snug fitting Capri jeans.

"Miss Mel?" A voice called, raspy and uncertain.

Melina turned. Her slanting gaze widened with happiness when she saw Pony Scoggins who served as caretaker of the waterfront ranch Yohan owned in a remote area outside of Ketchikan.

"Pony," she called, greeting the lanky fifty-something man with a quick hug. "It's been so long. How are you? How's Flora?" she asked, referring to the man's wife.

"She's real fine. Real fine, Miss Mel. Thanks for askin'." Pony went on.

"So," Mel said, slapping her hands to her thighs, "when do we head out?"

"In just a jif," Pony said, pulling the dusty cap from his tanned weather beaten brow and scratching at his receding hair line. "I'll be takin' you all out on one of the float planes to the ranch as soon as I make a few last minute checks."

Mel nodded as a frown marred the area between her brows. "Pony?" she called when the man started to turn away. "Um, did you say 'you *all*'?"

Pony responded with a bold, gaping grin, proof that he'd been in one bar fight too many. He nodded and glanced past her shoulder. "Mr. Yohan, ma'am," he said and turned away.

Blinking madly, Mel watched Pony stroll away. She wanted to run after him instead of looking behind her; knowing what she'd see–*who* she'd see. Struggling to catch her breath, she decided to meet her fate and turned to greet Yohan Ramsey.

No, it wasn't a hearts and flowers greeting as she'd predicted. Still, the electricity in their midst spoke volumes. It snapped and fired fiercely-intensely as their eyes greedily absorbed one another.

He was still as huge and as dark as she remembered. His rich, maple complexion was so close to hers but stretched taut over the bulging muscles of his arms, back and torso. He was a magnificent thing to look at-he'd always been. He was the epitome of strong and silent and Melina had been hooked from the moment she slammed into him while rushing to class during her sophomore year in college. She wondered if he was still soft spoken with that deep rumbling voice all warm and mellow. That voice was so similar to his incredible eyes-deep set and coaxing in their intensity. Their look instilled security and warmth upon first glimpse, but could turn fierce and menacing in an instant.

Say something fool! A voice ordered her. While neither spoke, Mel felt obligated to do so first. Of course that was to be expected. After all, the last time she saw her husband, she told him they needed to talk.

"What are you doing here?" was all she could muster, when she finally rose from under the spell his looks cast upon her.

Yohan's long lashes shielded his eyes from view when he glanced toward the ground and produced a double dimpled smirk. "Pony called," he shared, looking past Melina's shoulder.

"Why would he do that?" she asked with a quick shake of her head. Something told her she already knew the answer.

"He'd do that because I promised him a grand every time he let me know you were here," he admitted, folding his arms across the front of the heather gray crew neck shirt he sported.

Mel's lips parted and now she could barely hear over her heart pounding in her ears. "It's been eight years," she noted.

Yohan offered a one-shoulder shrug. "He's a very dedicated man."

Mel surveyed the lush green beauty of the place and knew her hopes of quiet thinking time had flown right up into the blue sky. "I was hoping for some time alone," she said, hugging her arms about her body. She looked up in time to see the warmth in Yohan's ebony gaze turn cold.

"Time alone?" he repeated, the muscle dancing a wicked jig along his jaw signaled his agitation. "So I take it you haven't been getting that in Memphis?"

Melina's gasp sounded against the wind.

"Your uncle," he supplied, anticipating her next question. "You didn't think I'd let eight years pass without knowing where you were?"

"I don't want to argue," she said in a whisper.

The glint in Yohan's eyes didn't diminish when he stepped close to tower over her. "I hate to disappoint you there, but an argument is definitely in our future."

"Han," she tried, cursing herself silently when she felt tears pressuring her eyes. She refused to let them fall, though. Instead, she leaned on her anger.

He read her emotions before she uttered another word. His uncanny ability to do that had always set her on edge. "I'm angry too, Mel," he told her, Melina fixed him with an accusing glare. "I offered to give you your freedom, Han."

"My freedom," he hissed, seeming to swell in the wake of his fury. "Dammit Mel, I don't want my freedom. I want my wife back." If possible, his voice was a soft roar-soothing yet terrifying. "I want you back on my arm, in my bed. Yes I'm angry," he admitted, blocking the sun as moved closer. "I'm damn mad as hell. I'm frustrated and God help me after eight years I still love you. Like a fool I've given you eight years to come to me when I should've come to you, beat down your door and made you tell me why you gave up on us."

"Mr. Yohan! Miss Mel! We're ready to set out over here!" Pony called, before heading back towards the landing strip along the river.

Yohan tilted his head in acknowledgement to Pony's announcement. Then he bent low to look directly into his wife's eyes. "I'm not letting you out of my sight. Not until I get some answers Mel and they better be damn good."

He brushed past her, barely touching her as he did so. Melina let her eyes drift close. She wanted nothing more than to melt against him. She wanted to beg him to forgive her. She wanted to tell him she'd go wherever he wanted as long as they were together. But, that wasn't to be. Could she ever hope for beautiful memories between them again?

Fool, she called herself once again. He had every right to be angry. *Every* right. How could she tell him everything now? She wanted no more secrets between them and now she carried one that would shake the very foundation of his life.

How could she tell him that Marcus Ramsey wasn't his father?

CHAPTER THREE

He hadn't meant to tell her about Memphis, Yohan thought as the floatplane carried them through the air towards the ranch. Telling her about Memphis was something he wanted no one to know.

How many times had he tried to reassure himself that he hadn't gone crazy? He wasn't stalking her, he swore to himself. He simply wanted to know how she was getting along. Instead, all he really did was torture himself into an enraged state of mind. For the past eight years he'd tried to make himself accept the fact that she needed to go. She needed to go and he had to accept that no matter how much it killed him inside.

But now ... now he wouldn't make the mistake of letting her go ever again. If it meant spending a year out here in the Alaskan outback, he'd uncover every secret she'd kept from him-no matter what it was. *Or who it was?* A voice inquired.

Yohan remembered his trips to Memphis then. On more than one occasion he'd seen her with a tall, well built white man. He was probably in his fifties. His hair was dark as crude oil, but Yohan could tell that gray was beginning to mingle around his temples. He figured the man was a co-worker. Boss maybe? Maybe more?

Shaking his head, Yohan pulled a hand across the silk waves of his hair. He wouldn't think about that part-the part that angered him most of all. If anything, this trip would tell him if there were any feelings-feelings of love-left between them. He knew there wasn't a woman alive who could replace her in his life. Perhaps that feeling wasn't reciprocated where she was concerned. Grimacing, his fist clenched reflexively at the thought.

"Mmm," he grunted, massaging the bridge of his nose while chanting for calm. Then he focused on her as she slept on the long seat opposite the swivel chair he occupied.

God she was still so incredibly unique. The China doll face and fragility still clung to her. The voluptuous swell and the adoring fullness of her bottom, however, threatened to make him hard in an instant. The moment she'd fallen asleep he'd allowed his arousal to take shape-literally.

The responsible side of his demeanor said-or rather screamed-*hands off!* It would be unwise to embark upon easing those needs—when so very much still lay unresolved between them. *To hell with responsible,* he decided. He was frustrated-sexually yes, but in so many other ways … if he touched her-just an embrace or forehead kiss. It would be the end of his restraint. He'd not stop until satisfaction arrived.

Melina shifted on the long seat. The glossy bush of her hair; held back by a pink and gray bandana, framed her face like a smoky cloud. Yohan knew that he had to touch her at least once-consequences be damned. He leaned forward. The cabin was small enough for him to reach out and brush his knuckles across her face. His fingertips traced the line from her high cheekbone and then down around the soft curve of her jaw.

"Approaching Black Summit!" Pony's voice blasted though the intercom as he informed his passengers.

Yohan began to cough and rap his knuckles against one of the overhead compartments in a none too subtle attempt to rouse her.

The noise gave Mel a start and slowly her eyes opened. She saw Yohan seated across from her. He stared silently out the window, his elbow propped on the armrest, his chin sitting on his fist.

Clearing her throat, Mel pushed herself upright. She wondered if they should risk conversation again. Discussing the weather might be a good way to break the ice. *We can't possibly argue over that,* she figured.

"I bet it'll be pretty chilly tonight," she said, smoothing both hands across her thighs.

"Probably."

"What's the ranch like now?" she tried. "Have you made any changes?"

"None."

"When was the last time you visited?"

"The last time you did."

Mel's eyes widened slightly. Yohan didn't need to see her face to know he'd stunned her.

"That surprises you?" he asked, still looking past the window.

"Well … I'm shocked and confused. It-it's such a beautiful place."

Yohan turned in his seat and regarded her closely. "Why confused?" he wanted to know.

Mel felt the familiar shivers kiss her arms beneath the intensity of his gaze. "It's a beautiful place, like I said."

"And you honestly believe I could come back alone after all the times we had out there Mel? You think I could enjoy the place after that?"

Melina took note of the flaring nostrils and the pulse beat at the base of his throat. Clearly their conversation was heading down an ugly road and Mel knew her saying 'I don't want to argue' would have them doing just that.

"What did my father do?"

Her stomach churned at his question. "Marcus?" she blurted, looking away when he eyed her strangely.

"Yes Marcus," he confirmed with a slow nod as though she were dense. "I know you left because of him."

Mel straightened and leaned back against her seat.

"I know about the letter," he continued, setting his elbows against his jean-clad knees. "Will you at least tell me what it said?"

Blinking madly, Mel realized she'd almost forgotten the note she'd left on his desk. He'd never received that letter. His … father had intercepted.

"Mel?"

"I was-I was only asking to speak with you," she explained uneasily.

Yohan spread his hands in a questioning gesture. "Where'd you leave it? And why didn't you just wait? Bren told you I wouldn't be gone long."

Mel massaged her neck with one hand. "It wasn't a conversation I wanted to have in your office."

"Why?"

Mel wished she could walk around instead of having to be confined in the cabin of the plane. "Things may've gotten out of hand and then your office wouldn't have been the best place to discuss it."

"Why would you think things may've gotten out of hand?" Yohan asked, dropping a huge hand to her knee to stop its fidgeting. "We'd argued before. What would've been so different about this time?"

Mel gave up on trying massaging the tension from her neck and shoulders. She decided to see if a modest amount of honesty would offer any relief.

"The reason I left had everything to do with Marcus," she confessed, her slanting stare challenging in its intensity. "But I'm sure you knew that already?"

Yohan leaned back in his chair. "Mmm, what I don't know is why? How many times will you make me ask you this, Meli?"

"Please fasten your seatbelts folks! We're about to make our descent!"

Pony's instructions forced silence between the couple. They did as they were told and waited for the plane to land.

Alaska summers were as beautiful as its winters were magical. Melina inhaled a deep refreshing breath of clean air the moment she stuck her head past the cabin door of the floatplane. For a while, her eyes feasted on the lush beauty of the sky. The foliage was a rich emerald color flecked with different hues of green. A calm, crystal clear blue river ran just past the ranch; helping to keep the breeze cool and steady.

The farm house itself sat majestically in a perfectly manicured sea of grass. It was nestled within a rather hilly area with a gorgeous view of the mountains in the distance. The two story getaway was a dark brick structure with A-frame roofing above wide windows. A protruding structure housed a two story glass enclosed balcony with a sitting room below it. Chimney tops peeked out from three places along the roof.

Melina accepted Pony's assistance and took his hand before she jumped off the plane. Yohan was already moving on. He deposited their baggage on the dock and waited for Melina and Pony to join him.

Mel gave the men a chance to talk, walking across the property to the dwelling in the distance. The calm and beauty of the place was already carrying her away from her concerns. She was almost halfway to the house when Yohan caught up with her. They journeyed forward in silence; each consumed by happier times they'd shared at Black Summit. They must have made love in every part of that farmhouse. Then, there was *outside* the house, the lake, the pool, the barn, the rooftop …

Melina cleared her throat to mask the unexpected moan that lilted.

"You alright?" Yohan asked, watching as she fanned one hand before her face.

Managing a quick smile, Mel only nodded. She slowed her steps and allowed him to walk on ahead of her.

"Damn," Yohan muttered once he'd set down the bags. The bolted door unlocked with a turn of the key, but more pressure would be needed in order to force it open.

Melina watched as he braced his shoulder against the weathered oak. She heard him grumbling about Pony neglecting to sand the door, but her thoughts were more focused on the powerful image he portrayed. She studied the definition of his body, taking her time in appraising every line and sinew that flexed as he worked at the door.

The sagging jeans and short sleeved crew-shirt he wore called attention to the extent of the biceps and chords of muscle that bulged in his forearms. She leaned against one of the wooden beams along the porch and imagined all that rock solid, chiseled strength covering her.

"Finally," Yohan snapped when the door jutted open. Waving a hand, he grimaced and urged her to precede him.

Melina stepped inside, closing her eyes to inhale the dewy aroma of pine and maple that had always filled the place. It was quite reassuring to discover there were some things that never changed. In spite of her surprise at seeing Yohan earlier than she'd expected, Mel celebrated the opportunity to spend a few days in such unique beauty.

The couple left the entryway and headed for the living room. Yohan set down the bags and massaged the tightness from his neck and shoulders. Mel's gaze slanted across the main room. The area was stylishly designed in oak. It trimmed the black and tanned plaid sofas and armchairs which sat atop the oriental carpeting that covered a portion of the polished oak hardwoods. Every piece of furniture was overstuffed and comfy.

The protruding glass encased structure was situated at a far end of the living room. It offered a dazzling view of the pool and the surrounding patio. Plush, sunken armchairs, bookshelves and magazine filled tables lined the room which housed the back stairway-a faster route to the master bedroom suite.

"It's nice out, but tonight could still be cold as hell," Yohan grumbled. He went to inspect the towering brick fireplace that sat nestled in a far corner of the cozy room.

Melina went to check out the kitchen. She'd always adored the layout of the area built around a wide kitchen island that served as both a prep area and dining table. She uttered a tiny gasp, surprised to find the step stool she'd always used to reach the lofty cabinets.

"Pony takes his work seriously!" She called out in a playful manner when she was but halfway through her perusal of their supplies. The cabinets were stocked with far more than they'd ever use or need.

Yohan didn't respond to her tease. He'd stopped working at the fireplace long ago and was now watching his wife. His smoldering pitch black stare revealed the raw desire that was scorching his soul. *They would make love before sunset,* he vowed, dismissing all the voices of reason that cried out—*bad idea!* No way would he share the place with her after eight years and not indulge in what tortured his mind every night.

Melina's hand paused over a can of tomatoes and okra when she felt his eyes on her. She'd always been able to tell if he watched her when she wasn't looking. A sudden feeling of self-consciousness washed over her. Reflexively, she smoothed both hands across the jeans encasing her thighs and bottom. Pressing her lips together, she realized the gesture was doing little to de-emphasize her curves to her husband.

She'd always considered herself to be far too skinny. Most men preferred their women thick-with an abundance of breasts, hips and behind she figured. She wasn't *abundant* in any of those departments-or so she believed. Her bosom however, was more than abundant in light of her slender frame. Her tush was full and rounded-though Melina took little pride in the fact. She felt those assets stuck out like sore thumbs instead of eye-popping provocations. Especially, since she had a weakness for clothing that did nothing to conceal the most alluring parts of her anatomy.

Men, of course, were quite pleased with all there was to see. They stared unabashed whenever she entered a room. Some just gawked while others very subtly verbalized their appreciation.

Yohan was the only man who never made her feel as though she were the star of some porn movie. What first endeared him to her was the way he watched in helpless fascination as though he were seeing more than he should when he looked at her.

Melina dismissed his staring, which was now more like the gawking she was so accustomed to. Inhaling deeply, she silently admitted that she couldn't blame him. After all, she'd been trying to project a mental image of his magnificent form without clothes, of course, for the better part of the day.

"Any ideas for lunch?" she asked, noticing as he left the fireplace and began to head towards the kitchen. "We've got so much," she reiterated, looking back inside the cupboards again. "Pony really outdid himself. Let's see … we could just have a couple of cans of soup and maybe some sandwiches. Or I could whip up something heavier if you're really hungry," she offered, acknowledging uneasily that he wasn't responding.

Melina was still talking when she felt herself being taken from the step stool and placed on the kitchen island. Yohan kicked a couple of the stools out of the way. He stood before her, his hands curving around her thighs to pull her close as he stood snug between them.

"Han-" was all she managed to say before her mouth was otherwise occupied. His kiss was deep and unrelenting. Hot, wet and seeking, his tongue thrust and stroked leisurely. His hands were everywhere once they left her thighs. They massaged her back before moving around to cup and squeeze her breasts. He took ample time reacquainting himself with the lush mounds, forcing desperate moans from her throat when he touched her. The pink hoody was unzipped and Mel let it slide down her arms to pool around her waist. The straps of the white scoop neck tank top she wore were tugged down. The built-in bra design of the top required no additional undergarment, leaving her bosom uncovered before his eyes.

Yohan was still kissing her deeply while removing her clothing. A helpless moan rumbled in his chest when he felt her bare skin against his fingertips. His hands weighed and fondled the bare cleavage and they both groaned when his thumbs grazed the firming nipples.

"Mmm," Melina grunted her disappointment when he stopped kissing her. She tugged her bottom lip between her teeth when she realized he'd only done so to kiss and outline her breasts with his tongue.

She whimpered then, thrusting her fingers into the gorgeous dark hair covering his head. Gently, she cradled his face more closely to her chest, obsessed with having his mouth touch every part of her. Suddenly, she had to feel his skin against hers and her hands disappeared beneath his shirt.

The rock hard abs and muscles in his back made her yearn to add sight to touch. Greedily, she pulled at his clothes, determined to view what felt like a concrete wall against her palms.

Yohan dutifully raised his arms to assist in her removal of his shirt. He stood there while she stroked and massaged his pects with the tips of her fingers and then her tongue. When she discovered *his* nipples, Yohan felt the strength leave his legs.

Any pretense at maintaining control became a non-issue for Yohan. His massive hands curved about her upper arms as his mouth trailed the line of her jaw, the length of her throat and collarbone. Their cries and groans of desire filled the lofty kitchen. Yohan cupped both her breasts for his mouth and alternated between lavishing each with the heated feasting of his lips and tongue.

Melina had lost control as well. She surprised herself by being so much the aggressor, but decided this was clearly no time for being shy. Pleasuring herself with memories of how they were together had lost its zeal so long ago. Now, she craved more-she craved it all.

Again, Yohan stood obediently still and allowed his wife to have her way with him. He watched; a bit stunned by the concentration on her exquisite face as she unfastened his jeans so that they fell around the rugged black hiking boots he wore.

She gasped at the image of his erection which threatened to burst free of his boxers. He slumped forward to brace his hands on the island when she touched him. Melina began to massage the stiff heaviness of his arousal beneath his underwear. She fastened her teeth to his earlobe when her hands ventured beneath the black cotton boxers to grip his bare anatomy. Her long lashes fluttered rapidly when her thumb brushed the silky tip of his manhood and felt the tell-tale moisture that revealed itself.

Yohan groaned this time he shuddered against the sweetly explosive caress. "I have condoms," he paused to swallow, "in-in my bag," he said.

"Later," she told him, meeting his kiss enthusiastically. She linked one arm about his neck, intentionally brushing her nipples against his chest. Her hand continued to work up and down his throbbing length.

"Mel," he whispered after breaking the kiss, "it's been too long. I can't … I can't hold out," he warned her.

Smiling softly, she stretched up to kiss his cheek. "It's okay," she spoke against his ear.

Yohan's chuckle was a mixture of relief and torture. Melina brushed her nose against his and then she was kissing him again. Tiny moans sounded in sync with the slow lunges of her tongue and her hand worked faster along his shaft. She felt him shudder once, then twice and she kissed his jaw in a lingering manner as his release rushed forth.

They rested awkwardly upon the island. Melina was on her back. Yohan was on his feet, but lying half across her.

"I wanted all of you," he said, squeezing her thighs that were still encased in the denim Capris.

Mel offered a lazy smile and stroked his temple. "You'll have me," she promised.

Yohan felt his heart thud hard beneath his ribs. "I thought I'd have to walk around pretending this wasn't on my mind."

"That wouldn't have been fair to either of us," Melina said.

Yohan groaned and pushed himself up over her. "You have no idea how much I need you," he confessed, his incredible deep-set gaze focused and intense.

Mischief sparkled in Melina's slanting stare and she pushed herself up as well. "So take me then," she challenged.

CHAPTER FOUR

The door to the master bedroom suite swung open behind a kick from Yohan's boot. He celebrated knowing the place by heart, for the moment he had Mel back in his arms, they were kissing fiercely. They were both fully clothed from the waist down. Of course, that fact did nothing to diminish the electricity the embrace stirred between them.

Melina kissed him with unmasked desperation fueling the passionate strokes of her tongue. She chanted his name amidst the lusty act, telling her husband that she was as starved for him as he was for her. The way she arched and rubbed against him caressed his ego like nothing he'd ever known.

Yohan's dimpled grin appeared when he saw that the huge sleigh bed was already turned down. *Good ol Pony*, he commended silently.

Melina sounded a contented hum when she felt the cool, crisp navy linens beneath her back. Yohan had placed her right in the center of the bed and settled to his knees beside her. Her eyes filled with wonder as she watched him, feeling as though she were in some sort of magical daydream. The reality of him being there beside her, loving her after so much had transpired between them was almost an impossible concept to grasp.

A sharp cry rose unexpectedly from her throat when he removed her strappy sandals and suckled her toes. He held her foot as though it were something fragile while he delighted her. Melina could feel herself growing wetter-drenching her panties shamefully. Yohan provided his pleasure slowly and eagerly, determined to please her until she was begging him to stop.

"Nooo," she commanded, when he left her foot and went to remove her jeans.

Yohan tossed the Capris to the floor and eased his fingers inside her panties. His nose nuzzled the undergarment and he smiled at their dampened state before sliding them from her body. Mel felt another powerful stab of desire as she watched him inhale the scent of her lingerie before casting them alongside the rest of her clothing.

He ravaged her with an explosive kiss deep within her sex. Melina grew orgasmic almost immediately as his tongue seemed to fill her. Impossibly, Yohan deepened the strokes and he was just as aroused by the feel of her moisture flooding against his tongue.

"Please wait ... Han please, just let me...." She couldn't complete the request that he give her time to ride out the overwhelming climax.

Yohan had no intention of stopping. Mel was practically spent when he turned her to her stomach. Her desire was renewed breathless cries rushing forth when he applied the same delight to the extra sensitive spot between her buttocks. Mel arched up to take more of the scandalous kiss, clutching fistfuls of the bed linens as she moaned into the pillow.

Yohan cupped her hips and positioned her to his satisfaction, spreading her thighs and taking her from behind.

Mel's cry was a cross between pleasure and pain she couldn't determine which she felt more of. She only knew that she didn't want it to end. Yohan's perfect white teeth, bit gently into the satiny dark flesh of her shoulder. His cries of pleasure sounded as helpless as Melina's. The stiff and very impressive length of his sex drove smoothly in and out of her body. At the same time, his fingers journeyed over her hip to fondle the folds of her femininity before they invaded her body from that angle.

Mel sought pleasure from both directions. Her hand curved over his massive thigh in a silent command that he increase the force of his thrusts. She had no idea where her strength was coming from, but she had no intentions of stopping. She met his power with her own in a continuous melody as they rediscovered the pleasure they'd been missing.

Later, they rested, nestled amidst the tangled covers. Mel was content, being lulled by the strong steady beat of Yohan's heart while her cheek rested against his chest.

Yohan was equally relaxed and at peace, holding the woman he loved. Slowly, however, reality took its place amidst the solitude. No matter how wonderful the last four hours had been, the state of things would not allow them to ignore what had to be said. Yohan decided to begin, collecting his thoughts regarding all he'd been told.

Dim afternoon light flooded throughout the room relaxing him further as he began the tale.

"Moses and Fern stopped by a few days ago. What they told me about Pop … I always knew he had secrets-bad ones. I never believed they were so … evil."

Yohan continued to speak, sharing the news his brothers had delivered. By the time he'd finished, Melina was resting fully across his chest and staring into his face. The expression clouding her features was beyond terrified. No words came to her mind or mouth for none seemed appropriate. Instead, she was focused on a young woman she'd lost so many years ago-a young woman who had been so very dear to her.

"Mel?" Yohan whispered, not liking the fear frozen on her face. His hands tightened on her arms as he gave her a tiny shake. "Meli?" he tried again. "What's wrong?" he asked, when she finally focused on him.

"The-your story," she managed, resting her face in the crook of his neck. "Do you remember Jahzara?" she asked.

Yohan frowned, toying with his wife's flowing hair as he concentrated. The name rang no bells at first, but soon his memory recovered. The girl, Melina's cousin, had gone missing sometime between their sophomore and junior years in high school. It all took place long before he'd met Mel.

"Zara," he said, "yeah I remember her," he added, smoothing his lips across her forehead. "Why?" he prompted, when she offered no further explanation. "Mel? What are you saying?"

Sighing nervously and feeling cold, Mel snuggled closer to Yohan. "The night I left, Marc … advised me not to forget I had the safety of others to consider. He wasn't talking about *your* safety," she told him and looked into her eyes then. "A minute after he left, Johari was calling me."

The cold sensation washed over Yohan then. He quickly recognized the name of Jahzara's sister. "What happened?" he asked, almost dreading to hear the rest.

Mel shook her head. "She said she'd called because there was a message on her service that said it was important for her to contact me at the hotel where I'd planned to meet you. She said she was supposed to remind me of something." She shuddered reflexively. "It only took a second for me to understand what she meant."

Yohan's features sharpened with something sinister. "Marcus ..." he breathed.

"Han?" Melina whispered, feeling his powerful arms flexing like steel bands about her waist. "Yohan?" she called again, this time tapping her fingers to his cheek to get him to snap out of his trance.

Yohan didn't respond. Instead, he pushed himself up, taking Mel with him when she would have toppled off.

"No one ever knew what happened to Zara," he said, as though he were speaking to himself. "It was like she fell off the face of the earth," he added.

Mel braced her chin to his shoulder while straddling his lap. "Back then," she said, sniffling softly as she remembered. "Even when it was clear she was gone, I never thought she was dead. I wouldn't believe it. I told myself she was alive somewhere. Now you tell me about what Fernando saw ..." she looked at her husband then. "Do you think she could be one of the women they took on that ship? Marcus was obviously involved in it back then."

Yohan only shook his head the look in his dark eyes offered no clue about his mood. A moment later, he planted a kiss to Melina's mouth and left the bed.

Mel remained seated with the covers wrapped around her otherwise nude body. She was immersed in her own troubling thoughts when a booming sound thundered close by. Whirling around on the bed, she saw that Yohan had put his fist through the wall. It was a deep blow-so far that she could see the pink puffs of insulation lining the framework of the house.

"Are you alright?!" she cried, rushing from the bed. She captured his fist in her hand and rubbed his wrist until he'd unclenched it.

"He took you from me," Yohan said, focused solely on Mel while she studied his hand. "He's responsible for Zara."

"We don't know that, Han," Mel said, trying to keep him calm even while she admitted her words were false.

Yohan smirked. "We know, Meli. We know. Hell, if I didn't already know Houston was to blame for Sera, I'd pin that one on Pop too."

Both Mel's hands went weak and then she was pushing Yohan back onto the bed. "I'm going to get something for your hand," she muttered and almost sprinted out of the room.

"I could kill him Melina," he confessed when she'd returned with disinfectant, gauze and bandages.

"You're just angry," she reasoned, focused on dabbing cotton balls; moist with peroxide, to his knuckles. "Marc's not worth you doing anything that'll put your life or your freedom in jeopardy. Besides, he deserves to rot in jail-not in a coffin. Hmph, not yet anyway."

"I don't care," Yohan's voice grated in the quiet room. "He won't stop unless someone stops him."

"Shh," she soothed, smiling in wonder at his hand. Aside from a few bloody scrapes, there didn't appear to be any extensive damage.

"The fact that he's my father doesn't even register anymore, Meli," he was saying, wincing when his bruised hand clenched into a quick fist. "Fern and Mo want him in jail, I want him dead and that scares me, Mel."

She could hear that fear in his voice and stopped working with his hand. She didn't think she'd ever heard him admit to being afraid.

"I could end the life of the man who gave me life," he said, sounding as though he were settling the matter in his mind.

Mel watched him leave the bed and pull on the jeans he'd tossed aside earlier. How could she tell him everything now? He wanted to kill Marcus and he didn't even know half of the story.

◆   ◆   ◆

Melina showered and donned a pair of red Yoga pants and a white halter tee. With her thick, coarse hair pulled into a flouncy high ponytail, she trekked downstairs. Her easy manner, however, evaporated when she became aware of Yohan's absence from the lower level of the house. Her steps quickened as she checked and double checked each room. Relief flooded her body when she passed the glass doors in the kitchen and saw him out in the backyard.

He stood holding a grizzly looking axe above a massive tree stump that was surrounded by heavy logs. For a while, Mel's eyes were glued to him as he swung the huge axe to chop wood into more manageable pieces. The wide plane of his back glistened black and packed with muscle.

What to do, what to do, she debated, leaning against the wall near the doors. She knew at any moment, Yohan would come to her. He'd ask if she'd told him everything or if there was anymore. It would be the moment of truth then-literally. Would she lie to him and prevent a potentially fatal event such as him killing Marcus and going to jail for the rest of his life? Or would she tell him the truth and risk losing him again anyway? The choices, or perhaps the quality of the choices, made her nauseas. She looked up in time to see Yohan headed back to the house with several heavy logs in tow.

"Do you really think we're gonna need all that?" she teased, eyeing the wood he carried upon his shoulders.

"Temperature will fall in spite of the fact that darkness won't," he cautioned, dumping the planks to the brick floor surrounding the massive fireplace in the living room.

"Right," she acknowledged with a slow nod. During that time of year, daylight in Alaska lasted for months. Her eyes fixed upon Yohan again and she noticed him staring. "How about some coffee? Tea maybe?" she offered, attempting to lighten the moment.

Yohan shrugged. "Coffee sounds good," he said and turned to grab the towel he'd left on the back of an armchair.

Mel ordered herself not to stand there gawking as he used the towel to dry the sweat from his glistening chest and arms. She went into the kitchen, stopping in her tracks when she looked upon the island where she'd touched her husband for the first time in eight years. She heard Yohan's steps in the distance and moved on towards the towering cupboards.

"I think we made things more complicated," he said, folding his arms across his chest and leaning against the kitchen's arched doorway.

Mel had climbed her stepstool and was searching for Hazelnut coffee amongst the sea of flavored brews. "How so?" she asked him.

Yohan massaged his jaw, his heavy brows rising skeptically. "Sex tends to complicate things, doesn't it?"

Mel had just grabbed the Hazelnut tin only to have it slip right from her hand. She uttered a whispered word of relief, thankful none of the contents had spilled on the counter. She couldn't think of a thing to say to him, especially when Yohan's hands spanned her waist before he pulled her from the stool.

Yohan trapped her between himself and the counter. One hand cupped her face to hold her still for his kiss. It was long and deep, his tongue rubbed around and beneath hers and he groaned when she reciprocated.

She was hungry for him again instantly, arching close as her hands stroked his wavy hair. Moaning helplessly, she became the aggressor in the kiss. Her arms were wrapped around his neck in much the same fashion that her legs were locked around his waist. She was seconds away from begging him to make love with her again, when she felt his hands patting her thighs. She recognized it as a signal for her to ease down. She could feel her cheeks heating and it was impossible for her to look up at him.

"So where are we gonna have this coffee?" he asked, his own words tinged with a hint of breathlessness.

"Um, the living room," Mel managed after a quick look towards the kitchen island.

"Is that all I get?"

"What?" she blurted in response to his question. Her entire body was still on fire with powerful arousal for him.

Yohan grinned, knowing how he'd confused her. "Are we gonna eat anything, is what I meant?"

Mel nodded, her cheeks burning now. "I um, I could maybe whip up a coffee cake or something before dinner," she offered, with a flippant wave.

"Sounds good," he said and put more distance between them. "I'll go up and take a shower," he added, before leaving the room.

Alone, Melina collapsed to the step stool.

◆   ◆   ◆

Michaela was reaching for paper on a high shelf from the book case. Quest stepped into his wife's home office to let her know he was on his way to a meeting at Ramsey.

"What the hell?" he whispered, his gray eyes darkening at what he saw. Uttering another soft curse, he went to Mick and took her down from the chair she was perched on. "What are you doing?" he asked when she stood before him.

Mick glanced toward the top of the shelf. "I needed paper," she replied simply.

"What for?" Quest asked, managing without effort to obtain an unopened ream from the shelf.

Feigning confusion, Michaela pointed to the labeling on the paper's packaging. "It's notebook paper, baby. See? It says so right here on the front."

Quest grimaced, quickly sparking his left dimple. "What's it for?" he asked,

"Uh … taking notes?" was Mick's sarcastic response.

Taking a seat on the arm of a loveseat, he smiled. "Notes on what?"

"Why?"

"Why won't you tell me?"

"Why are you so interested?"

"Because clearly you don't want me to know and now I'm suspicious."

Mick's amber gaze narrowed. "Suspicious?" she snapped, propping a hand upon her non-existent waistline. "What? Am I not allowed to take notes?"

"Depends on what they're about." Quest said with a lazy shrug.

"Well, if you *must* know, I'm putting down a few ideas on the next family I want to research."

Quest didn't miss a beat. "Do I know them?" he asked.

Mick went completely still. "Why are you being so difficult?"

Leaning forward, Quest tugged at the flaring hem of the light blue maternity blouse she wore and brought her close. "Because I don't want my pregnant wife dabbling in things that could get her hurt."

Mick shook her head, sending a hoard of curls flying into her face. "How can taking a few notes be harmful?"

Quest bowed his head, grinding the muscles in his jaw as he took a hold of his frustration. "If you're trying to play dumb, stop. You're doing a bad job of it."

"Quest-"

"You know *exactly* what I'm talking about."

Mick folded her arms atop her belly. "Contessa House is still looking for an author to take over the book."

"Tell County I said 'good luck'," he said and stood to pull his suit coat off the sofa.

"I never should've backed out on writing it," Mick admitted, one finger raised in the air. "I've done majority of the research, I've been on the story for years, I want to see this through." She followed behind Quest as he shrugged into his suit coat. "If those aren't enough reasons why I should author that book, then I've got plenty more."

Quest stopped and turned to look down at her. "Don't bother-my *three* reasons why it *shouldn't* be you are damn good and fully outweigh yours."

Mick remained quiet and searched Quest's now pitch black stare as he looked directly into her eyes.

"You're pregnant, you're my wife and I said 'no'."

"What about Sera?" She challenged her voice soft and coaxing. "Sweetie, don't you think that poor girl deserves to have her story told?"

"Dammit Mick!" Quest thundered, rubbing a hand across the back of his head. "Do you even remotely recall what Fernando told us about Marc's ship? I don't want you involved in that for anything or *anybody*."

Mick was unfazed. "Too many people have died already. Quest aren't you the least bit curious to know what *really* happened to Wake?"

"If it means you have to be involved, hell no."

"Quest-"

"I don't want to talk about this again Michaela, alright?" he prompted, his voice soft and polite as he waited patiently for a nod she had to force herself to deliver. A heart stopping smile came to his face when he spread his arms to beckon her hug.

Mick complied without hesitation, closing her eyes as she rested her cheek against his chest. Quest kissed the top of her curls and then placed another to her forehead. Then, he was gone.

♦   ♦   ♦

Yohan had drawn all the drapes-giving the illusion of nightfall inside the house while daylight still ruled the evening skies. The temperature had taken a drastic dip-yet inside the farmhouse things were cozy and warm.

Melina felt more content than she could recall being in such a long time. She and Yohan lay cuddled against one of the armchairs before the fire that roared in the living room's massive brick hearth. Though she was reluctant to break the silence, Mel cleared her throat and decided to speak.

"I never answered your question," she said, clenching her fist atop his chest.

"Which one?" he asked in a slow tone. His baritone voice sounded muffled as his face was partly buried in her thick hair.

"What you said about sex complicating things," she told him after a second's hesitation.

Yohan sat a bit straighter, taking Mel up with him. "And? Do you agree with me?"

She smiled sympathetically. "I fully agree. Sorry."

He stiffened, a glare adding a sour look to his face. "I'm not going to like the rest of what you're about to say, am I?"

"This has all been so nice," Mel sighed, forcing herself to finish, "but I have work to do in Seattle and I just don't think we should take this any farther than where it is right now."

"Have you lost your mind?" Yohan's voice grated in the fire lit room.

"Yohan you know I'm right," she said, her fingers curling into the neckline of his T-shirt. "We'd have so many questions to answer with everyone in our business and-"

"The only question I figure we'll have to answer is why it took us so long to come to our senses and try to work things out."

"Oh please, you know it wouldn't be that simple-"

"Marc's not there if that's what's got you worried."

Melina rolled her eyes. "Marc doesn't faze me, but I'm not up to handling a load of inquiring minds."

Yohan's expression was skeptical. "You know we'll have to answer questions whether people see us together or not, don't you?" he asked, trailing his thumb across her full mouth. "Hell, people will mostly want to know why you're back in town and if it has anything to do with me."

"I don't plan on being out and about that much," she replied with a shrug.

"That suits me fine," Yohan said, easing back into a more relaxed position against the armchair.

Mel couldn't resist smiling. Eight years hadn't caused her to forget how much the man protected his privacy. "We've still got so much more to talk about-maybe even argue about and you know we aren't even close to working out what went wrong between us."

"So there *is* more you're keeping from me?" he inquired, his deep voice going impossibly lower.

Mel shivered, realizing that the moment of truth had arrived.

"Meli?"

"No, no Yohan. I-I didn't mean it that way," she said, her voice breathless as she spoke the lie.

He cupped her face in his massive hands. "Then can we leave the past alone for a while and think about the now?" he pleaded, his touch becoming as pleasurable as his words.

"Yohan I-"

"Later," he commanded gently, easing her back to the floor. His mouth grazed her flat stomach, paying special homage to her bellybutton. The airy kisses drifted upward to shower the undersides of her bare breasts.

Melina shuddered, helpless to do more than moan and let her nails rake his chiseled torso and back. Yohan made sweet, slow love to her using only his hands and mouth. Melina begged him to take her completely as they lounged before the fire, but he wouldn't comply. When she thought she'd die from un-sated desire, he pulled her close and carried her upstairs to consummate the act.

CHAPTER FIVE

Crane Cannon's Charm Galleries could be found in New York, Atlanta, Miami, Memphis and Seattle. Each locale, boasted lucrative profits, exquisite pieces and highly publicized showings. The galleries had helped to launch the careers of many talented artists as well as the people who worked behind the scenes to make the shows a success.

Melina couldn't believe such a blessing had befallen her when she discovered how deeply Crane's interests ran in the art world. She'd obtained her art history degree about a year after she and Yohan married. Only to herself would she admit her fear that there would never be an opportunity to utilize her degree-her passion. She worked the Memphis art store one year before her natural flair for the business got her more notice. The knowledge and expertise landed her the position as art buyer for the galleries. While Mel believed the promotion was more about Crane's favoritism than her abilities, she was determined to prove that she deserved it.

The position was so multi-faceted it soon transferred into more of a PR job for Melina. She'd never admit it to Crane, but the trip to Seattle would give her the chance to really work in the 'art side' of the business. It was a thing she'd missed, but hadn't the time to dwell on with all her other responsibilities.

Besides, working on the gallery showing would help to keep her every waking thought off of Yohan Ramsey.

Do you really believe that? Melina's voice of doubt inquired.

"Oh shut up," she muttered, turning to survey her view from the windows on the corner office that had been reserved for her.

As the Seattle office had never been used; the showing would be the premier event at the newest gallery for Crane's company. Melina was already feeling like the place was her own.

"Don't get to comfortable, Mel," she warned, hugging herself while staring blankly at the downtown view from the floor to ceiling windows.

Again, Yohan crossed her mind. They'd enjoyed an entire week at the Alaska farmhouse. They indulged in pleasures so intensely, Melina thought it was a wonder that she could walk into the gallery that morning.

With a grimace, she took a gulp of the flavored coffee in her mug and set the cup back to her oak desk with more force than necessary. Unfortunately, nothing would keep Yohan off her mind now; not when he was so close and so wanting to see her-so wanting … her.

Pressing her lips together to stifle the moan that was desperate to escape, she tried to focus on work. The promotion packet lay unfinished on the desk and with the showing only two months away, the packet was definitely not something for the backburner

"Dammit," she hissed, when the phone rang seconds later. "Yeah Kate?" she answered.

"Mel, I've got a Josephine Ramsey on the line for you," the assistant announced.

Mel closed her eyes resolvedly. She had almost completely forgotten her other far more important reason for being there. Any hopes for keeping her mind off Yohan were pointless now.

"Well hello!" Mel greeted her mother-in-law, truly pleased to be speaking with her again. Regardless of what situations prompted her return to Seattle, Mel had missed Josephine terribly.

"Oh Melina, thank God!" Josephine cried, "Thank you so much for agreeing to come!"

"Josephine? Josephine, listen to me. I had no plans to do this," Melina tried to explain. "My boss needed me here, so it all sort of fell into place."

"I don't care. I'm just so glad you're here," Josephine went on, swallowing heavily. "Have you thought over what we discussed?"

Mel toyed with a fluffy tuft of her hair. "I've thought of little else," she sighed.

"Well unfortunately things haven't changed much since you lived here. Marc is still the same conniver. His latest scandal though … at least his evil is finally being uncovered."

"I know about the boat," Mel sighed, taking her seat as she spoke.

"But how? No one but the family-"

"Yohan told me," Mel shared, waiting for Josephine's explosion of happiness.

Of course, the woman was elated. "Well when? Where did you see him? Are you back at the house?"

Melina felt her head spin while Josephine rambled off the questions. "We spent a few days at the place in Alaska."

"And now you're-"

"We're the same place we've been for the last eight years Josephine," Mel firmly assured her mother-in-law. "Nothing's changed."

"Nothing except the fact that you've just spent time alone together for the first time in eight years. Melina you can't make me believe that didn't mean anything?"

"Of course I don't," Mel snapped, standing and in the process dragging a hand through her thick tresses. "It was wonderful. For a while, it felt like the last eight years had all been some bad dream," she said, her voice trailing to silence as she stared at an abstract painting that adorned a far wall in the office. "But don't get happy Josephine," she warned, the firmness returning to her voice. "My plans to head back to Memphis once I'm done here are still in place."

"But how can you …" Josephine was clearly stunned and seemed to need a moment to gather her thoughts. "Why would you leave now when the two of you have talked? Everything's in the open now."

"No," Mel sighed, massaging the bridge of her nose. "No Josephine, everything's not out in the open. We didn't get around to discussing it."

"But what-"

"Josephine, I haven't told Yohan *why* I left-I skirted around it … there's just so much to tell him." She closed her eyes. "There's so much more to this."

"I don't understand, baby."

Josephine's lost tone, filled Melina with a sense of foreboding. No aspect of this situation was going to be easy, including certain matters that needed to be discussed with her mother-in-law.

"Listen, we can't talk about this over the phone," Mel said, already punching into her calendar. "Let's have lunch-someplace we can talk."

"Why don't you come out to the house?"

The quick suggestion created a sinking feeling in the pit of Mel's stomach. "Joseph-"

"It's perfect and Marc hasn't been here for weeks. I'm not expecting him anytime soon."

Mel scratched the arch of her eyebrow. "Are you sure?"

"Trust me love, no way would he step foot back here when he knows what's waiting for him."

◆   ◆   ◆

"Are you serious?"

"Quite."

"This could be risky."

"I have no choice. Unfortunately."

Stefan Lyons grimaced, but kept his opinions silenced. Of course, he would've preferred to hear another reason for Marcus Ramsey to request his help, but he'd take what he could get.

"Have you told your top people?" Stef was asking.

"The ones who matter."

"And?" Stef prompted, when no other explanation came through the phone line. "What'd they say to the news that I'd be taking over your interests?"

"Stefan relax. They work for *me*, they have no opinions about the decisions I make."

"And the rest of your people? This could get messy when they find out I-"

"*Again,* relax. I assure you everyone who needs to be-will be informed of my decision before the executive staff meeting in a few months."

Stef nodded. "Right, the executive staff meeting," he parroted.

"Mmm, the elders should all be there. It'll be the perfect time and place to make this announcement."

"The guys won't like it," Stef predicted, referring to Moses, Fernando and Yohan.

Marc sighed across the line. "They won't care. They all practically told my team to go to hell when I sought their assistance."

Stef felt a stab of regret at the news, but refused to let that dim this shining moment in his midst. "I'll wait for your call, then," he told Marcus.

"Good, but now there's another matter I need you for."

Intrigued, Stef remained silent and waited.

"How much do you know about Fernando's latest piece of ass?"

Stef smiled at the question. "Contessa Warren," he said.

"Right," Marc almost growled. "This publisher," he clarified.

"I know Fernando keeps topping himself," Stef complimented, shifting in his seat as his trousers tightened across his lap in a telling manner. "She's gorgeous as hell," he said.

"And Fern's all caught up in her, I assume?"

"Damn right he is. She's a prime piece of tail."

"Yeah, I've met her and I pretty much figured that's all it was about. Still," Marc added after a second's hesitation, "she's dabbled a little bit too far in my business. Maybe it's time to give my sons an example of what happens when either they or their sluts meddle in my affairs."

"What can I do?" Stef asked, excitement beginning to well in his chest in anticipation of Marc's instructions.

"I need your help. I trust you know what I mean?"

Stef needed no further clarification and promptly answered. "You know I'll do anything for you Marc."

◆   ◆   ◆

"It's been a pleasure, Mr. Ramsey," the desk manager said to Quay once the last hotel receipt had been signed.

"Thanks Fred," Quay replied with a nod and handshake. Then he was reaching for Ty who stood close to his side. Playfully, he nibbled at her earlobe hoping to bring a smile to her face.

Tykira had been subdued much of the morning and barely managed a smile.

Quay's smoldering gaze grew stormier as he grimaced. "I shouldn't have brought you out here," he regretted.

Shaking her head, Ty smoothed her hands across the front of the casual black shirt he wore. "Don't feel that way. You know I wanted to come."

"Looking at your face doesn't convince me."

Soft, honest laughter passed her lips. "No really. I'm really glad I came with you."

"But?"

Ty rolled her eyes, "The whole situation's just so sad," she whispered, focusing upon the chandeliers that dotted the lofty ceilings.

Quay bowed his head. He wasn't a bit surprised by her admission. He'd felt much the same way since they'd visited his best friend's mother.

"Wake won't even be around to watch his sons grow up."

"I still can't believe he had kids," Quay sighed, rubbing one hand across the back of his neck. "That crazy fool was a father," he chuckled.

"Of twins," Ty added, brushing her lips across her husband's jaw. "Just like you and Quest," she added.

"Damn," Quay muttered, turning away from Ty as he smacked a clenched fist against his palm.

"Shh," Tykira urged, smoothing her hands across his back and resting her cheek to his shoulder.

"I have to admit things may've happened just the way they told us."

"What?" Ty inquired, making him turn around to face her.

Quay folded his arms across his chest. "No way would Wake fake a death and leave his sons behind like that."

Ty hesitated to remind her husband that his old friend had done many things over the years. Things no one may have been aware of. "Well, his mother seems capable of raising them," she said, offering a refreshing tone of voice.

Quay's tense expression softened, sparking his right dimple. "Yeah, she loved Wake. She'll make sure they know he was a good man."

"And what about you?" Ty asked, tilting her head in an inquiring manner. "Do you think he was a good man?"

"He was a good man," Quay told his wife without hesitation. "I think he was out there trying to gather the same dirt on Marc that we all were."

"Speaking of which, do you believe what Fernando found on that ship?"

"It's frightening how much I believe that," Quay admitted, with a haunted look. "What's more frightening is how many things from back in the day seem to be falling into place."

Ty's almond shaped gaze narrowed curiously. "You've lost me again. What things are falling into place?"

Stepping close, Quay cupped her elbows. His thumbs brushed the tassels that hung from the short sleeves of the fitted sandalwood dress she wore.

"Remember my curse?" he asked, his right-dimpled grin appearing at the confusion he saw on her face.

Ty only shook her head.

"At least, I *thought* I was cursed. All the time it was Marc."

"Marc?" Ty whispered, shaking her head a bit. "What do you-"

"The disappearances," he told her, "my not wanting to be with you back then had to do with a lot more than Sera."

"Zara?" Ty recalled, her breathing growing labored as she watched her husband nod.

"And there were other girls. At first, I thought it was because of me. I thought I'd pissed off somebody big time and this was the fool's way of getting back at me. I thought Wake was behind it once it seemed all the evidence and coincidence pointed to him." He looked at her and pulled her closer. "I didn't want you around because I didn't want whoever it was to even suspect how I felt about you. Hearing all this crap about Marc … it's scarier than thinking it'd been Wake who was responsible."

"Marc? Baby are you sure he could've … some of those girls were barely in their teens."

"And Fern said he was told younger girls were available if that's what he was into," Quay reminded his wife with an apologetic look.

Ty covered her mouth, unable to argue his point of view.

"Hey," Quay whispered, kissing her cheek before hugging her tight.

"Well, it looks like your worst fears are correct," she said, her voice muffled against his shoulder. "I'm afraid your father definitely has *two* monsters for brothers."

"And one will probably never be stopped," Quay said.

"Unless someone stops him," Ty added.

◆   ◆   ◆

"Dammit," Melina hissed, her slanting black gaze was so blurred with tears. They spilled onto the pages of the letter she held and the sound of the water slapping the brittle sheet of paper seemed to echo in the office.

Sniffling loudly, Mel refused to set the page aside and collect her emotions. Instead, she continued to read the words that she knew by heart.

I've grown accustomed to this life, I actually love it. I know it sickens you to hear me say I love prostituting myself, But Mel, I don't see it that way. The men I've met have been such gentlemen. Some only want companionship and a friend to talk to-a shoulder to cry on. Others … well, others want deeper communication, but as I said they're all such gentlemen, I feel like a queen every time. Melina please don't ruin this for me.
What's happened has happened and there's no going back. This has been my life for over eight years. If you betray this my life could very well be over.
Please do what you're told. Tell no one I've contacted you and please stay away from Yohan. My life depends on the way you live your life. I'm so very sorry.
All my love, Zara.

The letter slipped from Mel's hand and drifted to the floor. She began to cry with no thought of who might overhear her wailing. The tears flowed more heavily than usual that day and reminded her of the first time she'd ever set eyes upon the powerful message.

So much more drove her tears now. It was the first time she'd read her cousin's words since she'd returned to Seattle-returned to Yohan.

Zara's letter arrived a few months after Melina had left Seattle. Melina recalled how stunned and unnerved she'd been to realize anyone knew where she was. She'd been careful for the most part, hadn't she? Or perhaps not. After all, Yohan had discovered where she was. While she was certain her uncle would inform no one else; someone sent her that letter. Perhaps it'd been the same someone who took her cousin.

When Zara's letter arrived, it dashed any and all possibility of Melina returning to Yohan then. It was Mel's greatest regret and the one thing she desperately wanted to correct. She'd had every intention of doing that until the note appeared so mysteriously. It had been left inside the PO Box she'd been renting, until she'd gotten settled. She'd only obtained the box for hopeful correspondence from the numerous job applications she'd completed.

Melina reclined in her desk chair and fiddled with the cuff of the petal pink blouse she wore. She recalled the day so vividly. It was as though someone had simply placed the note inside without it ever going through normal postal procedures. It was a simple white envelope with only her name on the front.

Inside, however, were words and instructions so damaging they'd ruled her life right into the present. As painful as it had been to walk away from the only man she'd ever loved, that hadn't been the worst of it. Seeing him again, knowing the feelings were still there and as powerful as they had ever been, seemed to increase her pain ten-fold.

Melina jumped when the phone's intercom line buzzed. Smoothing her chilled hands across the front of the chamois bow pants she wore, Mel quickly reigned in her emotions.

"Yeah Kate?" she answered, a few seconds following the initial ring.

"Melina you have a guest out front."

"I'm sorry," Mel started, brushing the stray moisture of tears from her cheeks. "I didn't realize I was due for an appointment."

"Oh no Mel, the gentleman says he wasn't expected," Kate informed her softly.

Mel knew who her unexpected guest was then. Her heart thudded a singular powerful beat which caused her hand to weaken over the phone.

"Would you ask him to come on back?" Mel instructed her assistant, and then stood from her desk. She let out a long, deep breath before squaring her shoulders and heading for the door.

Finding Yohan in the office lobby brought a sweet smile to her face. As he crossed the room, Mel's smile faded a bit while she took in all the downright wanton female stares that followed him.

"Hey," she whispered, waving him inside the office. The door closed on the lingering gazes with far more force than was needed.

Yohan turned mid-stride taking Melina in an unbreakable hold. She gasped, allowing him the entrance he sought. His tongue thrust deep and possessively. Thankfully, his embrace was firm, for Mel had no strength left to stand. She tingled from head to toe and emitted soft, helpless whimpers of need as her tongue rolled leisurely and erotically around his. Her hands settled to his chest and she arched closer, deepening the kiss while emitting soft, helpless whimpers into his mouth.

"Come with me," he asked, still kissing her thoroughly. His tongue thrust longer and harder with every second that passed.

"Mmm ..." she responded, wanting so very much to follow him anywhere he wished.

"Is that a yes?" he queried, filling his hands with ample portions of her cleavage. "Mel?" he called, nibbling at her earlobe.

"Mmm ... no, no," she managed, trying to fight the strong urge to say yes. "No Yohan, I have to work. This showing-"

"It can wait," he decided, trailing his lips across her brow, along the curve of her cheek ...

"Han," she said with a bit more force then. Pushing him away; far as he'd allow, she fixed him with an incredulous look. "Why are you doing this?"

"What?" he asked, appearing confused, "wanting to sleep with my wife?"

Melina sighed and shook her head. "I've been your wife in name only for eight years."

"Exactly why I want you in my bed. Now," he teased, pulling her closer. "What?" he asked again when her expression remained solemn.

"This has all been so much aggravation-aggravation neither of us need. Especially you," she said, searching the gorgeous onyx depths of his eyes. "Clearly, any woman would kill to have you," she said, grazing his dimpled chin with her thumbnail.

Yohan's shrug was almost nonexistent. "What exactly do you expect me to say to that Mel?"

"You act as if you don't see the way women drool over you when you walk past them," she accused in an incredulous tone. "You're gonna be the talk of this building for the rest of the week," she predicted and pulled away from him.

Yohan grinned, stroking his jaw as he turned to watch her at the windows. "So is this your sly way of asking how many women I've slept with over the last eight years?"

Mel slanted him a tired glance. "Don't be stupid," she muttered.

"Because I'll have you know that I reserve the right to ask the same of you."

This time, Melina turned to face her husband more fully. "I haven't slept with *any* women over the last eight years," she informed him playfully and leaned back against the window.

Yohan's grinned intensified, while he folded his arms across the short-sleeved driftwood colored shirt. Melina commanded herself not to gawk at the display of his forearms and biceps glistening dark and powerful.

"I really don't want to know how many women there've been," she said, clearing her throat when her voice shook over the last few words. "Anyway, that's not what this is about," she grumbled.

"You're right, this is about my father." Yohan pointed out, his playful demeanor sobering into intensity.

Mel seemed to wilt at the observation. Of course, her husband immediately noticed her reaction.

"Dammit Mel," he hissed, folding his hands over the back of one of the chairs before her desk. "What the hell is it? What aren't you telling me?" he demanded, silently acknowledging that she was terrifying him by her behavior. He shrugged, forcing himself to use a different tactic.

"Maybe it's nothing," he said, pushing one hand into a pocket on his beige trousers. "Maybe you just wanted to leave back then, simple as that. Maybe you figured using Marc as the reason would make it easier or justified somehow."

"No!" Mel whispered fiercely, her slanting ebony stare filled with rage.

Yohan was just as enraged, when he turned to face her. "Then this has to end. After eight years this has to end," he said, pointing his index finger in her direction. Quickly, he curved his hand into a fist and banged it against his thigh. His temper was heating slowly, but definitely to that point of no restraint. The anger rose as much from the fear he saw on her face as from the fact that his father was at the root of it all. He bowed his head, brushing his thumb across the sleek line of his brow and debated. He should go, right then before he said or did something they'd both be sorry for.

Relief flooded Melina's body when the phone rang, interrupting the heavy tension. She practically ran to answer it, desperate to be rid of Yohan's suddenly disturbing presence.

"This is Melina," she greeted breathlessly,

"Hello Love, this is Crane."

An indecipherable sound passed her lips and she sank into her desk chair. She knew her voice had deserted her and she hadn't even tried to say another word.

"Melina?" Crane called, when seconds of silence passed.

"Hi," was all she could manage.

"Are you alright? Did I interrupt you?" he was asking.

Yohan's incessant staring mixed with Crane's voice on the phone, was a recipe for total unrest. Mel just managed to hold onto the phone.

"No," she cleared her throat, "no I'm fine."

"I'm only calling to find out how things are progressing?"

"Everything's on schedule," she said, her voice becoming more firm, "the gallery show should be quite a success," she said, knowing full well that wasn't what he was referring to.

Crane was silent for a moment. "So I take it there's nothing more to report?"

Mel shook her head and stood. "No, but I'll keep you posted."

"Mel-"

"I'm sorry it's just that I'm about to be late for an appointment so …"

"I see," Crane whispered, disappointment filling his soft voice. "Alright, well I'll let you go and we'll talk soon?"

"Mmm mmm," Mel confirmed quickly and set the receiver back to its cradle.

Yohan kept his gaze hooded and smirked when Mel ended the call.

"My boss," she saw fit to inform him.

"You two must be really close," he observed coolly while his fist remained hidden in his pocket.

The comment brought a curious frown to Mel's face. Folding her arms across her chest, she waited for him to clarify.

"He must really trust you," Yohan continued, loving the confusion in her captivating eyes.

Mel stood. "He does, but … why would you say that?"

What would she say if he told her he'd seen her with him? That he'd been *dropping in* on her for the better part of her eight years in Memphis. He wasn't ready to go into that. He wasn't ready to hear what she might say.

"This is one of Seattle's finest galleries," he said, waving his hand in the air for emphasis. "Your … boss must really trust you to leave it in your care."

"That's got little to do with trust," she said, reaching for a folder on her desk, "I'm just damn good at my job," she boasted wearily.

Nodding, his deep set eyes raked her figure a second longer. "I'll take that as my cue to leave, then," he said when she slanted him a look. "What time should I expect you at the house tonight?"

Mel gasped, hearing the comment clearly in spite of the fact that he called it across his shoulder. "You-you want me to … come to the house?" she asked, stunned he wanted to see her at the home they once shared.

His hand on the door lever, Yohan turned and regarded her curiously. "Yeah, why?"

The contents of the folder she held spilled to the floor. Her hands were shaking terribly. "Han, I-I don't know if that's-"

"Would you prefer me to come get you?" he asked, his baritone voice holding a softness that was more unsettling than soothing.

Mel knew she couldn't refuse the invitation. No wonder he stopped earlier, he had something far more explicit already planned for that evening. "I um, I should be there by seven," she promised quietly.

"Cheer up," he urged. The arrogant expression on his dark, handsome face made it abundantly clear that he knew exactly what had her on edge. "I promise you'll enjoy yourself," he said and left without a backwards glance.

Mel knew the implication of his words would've pulled a moan from her throat if she could have found her voice. Instead, she sank back into her desk chair and held the back of her hand against her forehead.

◆   ◆   ◆

Chicago, Illinois

"Don't stop yet."

"The doorbell's ringing."

"Let it ring."

Contessa laughed. She pushed herself from beneath the covers where she'd been using certain *skills* to awaken the gorgeous giant who'd been sleeping in her bed. With a wicked look on her face, she sank her teeth into his broad, muscular chest and squealed when he swatted her bottom.

"I promise I'll be right back," she whispered sitting astride him then.

"Just five minutes," he begged, his massive hands curving around her hips.

County shrieked. She barely managed to wriggle free of his grasp before he set-tled her to his erect arousal. "Be good," she ordered, once she stood at the foot of the bed. Grabbing his night shirt from the floor, she headed out to answer the ring.

She'd ordered out for breakfast as a surprise and figured it was the delivery. When she whipped open the door, nothing prepared her to find Stefan Lyons standing on the other side.

Stunned speechless, she couldn't respond with all the unwelcome greetings that flooded her mind. Stefan decided to take her silence as an invitation to enter.

"Contessa," he breathed, his eyes raking her scanty attire.

"Mr. Lyons," she managed coldly.

He made a tsking sound as he smiled. "So formal. Don't tell me you don't recall our meeting?"

County rolled her eyes. "I'm trying to forget it," she sneered.

"I'm sorry to hear that," he said, advancing a step or two.

County muttered a curse when she backed away. She'd be damned if she'd let him rile her in her own home.

Stefan's leering gaze was becoming bolder as it focused on her bosom. "I take it from your appearance, Fern isn't too far away?" His smile widened. "Or am I mistaken?"

"What the hell do you want?" she demanded.

Stef shrugged. "I have a delivery for him."

County shook her head. "And you came all the way to Chicago to hand deliver it? Must be mighty important."

"It's a last minute invite," Stefan shared, still moving closer to Contessa, "I wanted to be sure he got it ASAP. But if he's not … in," he punctuated the remark by curving his hand around a generous portion of her derriere, "I can try elsewhere," he added his fingers and massaged just slightly.

Stunned and wary, County caught her breath and practically flew from the room. All the while, she cursed herself for not slapping the grin from his face. She was still trying to catch her breath when she made it back to her bedroom.

Fernando was chuckling at the sight she made, until something told him she was truly upset. Contessa couldn't mask her unease and didn't notice Fernando watching her closely while he pulled on his sleep pants. When she moved past him, he took her arm and felt her jerk in response.

"Are you alright?" he whispered.

Running a shaking hand across her cropped cut, she managed a nod. "Your partner is um, he's out front."

"Stef? What the hell for?"

County shrugged. "I don't know, he said he had something for you."

Fernando's hold on her arm tightened when she tried to move on. "Are you alright?"

"Yes, yes Fernando I'm fine. I just don't like having that man in my house," she muttered.

Fernando watched her a while longer, his brows drawn close in concentration. Then, he leaned in to plant a kiss to her temple before heading out of the room.

When the door shut behind, Contessa expelled the breath she'd been holding. Hugging herself, she sat on the edge of the bed.

"What the hell are you doin' here?" Fernando demanded, finding his partner in the living room browsing the book shelves.

"Fern," Stef called, clearly taking no offense to the hostile greeting he received. "Hope you can make it," he said, passing Fernando a small envelope.

"The Sharpe Club?" Fernando noted when he saw the establishment's logo.

Stef grinned proudly, "I know you have to be a member to even stick your head in the place and well …"

Fernando shrugged. "So what? You announcing your membership or something?" he guessed in a weary tone.

Stefan grinned. "It's a little more than that, brotha. Hope you can make it."

"Don't come here again, man," Fernando advised, tossing aside the envelope.

"Why?" Stef retorted with a look of phony innocence.

"Because she doesn't like it and neither do I."

"Easy, big Fern," Stefan soothed, his hands raised defensively. "Damn man," he chuckled, glancing towards the rear of the living room. "She must be a damn good piece of ass to have you so possess-"

Fernando's massive hand encircled Stef's neck before the man could complete the sentence. Without a word, Fernando literally pushed him out into the hall.

When the door slammed in Stef's face, he leaned against the wall; coughing to catch his breath. He cast a murderous glance at the door and then continued on down the hall.

CHAPTER SIX

"Child!" Rita Hotchkiss' cry of delight filled the foyer when she opened the door to Melina later that afternoon. The Ramsey housekeeper had always felt a special closeness towards Marcus and Josephine's only daughter-in-law.

"Rita," Mel sighed, pulling the woman into a close embrace. "It's so good to see you."

Rita closed her eyes and relished the hug. "Same here love. Same here. How long will you be here in Seattle?" she asked, once they'd pulled apart.

Mel rubbed her hands over her blouse sleeves and watched Rita close the front door. "I'm not too sure of my plans yet," she said, offering the older woman her arm as they strolled out of the foyer.

"Please don't be a stranger while you're here then," Rita urged, patting Mel's arm in a motherly fashion.

"I promise," Mel whispered, pressing a kiss to the woman's cheek.

Rita escorted Melina across the beige and black speckled entry hall leading into the living room. Inside, Josephine Ramsey stood waiting. Her hands were clasped at her mouth and tears filled her eyes when she saw Melina.

No words were spoken mother and daughter-in-law closed the distance and met in a lengthy hug. Rita smiled and left them alone.

"Oh Mel, Mel thank you so much for coming back," Josephine sobbed, twin emotions of happiness and regret filling her mood. "I've missed you so."

"I've missed you too," Mel was saying, hugging Josephine more tightly.

"And you've seen Yohan," Josephine noted, pulling back to smile at Melina. "This is so wonderful. I can't tell you how much it means."

Sobering then, Mel's smile tightened a bit. "Why did you call me out here Josephine?" she asked.

The light in Josephine's bright gaze dimmed as the sobering feeling overcame her as well. "Marc's out of control," she hissed.

Melina grimaced. "Marc's always been out of control."

"This is different."

"How?" Mel asked, needing to hear the woman admit to her fear.

For a while, Josephine was silent. An absent expression fell over her face as she stood, toying with a lock of Mel's coarse, dark hair. Then, she turned away.

"Have you met Quest's wife yet?" Josephine asked, taking a seat on one of the loveseats filling the spacious front room.

The question stumped Mel, but she shook her head. "No, no I heard he was married but no I haven't met her yet."

Josephine nodded and smiled as a bit of the light returned to her expression. "Michaela's a lot like you. You'd like her I think. She came here to Seattle doing research for a biography on the family. She's very smart-very intuitive. It didn't take her long to dig up the truth about Sera Black."

Melina's heart lurched at the sound of the name. "Sera," she breathed.

Josephine offered a refreshing smile and smoothed her hands across the silky hose she wore beneath a lavender skirt suit. "Mick was the reason they know what they do about Houston's involvement."

"Houston's?"

"Yes Houston," Josephine confirmed, fixing her daughter-in-law with a knowing look. "*Only* Houston."

"And?"

"*And* Marc is on the verge of sweeping another incident under his dirty rug."

Mel leaned back in the armchair she occupied. Her dark lovely face was a picture of deep unrest.

Josephine sat forward. "Melina if you were to-"

"Hold it. No," Mel interrupted, quickly regaining control of herself. "Before you ask, no." She reiterated.

Josephine appeared to deflate. "But why? Why not?"

Mel raised her hand. "Josephine-"

"How could you keep silent about this any longer? Especially when you were so ready to tell Yohan before you left?"

"And I'm sure you've always wondered why I didn't?"

Josephine was quiet, observing the pensive young woman. "Yohan always believed Marc had something to do with your leaving," she said, sounding as though she were carefully choosing her words.

"Well, he was right," Mel confirmed while rolling her eyes. "Marc had everything to do with my leaving."

"That's impossible!" Josephine hissed. "No way would you let that bastard bully you into leaving your husband."

"It was easy for him to do," Mel admitted, standing and pulling something from her purse. "Once I received this. It came a few months after I left," she said, dropping Zara's note into Josephine's lap.

After scanning the brief, but explosive letter, utter shock took hold of Josephine's face. The question in her eyes was easy to read.

"He was responsible for that," Mel confirmed. "All that time we cried, wondered, mourned her and he knew." She turned and pointed down at Josephine. "So you see putting Marc behind bars isn't tops on my list until I find out where that son of a bitch is keeping my cousin." Mel slammed her fist to her palm. "I let all that time pass, afraid for Zara when I should've done anything I had to find her. Especially when Marc threatened Johari the very night I left," she confided, referring to her other cousin and Zara's sister.

Josephine was almost motionless with shock. "If you're not here to tell what you know about Marc … then why? Why have you come?"

Swallowing noticeably, Mel propped both hands on her hips. "I came on business for my boss … Crane Cannon."

If Josephine hadn't been seated, she would have surely fallen to the floor. "How?" was the only question she could form.

"He didn't know who I was when we met," Mel assured her.

Josephine's hands shook as she settled them to her lap. "How long have you known? You know, don't you?"

"That Yohan is Crane's son? Yes."

"He sent you here?"

"He did."

"What will you do?"

Mel pressed her fingers to the silver band holding back her hair. "It's what I need *you* to do," she clarified slowly.

Josephine began to shake her head. "No, no Mel I-"She looked everywhere but at Mel. "What you must think of me ..."

"Wait, shh ..." Mel urged, stooping before Josephine and taking her hands in her own. "I feel the same way about you that I always have. But why, Josephine?" she pleaded, giving the woman's hands a tiny shake. "Why would you jeopardize your family-your reputation by doing this?"

"Reputation? Ha!" Josephine snapped, jerking her hands from Melina's. "You must mean a reputation for being a fool. Trust me, love, with a reputation like that I didn't care much for maintaining it!" she cried, self loathing spewing from her voice and eyes. "Besides," she muttered, settling back on the loveseat. "I was so angry. I was so *angry* Mel. Marc had lied and cheated and ... humiliated me in every way a man-a husband could humiliate a wife."

Mel leaned close to kiss the woman's cheek and dried her tears when they rolled down her face.

"I always knew he'd had affairs," Josephine continued to confide, "even had children outside the marriage. I lived knowing that for years and I didn't do a damn thing. I never confronted him-never left him." A smile began to tug at her mouth then. "So one night I decided to follow him. I don't know why-I guess I just wanted to feel like I was *doing* something. Finally. I had to know who at least one of the bitches was. I only caught a glimpse of her once when she opened the door. She was married, but her husband was rarely there judging from the amount of times Marc visited her." Her smile widened. "But then, one day I met him. I'd driven by the house and he was backing out the driveway."

Mel perched on the edge of the coffee table and focused more clearly on Josephine as she spoke.

"I followed him-followed Crane to a warehouse. Inside it-it looked like some sort of gallery."

Mel smiled and shook her head.

"Anyway," Josephine sighed, looking off as though she were seeing into her past. "I pretended my car had broken down ... Crane was so sweet and he seemed so lonely. As we talked, I forgot all about Marc and Crane's ... wife. We never spoke of either of them. And for the longest time it never went farther than talking," she said, looking directly at Mel as though needing her to understand that what she'd shared with the man hadn't been something spontaneous and meaningless. "And then ... one day, I saw her in the park with a baby. I went over and pretended to want to fawn over the child. It didn't look like she or Crane, but anyway ... I knew Marc's visits to her had started to dwindle. The bastard stopped seeing her because she'd gotten pregnant." Josephine took a deep breath and shivered when she let it out.

"That was the day I told Crane about my husband's infidelities. I didn't implicate his wife," she said with a grimace. "It wasn't about that for me. I needed closeness and we acted on that closeness in a way that was far more satisfying than talking." She smoothed her hands across her skirt. "And then I found out I was pregnant with Yohan. Crane was so wonderful. He wanted to raise Yohan, Fernando and Moses," she laughed. "I knew it was impossible-*beyond* impossible. So did he I think. We were just hurting so much … At any rate, it could never be. He was white. I was a part of Savannah, Georgia's … *society.* Yohan was black as a panther. Marc was so proud," she reminisced, her face tightening with hate. "It was so easy to pretend. It felt like heaven to pretend. I watched Marc strut like a fool-doting over another man's seed. It made everything he'd put me through just a little more bearable."

Mel sat there clutching Josephine's hands. Her own head spun from the depth of the story. Crane's somewhat cursory explanation of the events leading up to Yohan's birth barely scratched the surface of the whole situation.

"And now Josephine?" Melina asked, finding her voice at last. "With the way things are? Yohan hates Marc and maybe … maybe if he knew Marc wasn't … maybe some of that anger I see taking over his soul might-"

"Might what?" Josephine snapped, bolting from the loveseat. "Might have him hating me too?"

Mel turned, raising her hands. "No, no Josephine-"

"Yes! Because that's all that would come of me telling him."

"Josephine-"

"How do you tell your child he's the product of revenge?!"

Mel looked down. "You have to."

"I can't! It'd destroy Yohan and *he'd* destroy Marc. I don't want my son's life any more ruined because of that monster."

"I don't want that either," Mel swore, pressing a hand to her chest as she stood, "but it may not be up to us."

The anger on Josephine's face cleared a bit. "What are you saying?"

"Crane's running for office. A senate seat in Tennessee. He's being threatened with this," Mel said, seeing her mother-in-law's light complexion grow flushed. "Someone else *does* know Josephine. It may come out whether we want it to or not. Better he hear it from us-from *you.*"

Josephine rolled her eyes and turned away. "Perhaps when you have a child Melina, you'll understand that you'd do anything to protect it."

Mel reached out and made Josephine face her. "This isn't protecting! If he hears this from someone else it could make things that much worse."

"Then *you* tell him!"

A knock rose from somewhere in the room and brought the argument to a definite halt. Melina and Josephine turned and shock took hold of their faces when they saw Yohan leaning against the living room doorway.

"Now why do I get the feeling you two are talkin' about me?" he asked.

◆   ◆   ◆

Tykira brushed both hands across her form-fitting calf length eggshell skirt. She closed her eyes and took a deep breath before stepping off the elevator and into the penthouse office at Ramsey Group.

"Quay?" she called out softly, while moving deeper into the dim overtly masculine office. She made a quick survey of the outer rooms before glancing inside her husband's abandoned office. "Damn," she sighed, then reached for a pad lying next to the phone and began to scribble a message. Only a second or two passed, when a smile tugged at her mouth when she sensed his presence in the room. "I thought I'd missed you," she called, tossing her lengthy tresses across her shoulder and glancing back at him.

Quay snapped his fingers. "How'd you do that? How'd you know I was here?"

Ty drew a pen mark through the note and turned to lean against the desk. "Your cologne," she said.

Quay's right dimpled grin flashed. "Sexy, huh?" he guessed.

Ty's arched brows rose a notch. "Mmm ... I was thinking more along the lines of *strong*," she teased, her laughter mounting when she found herself tugged into her husband's embrace.

"Joke's, huh?" he taunted, dropping soft kisses to the sensitive area below her earlobe.

"Quay," Ty gasped, feeling him tugging at the zipper lining the front of her white blouse.

"Shh," he urged, capturing her lips in a gentle kiss. His tongue eased inside her mouth as slowly as he pulled down the zipper.

Tykira arched into his solid frame, her arms encircling his neck as she deepened the kiss. Soft moans filled the office, growing louder when his hands were cupping her breasts only concealed by the lacy fabric of her bra.

"Wait," she murmured, even as she rubbed her nipples across the center of his palm.

"Uh-uh," Quay refused, stepping closer to force her back onto his desk.

"Wait please, I have something to tell you," she gasped, but allowed him to make her sit on the desk.

"Save it," he ordered gruffly, trailing his lips across her jaw, the line of her neck and the valley between her breasts.

"No, I mean it," she argued, pressing against the lapels of his black suit coat. "Please, it-it's important," she groaned, arching forward when his tongue stroked her nipple through the bra.

Quay chuckled, going to unhook the front clasp of the wispy undergarment. Suddenly, Ty slapped at his hands and cleared her throat.

"No Quay, this is too important and we need to talk about it. *Now.*"

"What's the rush?" he complained, moving to prevent her from leaving the desk.

"I got a call from Lena Robinson today," she said, pushing past him to fix her bra when she saw the stunned look on his face.

"Why would she call you?" he asked slowly, turning to settle against a desk corner.

"Due to the nature of what she wanted to discuss. I guess I was the logical choice," Ty said, while zipping her top.

Quay's dark gaze narrowed with unease. "And what was that?"

Ty folded her arms across her chest. "She's sick Quay. Terminal."

"What?"

"Her doctors can't say how long she has and with Wake being gone," she shrugged, "she didn't tell him about her illness. Lena's all the boys have."

"Jesus," Quay breathed, closing his eyes as he bowed his head.

Ty pushed a lock of hair behind her ear and stepped closer. "Baby, Lena wants us to consider taking the boys. She wants to keep them with her until ... well, anyway, she wants us to visit as much as we can in order to bond with the twins," she explained, her expressive gaze focused and unwavering as she studied Quay's reaction. He was quiet-too quiet for Tykira's liking. She wasn't sure what to expect with regards to his reaction and decided that she wasn't in any mood to find out.

"You don't have to give an answer yet," she told him, stepping closer to pretend at straightening his navy blue tie. "Just think on it," she urged in a bright tone.

"I don't need to think on it."

Ty's hands fell away from the tie and she backed off. "Well, before you ... decide Quay just please keep in mind that anything could happen to those babies and none of it good," she warned, a ball of emotion swelling in her throat. "They could be sent to foster homes with people that might do all sorts of terrible things to them. They could be split up and raised without ever knowing the other existed. They'd be strangers who know nothing about their family …"

Quay watched his wife, falling more in love with her every second she spoke. Finally he smiled and walked over to take her hands.

"I'm sorry," she whispered, closing her eyes and forcing a few tears to trickle down her cheeks. "I shouldn't try to force your hand with this. It's a decision we should both be clear and in agreement on."

"That's true," he agreed with a solemn nod. "But you forgot to mention one very important thing during your speech."

Ty was stumped. "What?" she blurted.

Shaking his head, Quay stepped close and cupped her face in his hands. "That it's the right thing to do."

"Quay … Oh Quay are you sure?" Ty whispered, her brown eyes widening. "Are you really sure because you don't have to decide now."

His hands moved from her face to massage her shoulders. "Now or later, my answer will be the same," he stepped back and looked at her. "Are *you* sure?" he asked.

Ty nodded, her lips trembling when she smiled. "I couldn't stand not know-ing if those babies were being properly cared for or if they're even together."

Quay laughed completely in awe of her nurturing tone, her concern and the happy tears in her eyes. "I couldn't stand it either," he said, giving her a tiny shake.

Ty threw herself against his chest. Her arms locked around his neck as she pressed dozens of quick kisses to his face. "Thank you, thank you," she sighed, laughing when they hugged.

◆   ◆   ◆

"So?" Yohan inquired, casting his charcoal gaze from his mother to Melina.

Both women remained quiet. Aside from Yohan's lone inquiry, the silence in the room was heavy as a morning fog.

Suddenly, Josephine cleared her throat and moved towards the front of the room. "I'll just leave you two alone. Baby this is really something you should dis-cuss with your wife," she said, kissing Yohan's cheek before she all but ran from the room.

Stunned, Melina could barely swallow or blink. From the corner of her eye, she could see Yohan watching her. He was waiting for her to turn and face him. She stood there praying that he'd go after Josephine. It didn't take long though for her to accept the inevitable. This was her burden to bear-alone. In truth, things were really no different now that they had been for the last eight years. Besides, he'd waited all this time for her to talk to him, hadn't he?

Yohan rolled his eyes, tiring of waiting for his wife to speak. He closed the distance between them and came around to face her.

"How much longer, Mel?" his voice grated, its baritone octave rumbling louder in the lofty room.

Melina winced, and then stiffened while a glare darkened her face. "As long as it takes for me to be sure that what I tell you won't send you running off furious after Marc." She said, losing her courage to confess all now that he stood before her.

"I told you he was gone."

"And I wouldn't put it past you to go trying to hunt him down." She said, beginning to share Josephine's fear. In that moment, he appeared absolutely livid.

Yohan's midnight stare sharpened and Melina stilled herself from flinching when he moved close.

"Do you realize, the longer you keep these secrets, the angrier I become?"

Mel's lips thinned. Of course, she could see that without having to hear him say it. His body was drawn taut with an anger that seemed to hover invisibly around him.

Softly, she cleared her throat and fixed him with a pleading expression. "Just promise me that-"

"Hold it," he ordered, shaking his head, "don't ask me to do that. I won't. I won't make you that promise, Meli."

Melina did step back then, watching him as though he were a stranger.

"I'd do anything for you," he swore, pressing his hand to his chest for emphasis. "I'll do anything except promise not to go after Marc."

She bowed her head, able to accept the words that seemed to pain him to speak. "Then promise not to do anything until you hear everything I have to say. Take *real* time to think over it before you let your anger take over," she asked.

Yohan took time to respond. He stroked his jaw while pondering her request and finally met her expectant stare. "Alright. Start talkin'."

Mel ignored the cold shudder that lilted up her spine and began to put space between her and her husband. "Remember what I told you about Johari calling the night after Marc left my hotel room?"

Yohan began to nod when Mel mentioned her cousin. "I remember," he said.

"Three months later the shock of ... your father's subtle threat wore off and I realized I made the biggest mistake of my life by leaving you," she faced him then. "Leaving our marriage and letting Marc win-it almost killed me Han. I don't expect you to believe me but it's the truth," she sniffled and cleared her throat. "Anyway, I decided that I wasn't going to let him win any longer. I was coming home," she said, turning back to stare out over the gorgeous back lawn. "I couldn't stand it anymore and I was going to chuck it all and head back when I stopped to check my PO Box." Her slanting stare took on a far away gleam as she reminisced. "It was almost as if he knew I was coming back that very day."

"Mel?" Yohan called, tilting his head slightly. The absent tone carrying on her voice held a haunting quality.

Mel turned quickly, realizing she'd spoken aloud. "I already told you I suspected Zara could've been on that ship after what you told me. I asked your opinion, but I already knew Marc had taken her."

Yohan's long lashes fluttered, nearly closing over his deep-set eyes. The rage boiled inside him like a living thing. "How?" he managed to ask.

"That day, Zara sent me a letter. I don't know how anyone knew where I was so soon after I left," she smirked and fluffed out her coarse hair. "I hadn't even told my parents. Anyway, there it was lying in my PO Box. Zara never mentioned Marc by name, but after his ... threat everything became crystal clear. What she *did* tell me, was that she was pros-prostituting herself-" Her words broke and she began to cry.

"Son of a bitch," Yohan hissed.

"Said she loved it, that she was being treated very nice."

"'Very nice', she was probably rotting on that slave ship," Yohan pointed out darkly.

Mel swallowed. "That's what I believe. But it was the way she ended her letter that told me I could never go back to you."

Yohan simply folded his arms across his chest and waited.

"In her letter, Zara told me I had to stay away from you or her life would be over."

Her eyes narrowed again, this time Yohan didn't bother to conceal his anger. The heavy arm chair he stood next to was suddenly turned on its side. Then, his anger redirected towards Melina.

"Why the hell didn't you come to me with this?!"

Mel could barely see him through her tears. "Things just happened so fast at the cabin and I-"

"Dammit I'm not talking about Alaska! Why didn't you tell me before? Before you ran off without ever telling me what the hell was really going on!"

Mel was crying frantically now. "I knew Marc would-"

"I'm not afraid of my father, Mel!"

"But I was!" she cried, slapping tears from her face. "I believed and *still* believe he would've killed her."

"Ah Mel, my father used Zara to scare you into doing nothing," he cast off with a wave of his hand. "Damn I wish you had just called his bluff."

"I would never have done that," Mel told him simply.

Yohan shrugged. "And Pop knew it."

The distinctive screech of car tires rang out and all conversation ceased. Yohan and Melina ran out of the living room, arriving on the front porch just in time to see a black Sedan spreading down the white brick driveway leading from the house.

"She wouldn't listen! She just wouldn't listen!" Rita Hotchkiss ranted, her brown face appearing puffy in the wake of extensive crying.

Melina and Yohan joined the hysterical woman on the bottom porch step. "What happened Rita?" Mel asked.

"She wouldn't listen. She just wouldn't ..." Rita continued to moan, as though she hadn't heard Melina's question.

"Miss Rita?" Yohan called, taking both the woman's hands and squeezing them firmly. "Miss Rita, who? Who wouldn't listen? Ma?"

Rita blinked. "She's gone." She told Yohan, looking directly into his eyes.

"But why, Rita?" Mel urged.

"She's had these plans for months. Plans to leave," Rita confided looking away from Melina and Yohan's shocked expressions. "I thought she'd changed her mind after your father left," she glanced at Yohan, and then shook her head. "I guess she hadn't. She ran upstairs and told me to get the suitcases already packed in the closet while she called for the car." Rita quickly explained, her chest heaving frantically beneath the crisp black uniform.

"Miss Rita, where's she going?" Yohan asked, taking the woman's arms in a gentle hold.

Rita shook her head. "I don't know," she whispered, her brown eyes pooling with tears once more. "I'm scared, I'm so scared," she admitted, crying into Yohan's shoulder.

Mel walked over to rub a reassuring hand across Rita's back. "Shh...." She urged.

Rita pulled away. "You two don't understand. Josephine is not a well woman. It was one reason I insisted on staying here with her fulltime instead of coming in each day.

Mel exchanged a quick, uneasy glance with Yohan. "Why was that necessary?" she inquired slowly.

Rita looked toward Yohan as well, before she buried her head. "She tried to kill herself. More than once and now she's gone God knows where with no one to look out for her."

"Han," Mel gasped, growing as unsettled as Rita.

Rita began to tremble and Yohan pulled her closer. "Miss Rita will you be alright here?" he asked, prepared to close the house and take the woman back to her home in the city.

Sniffling softly, Rita managed a nod and cleared her throat. "I'll be fine."

"Can we take you home?" Mel asked.

Rita shook her head. "No child, I'll wait right here. Someone should be here in case she calls," she cast a lingering look back at the house.

"You know you don't have to do that. We'll get on this," Yohan promised her, "We'll find her."

Rita patted his chest. "I know baby, I know. But I need to be here. I'll go crazy with worry at home."

Nodding resolvedly, Yohan kissed her cheek, and then turned away to find his cellular. Mel pulled Rita into a hug.

"You call if you need anything," Mel whispered.

"I will, I will," Rita promised, "I hope they find her," she added, watching Yohan as he spoke on the phone.

Mel nodded. "They will," she promised, then escorted her across the few steps to the front door. "You get inside now and don't worry."

Mel waited for the front door to close behind Rita before allowing her own worry to resurface. She'd known Josephine was upset-so was she. But to run the way she had … Mel shook her head and told herself everything would be fine.

"Let's go."

Forgetting her worry, Mel turned to Yohan. He'd finished his phone conversation and stood watching her with a closed expression.

"Go?" she parroted, glancing towards the house. "But we can't just leave with everything that-"

"We can't do anything from here and we've got a conversation to finish."

The look in Mel's eyes mirrored the surprise in her voice. "You can't be serious. What about your mother?"

Yohan pulled keys from his pocket. "We'll find her, but we need to finish this."

"Why can't we talk here?"

Yohan's smile was not reassuring. "I have a better place in mind."

Mel decided not to argue further. Casting one last look at the house, she shrugged and turned to head for her rented Acura.

"I'll have it sent back to the Montgomery," Yohan offered, extending his hand for her keys.

Stunned that he even knew where she was staying, Melina nodded. Absently, she dropped her car keys into his palm. Her ears filled with the sound of her heartbeat, the instant his hand cupped her elbow. She remained quiet, focusing on the birds singing in the air amidst the rustle of wind in the tree leaves. Unfortunately, the soothing sounds did nothing to diminish the nervous rumbling in her stomach. Finally, she gathered her courage to ask the question screaming inside her head.

"Where are we going?"

Yohan said nothing. He continued to lead her towards the mammoth-sized olive green Hummer; parked diagonally along one side of the wide driveway.

Melina braced herself, refusing to take another step until he gave her an answer.

Accepting her stubbornness, Yohan simply leaned down and neatly drew her across his shoulder. Mel was so stunned, she couldn't even gasp. Opening the passenger side door, Yohan deposited his wife on the seat.

"We're going home," he informed her quietly, then slammed the passenger door shut.

CHAPTER SEVEN

Once Yohan had angled his Hummer into the driveway, Melina just managed to open her door. Beyond that, nothing happened. Her voice had jaunted off for parts unknown and her slanting stare had stretched as wide as it would go. There before her was the house-the home she left eight years ago. The beautiful gray brick dwelling; with its deep porches, man-made pond in the center of a gorgeous horseshoe drive was a place created for comfort. It was the mark of two people who adored being home-alone.

A wave of dizziness overcame Mel as she recalled almost every intimate moment. The days and nights inside the spaciously cozy ten bedroom house, had been filled with more than its fair share of love, laughter and passion.

Her eyes were still devouring the gargantuan trees that provided graceful privacy, when Yohan came round to escort her from the SUV. He was silent as well-knowing how affected she had to be by the sight of the place. He was just as affected. Not a night went by that he hadn't envisioned the day when she'd be there again. Back in his life-as his wife. His lips twisted into a cold smile, they were a far cry from that he acknowledged. There were still secrets remaining between them-secrets he silently admitted he was terrified to hear her reveal. Still; he understood that until they were uncovered, a life-*any* life together would be a vain hope.

A growl of aggravation was forcing its way up inside his chest. Massaging his neck, Yohan closed his eyes and ordered himself to be patient. The last thing he wanted was to frighten her-well more than he already had. As anger-filled as he was toward his father, it would take all his strength to abide by her request that he hear everything she had to say before he flew into rage.

Melina tensed as they approached the front door. They would be there *alone* for hours at least. There would be plenty of time to tell him everything. Even about Crane? A voice inquired. There'd be no interruptions and she could get it all out in one fell swoop.

She knew she wouldn't tell him about Crane. That wouldn't happen, she decided with a resolving smile coming to her mouth. Knowing how on edge he was … in spite of the fact that Marc had disappeared … someone needed to be there. Fernando and Moses would have to be present-anyone aside from just herself. Besides, she wasn't ashamed of the fact that she hadn't the desire or the courage to tell him on her own.

Unfortunately, that only left her with one story to tell and it was just as devastating-maybe more so. Yohan's cellular rang just as he was pushing open the door.

Mel's lashes fluttered close as she celebrated the interruption. She uttered a relieved sign and walked deeper inside the house while he handled the call. Her lips parted as they often did when ever she studied the lofty ceilings that still managed to fill the rooms with a distinct sense of intimacy. She'd missed her home terribly. Here were all the touches-the personal attentions that made a house a home. No matter where she lived nothing-no place would ever instill completeness the way this place did.

"Man, what the hell is this invite from Stef Lyons about?" Moses was asking his youngest brother.

Yohan frowned, glancing across his shoulder at Mel strolling towards the living room. "No idea-I didn't get one, thank God."

Moses uttered a chuckle. "Hmph, not yet. I can't understand why I'd get one. I'm not involved with Ramsey that way."

"You got me, man," Yohan said.

"I got too much on my plate to be attending some stuffy business party anyway."

"So what's up? Anymore news on Pop?" Yohan asked.

Moses signed. "Hell no, it's like the man just fell off the damn face of the earth. Probably just as well anyway."

"Nah. Marc's got too much to pay for." Yohan argued, strolling slowly in the direction he'd seen Melina headed.

"What's that tone about, man? Somethin' else popped off that I need to know about?" Moses questioned.

Yohan's hand clutched reflexively around the thin phone. He couldn't tell him about Zara anywhere but in person. "We need to talk, face to face."

"Just name the time and place, man."

"Later. Right now, I need to tell you about Ma."

"What about her?" Moses asked after brief hesitation.

"Disappeared. According to Miss Rita, she's been plannin' it for months. She says Ma's tried to kill herself ... more than once. I want you to put someone on it. It's probably nothin' to get crazy over-"

"You're right. So you'll understand if I don't waste any of my man hours on it."

Yohan closed his eyes, having expected the reaction. "She's your mother, man," he noted softly.

"Mmm and I'm sure she would've changed that any day of the week."

"Mo-"

"Hell man, don't try to act like she's treated me with anything but contempt and coldness. All because I looked like Marc-what kind of crap is that?"

Yohan had no response.

"I'm sorry," Moses groaned and then laughed shortly as though he couldn't believe he'd gotten so carried away. "Just please forgive me if I'm not all upset and worried because she's run off in some emotional stupor."

"I understand, Mo," Yohan whispered, knowing the hurt and possibly the hate between his brother and mother ran deep. The seeds were possibly planted before he was even born. "Just do what you can, Mo. For me," he urged and then ended the call.

Melina was still inspecting her home-or more accurately, *Yohan's* home. It was clearly a man's lair now. Every square foot was beautiful and dark like him. All the chairs were gorgeous and monstrous-large enough to swallow her. Mel smiled and closed her eyes, admitting that she'd relish being consumed by the exquisite luxury of each cushiony, black armchair, sofa or recliner. She peeked into a den that housed the most impressive movie collection she'd ever seen. One complete wall was stocked floor to ceiling with DVDs. He'd also acquired several older movies which were on reels for the screen and projector she knew he owned.

She looked into the reading room-still the same as she remembered. There were probably only a few more hundred books and magazines littering the place, she acknowledged with a whimsical smile. The room was still full of beanbags and futons. Her contentment settled warm and sweet within her heart in response to the erotic memories that rose to the surface of her mind. Clearing her throat hastily, she hurried from the room before more of the lusty memories rushed forth.

Her tour led her to the ground floor which housed Yohan's gym, sports bar and Rec Room. In spite of their love for privacy, Melina could recall several Saturday afternoons there with Yohan, his brothers and cousins enjoying a strenuous workout session, then drinks and a televised ballgame. How many women would pay good money to see the Ramsey gods sweaty and half-dressed? She often mused.

Her steps slowed as she approached what looked like some sort of punching bag meat rack. There had to be at least eight of the towering black bags hanging from the ceiling. Her gasp resounded in the room as her inspection revealed the slaughtered appearance of the equipment. The stuffing poked out from the various slices in the sturdy material. In some areas there were full sized holes. Unsettled by the grizzly condition of the scene, Melina backed out of the punching bag forest, until she bumped to a stop.

Turning, she found Yohan right behind her and a soft laugh escaped her. "I guess I know what you need for Christmas-new punching bags," she teased. "Lots of frustration to work off, I guess," she cleared her throat.

Yohan's deep-set gaze didn't waver from his wife. "Yeah, I'm frustrated about a lot of things," he said, stepping closer.

Melina managed to retreat only a few steps when he caught her-lifting her high against his broad chest. Shocked, yet instantly aroused by his touch, her lips parted as she watched him. Her reaction gave Yohan the perfect opportunity to kiss her. Deep and forceful, his tongue thrust and caressed, his arms flexed possessively around her minute waist. Melina could scarcely moan amidst the crushing embrace mixed with the savage lunging of his tongue as he carried her deeper into the darkened gym.

Her hands were trapped between their bodies and she could only communicate her need through the desperation in her kiss. Unexpectedly, she felt them drop and she opened her eyes to find that Yohan had settled them to a deep, tattered burgundy armchair in a far corner of the room.

"I thought you wanted to talk?" she asked, when he released her mouth. Her heaving breasts nudged his fingers as he undid the buttons along her blouse.

His dark stare never rose from her chest. "Later," he decided.

The scene progressed at a fevered intensity Yohan practically ripped the blouse off her back, and then proceeded to kiss her out of her bra. His perfect mouth suckled her nipples as he unfastened the bra clasp with expert skill.

Mel's fingers trembled against the chords of his neck while she arched into his touch and cried out. She ground herself against the rigid power below his waist, until he pushed her to stand before him. She felt like a rag doll as he took her out of the stylish trousers and remaining undergarments. Quickly, she was nude-while he remained dressed and continued to pleasure her without shame. His nose outlined the curve of her belly and then tongued her navel while massaging her thighs.

A helpless cry lilted in the air when his hands cupped her bottom and his middle finger entered her from behind. Her next cry was bold and wanton-hungry for whatever he chose to do to her. Yohan would only pleasure her with the scandalous fingering for a few moments longer before depriving her of the touch.

"Han," she sobbed, pounding her fist to his shoulder.

He lifted her high above him and feasted on the now moisture-rich center of her body. At such an angle, Mel vaguely feared the chair would take a tumble, but she was with Yohan Ramsey and the chair was going nowhere. Mel ground into the savage thrusts of his oral kiss. She was so sensitive to everything he did that she could actually feel his tongue rotating deep inside her.

Yohan's low rumbling chuckle filled the gym when he heard the disappointed whimper she uttered. He ended the intimate stroking before she could orgasm.

She should have been limp with unsatisfied need, but her only desire was to have him out of his clothes. Straddling his lap, she kissed herself from his tongue in the midst of removing his shirt. Her fingers splayed across the heavy slabs of muscle in his chest and back. Grazing her nails across his chiseled abs, her fingers curved into the waistband of his pants and she tugged-forcing him deeper into the kiss they shared. Feeling him rise more insistently against her thigh, Mel broke the kiss and focused on undoing his trousers. Once accomplished, she groped for the part of his anatomy she yearned for most of all. She freed him from his boxers and kissed him passionately when he assumed control and lowered her onto his steel length.

Mel let her forehead rest against his, her eyes closed tight in concentration. She felt as though she were experiencing the hypnotic affects of a drug she had no intention of ever giving up. It was true. She couldn't survive losing or leaving him again.

Yohan's fingers left impressions in the flawless dark skin of her hips and back. He held her desperately, as though fearing she'd vanish if he eased his grip. He let his head rest on the back of the armchair and thrust upwards with reckless abandon. Mel increased her speed as she rode him in circular sweeps of her hips, before bouncing up and down along his powerful stiffness. The air mingled with tortured sounds of male desire and feminine cries of delight. When they were spent, they rested on the chair. Their bodies were still connected.

◆   ◆   ◆

Taurus Ramsey was in no mood to charm any of the dozens of female officers and executive assistants who filled the halls of King County correctional facility. With his suave and subtly mesmerizing persona, heavenly features and quietly rough voice, the man had an arsenal of seductive weapons that always provided favorable results. Alas, he felt far from any sort of Casanova that day. For weeks, he'd avoided calls from his father's attorney requesting that he pay a visit. Taurus decided to give in that day simply to have it over and done with.

"Taurus! Good to see you!" David McNeil greeted, grinning broadly while shaking hands with his client's only son. "Thanks for coming, man. It'll mean a lot to Houston."

Taurus's expression was unreadable. "I'm not here to make him feel better," he explained coolly, "I'm here so you'll stop filling my damn answering machine with calls begging me to come visit this bastard."

David cleared his throat and bristled noticeably but managed to maintain an easy smile. "I'm sorry you feel that way, but Houston is still your father."

Taurus's light eyes twinkled mischievously. "Remarks like that only lessen my desire to cooperate."

David nodded, deciding to be thankful for the young man's presence and let the rest be. He led the way into the facility and assisted Taurus with checking in with the guards. Then Taurus headed back alone to see his father.

His attempts at remaining unfazed by the sight of the man dissipated when Houston was right before his eyes. The man looked like only a shell of himself-gaunt, tired and on edge. His calm, usually unfettered demeanor held a blatantly paranoid aura. His eyes were wide as though he were suspiciously surveying his surroundings and every living thing that entered his space.

Taurus couldn't prevent his surprise from showing. After all, his father was always impeccably groomed be he in an office meeting or going to the grocery store. Soft laugher escaped his throat at the thought. As if Houston Ramsey had ever visited a grocery store in his life. Taurus's soft chuckling, caught Houston's ear and he looked up. Happiness replaced the paranoia in his eyes when he saw his only son.

"Taurus," he whispered in an eager tone, rising just slightly from the gray folding chair. He quickly resumed his seat and nodded humbly. "Thank you so much for coming, son."

"Don't get excited. I'm only here to get your lawyer to stop calling."

Houston nodded, the hope in his eyes now mingling with sadness. "I understand, I understand ... so, how are your mother and sister?" he asked, his tone pleasant.

"My mother and sister?" Taurus hissed, enraged that Houston could even speak of them especially to ask such a question as though he had no idea. "Dena is hold up in her house," he said of his sister, "everyone from her family and friends to her employees and the mailman is upset about how withdrawn she's become. As for my mother," he sneered, bracing his hands on the chrome table and fixing his father with a hateful glare, "she could be who knows where. I haven't heard from her in weeks. My guess is she's trying to get as far away from this mess as possible. As for me, I'm on my way out as well. I'm gonna check in on Dena down in Carolina before I leave."

Houston blinked. Obvious concern tightened his haggard face. "I'm losing my family," he noted absently.

"Losing us?" Taurus snapped his handsome features contorted into something sinister. "You never *had* us. You paraded us-trying to make yourself look far better than you were by demanding no less than perfection from the rest of us."

"I'm sorry, son," Houston said, looking as if he knew the apology were pathetic.

Taurus rose to his full height. "Save it. You know, I think about all the times you forced the best out of me-saying you weren't gonna be shamed by your son's inadequacies when it was *me* who should've been saying that to you." Taurus rolled his eyes, folding his arms across the front of his broad, heaving chest. "I should have been talkin' about *your* inadequacies to keep it in your pants-at least around your little girl's friends." He braced his hands on the table again, the chords in his forearms bulged threateningly below the rolled sleeves of his maroon shirt. "If you go near Dena or call me again, I'll kill you."

Houston blinked as though summoning courage to face his enraged child. "I know I don't have a right to expect ... anything from you, but Taurus I need my family. If ever there was a time I need-"

"What you need is to pay for what you've done. Stop hiding behind your law-yers and the loopholes you're praying they can find to dig you out of this crap. As for having us in your corner," Taurus's expression darkened with an almost frightening intensity, "well, I suppose in a place like this a man needs to have a dream, so you hold on to than one. Guard!" he called and soon left the room without looking back.

Shortly following Taurus's departure, David arrived to find his client crying and faced down on the chrome table.

"I'm sorry Houston," David was saying, pushing a handkerchief across the table. "I shouldn't have pushed for this. I knew it wouldn't go well."

"No David, no," Houston sighed, dabbling the kerchief at his face reddened by emotion. "I wanted to see him in spite of his anger."

"But that's the last sort of frustration you need now, further condemnation from your son."

Houston waved his hand. "But he's right. He's right, Dave. I have to pay."

David cleared his throat. "Houston think about what you're saying."

"Call the detectives."

"Houston-"

"*David.* Call them," he urged, his face holding a calm that had been lost for weeks. "It's time I told everyone what really happened to Sera Black."

◆   ◆   ◆

Melina believed she could have relaxed amidst the bubbling water forever. Yohan brought them into the Jacuzzi after the glorious love session in his gym. Now, they reclined in the ten person tub-Yohan was settled against the black por-celain surface with Melina resting on the unyielding muscular expanse of his chest. She sighed long and deep, overwhelmed by pleasure and contentment as Yohan cupped and massaged her breasts. His thumbs grazed her nipples that firmed instantly within the roaring water.

"Are you ready to tell me the rest?" he asked, still weighing her breasts in his palms.

Reluctantly, Mel moved out of the embrace. She turned to face him across the water from the other side of the tub.

Yohan's heavy brows rose. "That bad?" he predicted.

Melina pressed her lips together. "It's very bad," she confirmed.

Folding his arms across his water-slicked chest, Yohan shook his head. "Why are you so afraid of me? To talk to me?" he asked.

Mel smoothed her soaked hair across her shoulder. "I'm not afraid of you. It's what you might do that I'm afraid of." Her slanting black stare narrowed towards the door of the Jacuzzi room. "Those massacred punching bags in your gym ... I'm afraid you'd do the same to Marc."

"So this is *still* about my father?" he asked, thinking-almost hoping it'd been about her ... boss.

"Yes," Mel whispered, drawing her knees to her chin. "I'm so scared you'll do something, something that'd rid us all of Marc yes, but also take you away in the process." Her words silenced as tears pooled her eyes and mingled with the moisture already present on her face from the steam of the water in the tub.

Yohan offered his hand, pulling her close when she accepted. Mel clung to him-almost desperately. Her face rested near the crook of his neck. Then, she began to speak.

CHAPTER EIGHT

"I finished my last two years of high school in China," Mel began, her chin still resting on Yohan's shoulder while she stared blankly across the room. "We'd heard about Zara and I begged my parents to come back so I could be with Johari." She smiled as the memories returned. "The first few weeks were so great. All Jo could talk about was this great party Quay threw at the end of every year since they'd been in high school. I think much of her excitement had to do with Moses. I think he was supposed to be going to the party. Anyway, this year would be special because it'd be the last party and was going to be in a hotel downtown. Apparently, Quay had a reputation for giving great hotel parties."

Yohan chuckled. "Yeah *great*. Half of 'em were so wild, I think the trouble he got into because of them outweighed all the fun he had."

Melina smirked. "Well, I couldn't wait and the party was definitely lots of fun. I had the best time," she sighed, her dark eyes twinkling with remembrance when she looked into her husband's gorgeous face. "I think I would've had an even better time if I'd met *you* that night," she whispered.

Yohan pressed a kiss to her cheek. "I'd gone off on a fishing trip with the friends I'd be attending Hampton with in the fall," he recalled.

Melina smiled. "I'm so glad you decided to attend Hampton that fall," she said, referring to the day they met on the college campus. "Best day of my life when we met and so were all the days that followed," she admitted in a dreamy tone.

Yohan's entrancing stare narrowed as he leaned in to brush his mouth across hers. Melina heard herself moan above the bubbling water and returned his kiss eagerly when it deepened. Too soon, he was pulling away and Mel knew it was time to continue her story.

"When the party started to wind down, Jo and I went to get ice cream at this shop a few blocks away. We were going to talk a little more, maybe drive around for a while. Then I remembered I'd left my jacket and we went back to the hotel. I was about to knock, but the door was cracked so I just went on in and headed to the bedroom where all the things had been placed." Her expression softened more. "I probably would've gotten it and gotten right out of there, but I saw someone in the bed. Quay." She said, humor filling her slanting stare. "Stark naked in the middle of the bed and holding a bottle-a quarter filled bottle of gin. Anyway, I ran over and threw a sheet over him. I was on my way out when I heard Sera's voice." Melina winced, feeling Yohan's arms flex about her waist. "She was walking into the room or letting someone in, I don't know which. I was sure *she* knew who it was because she was laughing. I waited for them to move on before I came out." Her expression tightened and she bowed her head as if trying to ward off sickness.

"I was on my way out the door when I heard her scream and-and there was a thud-like something had hit the floor. I remember I wanted to run, but I had to see and-oh Han," she breathed, her voice shaking too badly to continue.

"Shh," Yohan soothed, pulling her into a tight squeeze, "tell me," he urged, "tell me all of it Mel. I'll be damned if I let you continue to keep carrying this on your own."

Mel nodded, wanting to share the rest and dried her tears with the backs of her hands. "Sera and Houston were on the floor-he was raping her."

Yohan eased his hands up and down her arms which were riddled with goose-flesh in spite of the heat. "Love, you know they were having an affair," he interjected softly.

Melina shook her head. "She was trying to scream and he was holding his hand over her mouth. He was raping her." She swore, pinning Yohan with a defiant gaze.

"I believe you," he whispered against her temple and relishing the silence before asking the one question he didn't want an answer to. "Meli ... what does this have to do with my father?"

"Sera opened the door to two men that night. The other was Marc. He stood there watching the entire thing."

Yohan slumped against the tub. "Did he?" he couldn't finish.

Mel closed her eyes. "I don't know if he touched her. I don't think so. I got the hell out of there. By the time I was in Jo's car and we were speeding out of the parking lot, Sera was on the ground." Her voice broke on the last word and her tears would not be silenced then.

"I hated myself for running!" she raged amidst her tears. "I hated myself. I still do! I should've done something! I should've-"

"Stop, stop," Yohan ordered, giving her a tiny shake. "You didn't do a damn thing wrong. Do you hear me? Mel?"

"I should've told," she chanted, "I should've said something. But I never did. I *never* did. I was too much of a coward, too afraid."

"Mel?" Yohan called, propping his thumbs below her chin to make her look up at him. "Did they see you?" he asked, Melina blinked. "When I turned to leave the room, my elbow hit the wall and they looked up. Marc looked right at me." She shuddered and moved closer to Yohan. "I had no idea who they were. I'd never met Houston and-well, the first time I met Marc was when you were introducing me to him as your wife."

Yohan whispered a curse. It all made sense now-perfect sense. Melina and Marc's intense dislike and unease around each other. God, she'd been living in fear practically since the day they married. They may never have married had he taken her to meet his family during the years they were dating. Thank God he'd followed his mind and kept her away from them-from Marcus.

"When I found out who they were," she was saying, "I knew no one would ever believe two members of the Ramsey family would be involved in something so vicious."

"And this is what you were coming to tell me that night." Yohan figured.

Mel managed a wavering smile. "Brenda said you were in a meeting. I didn't care. I didn't want to talk at your office anyway. So I left the note ... Marc got to it before you-"

"Son of a bitch," Yohan muttered, frowning as he remembered.

Melina cleared her throat. "I got a hotel room and rehearsed how I was going to tell you all this while I waited for you to get there," she shrugged. "Imagine my surprise when I opened the door to Marc instead of you."

Again, Yohan's arms tightened around his wife's slim frame. "Did he hurt you?"

Mel cupped his cheek. "Not the way you mean."

"He used Johari and Zara to keep you quiet."

Mel could only nod.

Yohan's magnificent dark features were drawn tight with the anger roiling inside him. His murderous emotions quelled when he heard Melina sobbing. He rocked her slow and assured her everything would be alright.

"I'm sorry Yohan, I'm so very sorry," she cried into his chest. "I ruined us, I ruined us …"

"Shh … stop Mel. Stop. Forget this, you hear?" he ordered, tightening his hold about her. "It's done. It's over."

"I ruined us because I was a coward."

Yohan closed his eyes. He felt her pain as though they were one and realized what he had to do. Somehow he would convince her that she'd handled this as best she could. He had to be there for her-to love her and give her the security she thought she never had from him. He would focus on Melina and only Melina. As for his father, Yohan knew the next time he saw Marcus Ramsey, he would kill him.

◆   ◆   ◆

The following week flew by in a blur. During that time, Melina dove into the gallery show with a renewed sense of purpose. Having told Yohan about Marc's role in Sera Black's death, lifted such a weight she'd never felt more at peace. Of course, the fact that she tried not to think of that one last secret she harbored, made things far easier as well. Additionally, Yohan had promised a long weekend and Mel couldn't wait for the chance to enjoy more 'alone time'.

"Lisa! I want these press releases out by Thursday!" Mel called as she issued orders to her staff that were scattered across the conference room. "Let's start to whet their appetites with just a little info and see if that generates a buzz. Casey, don't leave today before you get Faith Merel on the phone. I want Josh on her show ASAP!" she said, referring to the new artist they were featuring at the opening.

"Mel?"

"Yeah Kate?" Melina spoke to her assistant in the general direction she recalled seeing the speaker phone.

"You have a guest waiting in your office."

Mel cursed and glanced at her watch. "Did I miss an appointment?"

Kate giggled. "No, no she's an old friend. Tykira Ramsey?"

Shrieking, Melina dropped the folder she held and raced out of the conference room and into her office. Ty's full laughter filled the room when Mel wrenched her into a hug. They embraced for the longest time-happy tears mingling with their laughter. The two hadn't seen each other since they'd both graduated college.

"Why didn't you tell me you were coming?!" Mel cried, kissing Ty's cheek again.

Ty's eyes were filled with happy tears as Melina kept her bent low in the hug. "I wanted to surprise you."

"It's so good to see you." Mel whispered, pulling away to search her friend's face. "It's been so long."

"Too long," Ty emphasized, folding her arms across the front of the lavender button down sweater she wore with a matching duster. "You're heading up a gallery and"-

"*You're* married. To Quaysar Ramsey no less!" Mel blurted, more laughter filling her voice. "You finally got that fool to wise up."

Ty shake her head. "It wasn't easy, but he's shaped up nicely," she sighed, joining in when Mel laughed aloud.

Arm in arm, the two friends took seats next to one another on the butter cream suede sofa in the office.

"Quest and Quay married …" Mel closed her eyes. "I can imagine the hearts that broke all over Seattle at *that* upset," she teased.

Ty playfully flicked a lock of hair across her shoulder. "Somebody had to settle down those two."

Mel's brows rose naughtily. "Mmm … I hear you. So what's Quest's wife like?"

"Mick? Oh, she's great. It's amazing how incredible they are together. They're about to have a baby. Due the end of July." Ty shared.

"That's wonderful." Mel sighed and shook her head. "The first Ramsey grandchild-lots of pressure."

Ty's brown eyes narrowed secretively. "Well, hopefully Quay and I can help take off some of that pressure."

Mel's mouth fell open as her eyes fell to Tykira's almost nonexistent waistline. "No," she breathed.

More laughter erupted when Ty realized how Melina had misunderstood. "We're adopting! Twins!"

"Ty …" Melina whispered, pulling her friend into a rocking embrace. "I'm so happy for you … you guys are gonna be great parents." The happiness in her ebony gaze misted over with something more solemn. "Yohan and I would probably have a little one of our own if …"

Ty eased back, tugging on a lock of Mel's coarse hair. "How are things going with you being back and all?"

Mel looked up and blinked as though trying to keep tears at bay. "Oh Ty … things are incredible, beautiful, passionate, messy and scary. Does that sum it up pretty good?"

"Mel, do you need someone to talk to?" Ty asked concern evident on her dark, pretty face.

"How much time do you have?" Mel asked, with a lopsided grin.

"As long as you need."

"Okay …" Mel groaned, reclining on the sofa to fix her friend with a challenging stare. "How about we start with my telling you that Marcus isn't Yohan's father."

Tykira knew she would've dropped to the floor had the sofa not been supporting her.

◆   ◆   ◆

"Did you tell Fernando? County?"

"No, not-"

"No?! What the hell are you waiting on?!"

"Calm down, just calm down," County urged, switching her receiver to the other ear as she rolled her eyes over Mick's outburst. "Please, I don't need you going into labor over the phone. I just had to tell someone about Stefan and Fernando was definitely *not* the best choice."

"I'd have to disagree with you there," Mick retorted.

County huffed. "Please, telling Fernando could've only resulted in him heading off to jail and Stefan heading off the morgue. I'm sure the jackass was just testing me. You know how they do-trying to see how loyal I am to his boy."

"Oh my goodness," Mick groaned, holding her forehead against her palm. "What the hell happened to all your common sense? How could you think something so stupid when he did so much scheming to have you find out Fernando owned half of Dark Squires?"

County was silent.

"You shouldn't underestimate him." Mick warned as though she hadn't noticed. "Quest told me how he always got a bad vibe from Stef. He sounds like a dangerous man."

"He said he stopped by to deliver an invite to some business party out in Seattle."

"Yeah Quest got one of those but he said he didn't have a clue to what it was about. Are you coming?" Mick asked.

County shrugged while reclining in her desk chair. "Fernando asked me to and since it's so close to your Fourth of July bash, it'll give us longer to visit."

"Yaaay!" Mick cried, the flaring sleeve of her powder blue swing blouse flying when she waved her hand in the air. "County seriously though keep your guard up around Stef," she warned, becoming serious again. "If he tries another thing *I'll* go to Fernando," she threatened.

County bumped the toe of her petal pink pumps against the edge of her desk and smiled at friend's concern. "Thanks girl," she whispered, reluctantly moving to a less relaxing position in her chair. "I guess I'll talk to you-"

"Wait, wait," Mick said, whispering the second time. "What news of the book?"

"Jeez Mick," County hissed, massaging her neck beneath the collar of her cream blouse. "Can we have *one* conversation without you bringing that up?"

Michaela rolled her eyes. "Can you at least tell me if you've settled on another author?"

"No. We haven't."

"Why?"

"Dammit, you know why." County snapped, standing behind her desk. "No one has your flare. No one writes like you. It takes a special writer to bring true excitement to those biographies."

Since little prevented Mick from tearing up those days, her emotions elevated over County's praise. "Thanks girl."

"Oh hush, it's true," County said and then shrugged. "But there's no sense in crying over it now. Quest won't allow you to touch the story and I can't say that I blame him."

"Well, what if-?" Mick silenced the question when her husband walked into the den. "Um listen County, I'll talk to you later alright?"

"Sounds good. Love you."

"Love you too," Mick said, kissing into the phone before she hung up.

"How's County doin'?" Quest asked, while standing at the message desk and shuffling through mail.

"Great."

"You called?"

"She did."

"Why?"

"To discuss the barbeque."

Quest nodded, still focused on the mail. "You sure you'll be up for that? The baby comes in July, remember?"

Mick's amber gaze widened as she clapped both hands to her face. "Nooo," she wailed. "You're kidding. I forgot all about the baby."

Quest shook his head and chose not to respond.

"I'll be fine." Mick said, setting the cordless to its cradle before folding her arms atop her belly. "I can't write. Hell, the least I can do is have a party in my own damn house."

This time, Quest tossed aside the mail. His gorgeous gray black stare was narrowed and probing as he watched his wife.

"Forget it," Mick ordered, not allowing the haunting intensity of his eyes to rile her. "Just because you've issued these rules doesn't mean I have to like 'em."

Quest leaned against the message desk and eased his hands inside his slate green trousers. "Can't you at least-in the *smallest* way possible-see my point?"

"I see your point, but *my* point is that it's unfair of you to ask me to give up something I did years before I ever met you."

"Did I ever ask you to stop writing?"

"No."

Quest's broad shoulders rose in a lazy shrug. "Well then, feel free to write. Write 'til your heart's content," he stood and grabbed his mail from the desk. "Just stay away from anything that has to do with this family," he tacked on in a soft voice.

"Ugggh!" Mick raged, clutching fistfuls of the glossy curls that framed her lovely round face. "Do I have to remind *you* that *long* ago you promised you were over this thing about me writing the book?"

"I remember," he said, now making sure the battery was charged on his cellular, "but that was before I found out how low and ruthless my uncles really were," he eased the phone into his pocket. "And it was before you were pregnant with my child." He looked up and winked. "*Our* child," he rephrased. "Now get over this Michaela, because there's no way in hell that I'll be changing my mind."

Mick rolled her eyes, but didn't think of resisting when Quest pulled her close. She shuddered as much from desire as anger at herself when she responded to his kiss. A lilting cry escaped her lips when he deepened the slow thrusting of his tongue.

"I'll be home early," he promised, making no move to go as he continued to kiss her. When Mick's cries gained volume and she began to participate more eagerly, he pulled away; tugging on her curls before he left the room.

Mick grabbed a pillow from an armchair and threw it against the door.

◆   ◆   ◆

Tykira still sat in a stunned stupor once Mel was done baring every secret she had. "I can't believe you survived the last eight years carrying all this on your own," she marveled.

Mel pushed her thick hair back from her face and smiled wearily. "I'm sure you can understand why I had to keep it?"

"How could Josephine just leave you to deal with this?"

"Aw Ty," Mel sighed, "Josephine's always been terrified and now she's just too far gone to even think rationally."

Ty leaned back on the sofa and crossed her legs. "You know Yohan has to be told."

"I'm too scared of what he might do," Mel confessed, rubbing her hands along the sleeves of her black linen blouse. "I feel like a fool for saying that, but I just don't know if I can tell him on my own."

Ty nodded, tapping a nail to her chin as she concentrated. "What about Fern and Moses-they should be there anyway," she suggested.

Mel nodded. "I thought about that and then I remembered that they've always hated Marc-probably more than Yohan. They'd back him in whatever he decided to do to Marc. Especially Moses."

Ty expelled a deep breath. "When Moses finds out about Zara ... Do you think he ever suspected? Maybe that's why he broke up with Johari?"

Melina focused on her view from the windows. "I don't know, but I'd feel much better with a cooler head in the room."

"Well we definitely can't go to Quay."

"I was thinking of Quest."

Ty nodded at the idea. "I don't know anyone cooler," she winced. "I don't know Mel-this is a tense situation. I mean, Quest stood right there and watched Quay almost beat Marc to death at Mick's shower."

Melina groaned and buried her face in her hands. "Someone else needs to be there Ty. Yohan is going to go crazy when he finds out. Marc being his dad is the only thing restraining him."

"Maybe we need another opinion."

Confused, Mel shrugged. "Who?"

Ty grabbed her purse and stood. "Come with me."

◆   ◆   ◆

Moses and Fernando met at their younger brother's house to discuss their father. This time, it was Yohan who came with the answers. Moses and Fernando listened quietly. Then Yohan and Fernando watched Moses to judge how he would react to the news about Zara.

"She's alive?" Moses breathed, as though he couldn't believe it. He stood, pressing his hand against the gray skull cap covering his bald head. He was frowning as though struggling to absorb what he'd learned.

"According to the letter Mel got, it seems we were wrong to think she was dead." Yohan said.

Still frowning, Moses went to stand at the short brick wall that lined the patio where they talked.

"Johari has to be told," Fernando decided, before his translucent brown gaze slanted toward his brother. "Unless Mel already did?"

Yohan shook his head. "No."

"Moses?" Fernando called. He had to speak his brother's name several times before the man tuned in.

"Maybe it should come from you," Yohan suggested.

Moses looked as though he didn't recognize either of his brothers. "She'd never listen to a thing I have to say."

"This is her sister we're talkin' about," Fernando argued.

Yohan nodded. "She'd listen to anyone who had word about her."

Moses grimaced. "Not me."

"Mo-"

"I said no!" He thundered, his fist smashing into a ceramic planter set atop the wall. "Dammit," he hissed, shooting Yohan a smile. "Sorry man."

"That's why I don't have company, too destructive." Yohan teased, clapping a hand to his brother's shoulder and urging him to take a seat.

"I never told y'all why I broke up with Johari, did I?"

Yohan and Fernando exchanged glances and shrugged.

"We always thought she was the one who dumped you?" Yohan said.

Moses nodded. "That's because I made sure she would. I knew I had to the day I turned twenty one and Pop gave me my ... present," he stood and shoved both hands into the pockets of his sagging jeans. "A trip to that very boat you were so lucky to find, brotha," he shared.

Fernando stood. "You knew?"

Moses closed his eyes. "I didn't know what it really was-with the underage girls and all. I knew there was prostitution, drugs … and that Pop was right in the thick of it and reaping *all* the benefits while Ma was home dyin' a little every day because of him and growing to hate me more in the process."

"Man, she never meant-"

"No Fern," Moses said, waving his hand for silence. "I'm the splitting image of that fool and she treated me like I was him every day of my life." The expression on his dark handsome face was sinister with hate. "I didn't want Johari involved with a family like ours. I was starting to believe everything Ma said when I fouled up-which seemed like every day. Perhaps I was more like Marc than I realized … I didn't know and I'll be damned if I wanted Johari to find out. You know what I mean," he said to Yohan-who nodded. "I would've done anything to keep her away from this." Moses added.

Fernando smoothed his hand across his beard for several moments before he spoke. "She still has the right to know her sister's alive."

"'Course she does," Moses agreed, his voice holding a strange quality. "She not only has the right to know, but she has the right to see her."

Fernando looked over at Yohan; who stood from the lounge chair he occupied.

"What are you sayin' man?" Yohan asked.

Moses leaned against the patio wall once more. "I'm going to do everything in my power to make that happen."

◆　　　◆　　　◆

Michaela couldn't have been more surprised when she fluffed her curls and whipped open the front door to find Tykira on the porch. She was thrilled to finally meet Melina. After Ty made the introductions, the two hit it off like they'd been friends for ages. For a while, the three women sat chatting about this and that. Much of the conversation revolved around Mick's mother-to-be-status and Ty and Quay's adoption of Wake Robinson's twin sons. At last, Ty came to the real point of her visit.

Needless to say, Mick was as shocked as Ty had been once the secrets were shared. Of course, Mick's highly inquisitive nature wouldn't allow her to sit in a stupor for long. Eventually, her mind flooded with questions. Her only regret was she didn't have a recorder handy to capture the entire conversation.

"Has Josephine always known that Yohan belonged to another man?" Mick asked her eyes wide as they fixed on Mel who nodded.

"She's always known."

"And he lived in Savannah?"

"Mmm hmm with his wife."

Mick rubbed her tummy with quick strokes she was so enraptured by the story. "Well? Who is he?"

"My boss," Mel said, getting up to fix herself another glass of iced tea. "Crane Cannon."

"'Scuse me?"

"Crane Cannon, the man I went to work for in Memphis. He didn't know who I was when we met," she told Mick.

"Hmph, she's as shocked as I was," Ty mused, watching as Mick shook her head in wonder.

Michaela; however, wasn't as much shocked as she was stumped. She'd heard the name Crane Cannon before but she had no idea where. "And you're wanting Quest there when you tell Yohan about his father?" she asked, turning back to Mel and Ty.

Melina sent Ty an uneasy look, then smiled at Mick. "We know he's got issues with Marc too, but we need muscle in addition to a cool head. Quest may be our only choice." She said with a shrug.

"Is it at all possible that you could be overreacting?" Mick asked, inching forward on the sofa she occupied. "I mean, given the way Yohan feels about Marc, he may be happy about this, you know?"

"Mick, Yohan as much as told me that the *only* thing keeping him from going after Marc is the fact that he's his father." Mel's slanting gaze held no trace of doubt. "Mick, he's not bluffing. I think he'd kill Marc and worry about the consequences later."

"And we can't let that happen," Ty, trailing both hands through her lengthy tresses. "Yohan's too good a person to ruin his life over a piece of trash like Marcus Ramsey."

"Exactly," Mick said, pushing herself off the sofa just as her guests rushed over to help. "I know Quest will do whatever he can. I'll talk to him."

Mel slapped her hands to her thighs. "The only question is when."

"Probably after Stefan Lyon's has his meeting. Maybe you and Yohan could come out to the house?"

Twin expressions of joy illuminated Melina and Tykira's faces. They hugged Mick and thanked her heartily before heading out. Mick escorted them to the front door and leaned against the polished oak when it closed behind them.

"Crane Cannon," she whispered, "where have I heard your name before?"

CHAPTER NINE

"This calls for a celebration. Dinner, maybe a party ... no dinner-you, me, Mick, Ty-"

"Q, hold up man. It's not a done deal yet," Quay tried to calm down his brother who was ecstatic over the news of the adoption.

Quest waved off his twin's words of caution. He strolled the main room of their office suite, stroking his jaw as he contemplated ways to celebrate. "I think dinner out somewhere is best. Someplace where we can all kick back for a few hours. Maybe a place with dancing and live music."

Quay laughed. Usually, *he* was the one jumping off the walls when the smallest reason to celebrate presented itself. He loved Quest more then for being so happy for him.

"Fernando said County was coming out in a few days-they could join us. Hell, we could invite Yohan and Mel too," Quest went on.

Quay shook his head. "I still can't believe those two found their way back to one another after all these years."

"Yeah," Quest acknowledged, a smile spreading across his face as he thought about his cousins. Then, he fixed his brother with an adoring look. "What I can't believe is that you're about to become a father."

Quay closed his eyes, looking as though he couldn't believe it either. "It feels unreal Q, you know what I mean?" He asked, smiling when Quest nodded. "Unreal in the best way," he added, and then sent his twin a sly grin. "Is this how you feel?"

Quest rubbed his hands together. "Everyday. Nice, huh?"

"Damn right," Quay replied without hesitation.

"So how's Ty?" Quest asked, leaning against the back of a sofa and rolling up the sleeves of his heather blue dress shirt. "She jumpin' off the walls too?"

"Hell yeah, I think we're vying for the title of who can be more excited," Quay teased, before his dark eyes clouded with memory. "I guess we've both been thinking if things hadn't gone so wrong for us before, we'd have a family of our own by now," he said, easing both hands into the pockets of his butter rum slacks while strolling towards his brother. "We get to live our dream and do what's right at the same time."

Quest's left-dimpled grin appeared. "God is good."

Quay nodded. "All the time," he agreed chuckling when he and his brother hugged.

"I'm proud of you, man," Quest said.

"I'm proud of myself," Quay sighed.

◆   ◆   ◆

Yohan's already dim office appeared darker and mellower with the drapes drawn and the sound of the central air system cooling the room. On one of the long, overstuffed black sofas, Yohan held his wife a willing captive. They cuddled and kissed slowly. Melina was having a delightful time, but pushed against her husband's chest when he began to unbutton her blouse.

"We can't …" she mused, arching closer when his lips suckled her earlobe. "I have to um … get back to the gallery. Yohan I have so much to do," she said, gasping when her blouse parted and cool air brushed her bare skin. "Yohan please …"

"Mmm hmm," he agreed, his tongue tracing the shape of her breasts covered with the lace of her bra. Then, he expertly unsnapped the front hook and buried his handsome face in the valley between. His thumb brushed repeatedly across one nipple as his lips and tongue began to feast upon the other. The intermitted nibbling and suckling almost drove Mel crazy with desire.

"I really do need to get back."

"And I really do need *you*."

Mel trailed her fingers through his gorgeous hair and winced at the pleasure of his mouth on her body. "You have me every night."

"And it's not enough," Yohan complained in a growling tone. He settled his massive frame more securely between her thighs. "It hasn't been nearly enough."

Mel refused to give in and pressed more firmly against his chest. "Come on now, enough. I'm serious," she tried to sound firm.

Yohan groaned, bathing her nipples with one final stroke before straightening her bra and her poppy colored blouse.

Mel smiled and would have thanked him, but his mouth crashed down upon hers and he proceeded to kiss her deeply. A new wave of desire filled her as she suckled his tongue amidst its heated thrusts. His fingers grazing the edge of her panties beneath her khaki skirt provided an unexpected yet incredible sensation.

"I said no," she pleaded, this time bumping her fists against his chest.

In response, Yohan captured both her wrists in one hand and held them above her head. Of course, the positioning moved her breasts to a more prominent and vulnerable location.

A devilish smile sharpened his fantastic looks. "Damn, why didn't I think of this before?" he asked.

Melina braced against his hold, but couldn't hide her smile. "This isn't fair."

"But it's fun."

"Mmm," Mel replied, when their lips connected in another kiss. She arched into his chiseled torso when his fingers disappeared beneath her panties and sank into the wealth of moisture he found there. Eventually, she broke the kiss while crying out her pleasure as his thumb and middle finger assaulted the most sensitive areas of her womanhood. The phone ringing on the table closest to the sofa they occupied could barely be heard above her moans.

"Yohan," she called when he clearly made no indication of going to answer.

His perfect teeth fastened to her earlobe again as his thrusts grew deeper inside her. The phone rang three more times.

"Don't you have voice mail?" Mel snapped, now agitated that anything was interfering with her pleasure.

Yohan continued to suckle on her earlobe. "Must be the private line."

Mel cursed when her better judgment overruled her desire. "There could be word on your mother," she cautioned.

Yohan continued to enjoy his wife until her words began to penetrate his logic. Frustrated, he released her wrists and snatched the receiver from its cradle. "Yeah?" he practically snarled into the receiver.

"Yohan? Baby is that you?"

"Yeah," he said, his voice softening. "Yes ma'am. Sorry Miss Rita," he said, ignoring Mel's *I-told-you-so* expression.

"I'm so sorry to bother you at work, baby."

Yohan smiled and moved to sit on the sofa. "That's no problem, Miss Rita and no bother. Everything alright?"

"Well, I wanted you to know that your mother called."

Again, Yohan glanced at Mel. "She did?"

"Yes, she's at a clinic in California."

"Clinic?"

"Yes, it's a type of retreat. She'd talked about going down there once before, but it was always understood that I'd be going with her," Rita explained. "Anyway, it's water under the bridge. Just wanted you to know she was alright, baby."

"Thank you Miss Rita. Thanks for letting me know. If you talk to her, ask her to call?"

"I sure will, Sweetie. Kiss Mel for me, you hear?"

"Yes ma'am … yes ma'am … I will. Bye."

"See?" Mel challenged, when Yohan put down the phone.

"Ma's at some retreat in California. She and Miss Rita talked about it a while back."

Mel nodded, happy there'd been word on Josephine. Still, the news was bittersweet. She was thrilled to know her mother-in-law was safe. Unfortunately, with Josephine gone, it pretty much sealed her fate that telling Yohan about his true paternity would be *her* responsibility.

"Thank God," Yohan groaned, bracing his elbows on his knees and burying his face in his hands. "I won't have to ask Moses to help look for her again."

"You say that like he wouldn't do it."

"Hmph, I have my doubts that he would."

Mel fixed him with a curious expression. "But she's his mother … Yohan?"

"Listen," Yohan said, turning to take one of her hands in both of his. "Mo and our mother have drama that dates back to his childhood. The fact that he does and has *always* looked so much like Pop has made his life pure hell with her."

Mel sat straighter on the sofa. "How?" she whispered.

Yohan shook his head. "It's not worth goin' into," he decided, and then forced a refreshing smile to his face. "At least he's got another crusade to keep him busy. He's gonna find your cousin. He says he's gonna find Zara."

◆   ◆   ◆

David McNeil had stopped taking notes long ago. He was thankful that the recorder was still doing its job. Hearing the tale told by his client just then in the cold confines of the cement-walled room, almost gave him a case of the shivers. "Are you sure about this Houston?" David asked for the tenth time since his client began the confession.

Houston laced his fingers together atop the chrome table. "Do you really think my brother concealed *all* that evidence because he loves me so much?"

David massaged his forehead in hopes of preventing pain from forming at his temple. "An admission like that won't do a damn thing to help your case."

Houston grimaced, his honey-toned face appearing gaunt and ashen. "I don't care about that. Seeing Taurus ... the look in his eyes-cold; no feeling ... no love. You know the sad thing Dave?" he asked his attorney, wiping away tears with the sleeve of his orange jumpsuit. "He's always looked at me that way I just never saw it before. There's no way I could ever *make up* for all I've done, but I can at least own up to it."

"And what about your brother?" David asked, as he stood from the table. "If Marc's as dangerous as you say aren't you rattled about calling him out?"

A smile that was cold and hate filled, yet desperate at once came to Houston's face. "The man stood and watched me rape his daughter. No David. No way in hell am I afraid to call him out."

◆   ◆   ◆

A few days later, Michaela was hugging County after she and Fernando arrived at her home that afternoon. Quest took his cousin to the den for drinks while Mick caught up with her best friend. Once the small talk was out of the way, Mick made sure her husband was out of ear shot.

"Now let's talk about the book," she decided, pushing her hands into the side pockets of her yellow housedress.

Contessa rolled her eyes. "Not this again," she breathed "don't do this to me Mick," she begged, pulling off her white open-toed heels as she headed for the living room.

Mick wasn't about to give up. "I want in."

"I'm not discussing this."

"Count-"

"Shut it." County urged, with a raised hand and a furious glare at her friend. "What the hell am I gonna say to Quest when your name shows up on the front of a book he forbids you to write?"

Mick extended her hands in a pleading gesture. "If you'd just let me tell you-"

County raised both hands then. "Save it. I don't even want to know how you plan to make this happen." She softened in response to the disappointment on Michaela's face. "Don't worry girl, the book will be well written and well produced. I promise it'll make both you and Johnelle Black proud."

Mick blinked and stood staring at Contessa with a closed expression plastered on her face.

"Oh God," County gasped, jumping off the sofa. "It's time, isn't it? It's time, you're going into labor aren't you?" she panicked.

"No," Mick hissed, catching her friend by the belt of her red sundress before she could run off to Quest. "No I'm fine," she said before turning away.

"Then what is it, dammit?" County demanded, not liking the look of Mick muttering to herself.

Michaela thrust one hand through her curls and held it there. "I know who he is. Oh no ... County I know who he is."

◆   ◆   ◆

Melina woke with a jerk and found herself alone in the spacious bed she'd shared with Yohan every night since the first day she stepped foot back inside their home. This, however, was not the room they'd shared as man and wife, but a guest room. Something wouldn't let her step inside the master bedroom suite and she loved Yohan even more for not pushing her to do so.

Now, in the wee hours of the morning, she woke confused by the eerie silence and the fact that he was not lying next to her. She shivered, acknowledging her nude state. But Yohan would have her in bed no other way. It had become customary to feel her most intimate parts ache with the sweetest pain once they'd reached the conclusion of a lovemaking session.

"Han?" she called out to the darkened room, not surprised to receive no response. Concerned, she grabbed his T-shirt that had been tossed across the bench at the foot of the bed and pulled it on as she left the room.

The house was dark with the exception of the tiny track lights which were embedded into the carpet lining the hallway and staircase. She knew he'd ventured down there, but didn't call out as she made her way to the first floor. The living room sat just off from the staircase and she checked there first, spotting him the moment she stepped into the spacious area.

His nude frame was outlined before one of the tall windows where he stood-staring past the spotless panes. His arms were folded across his massive chest while Melina watched, uncertain of whether to disturb him.

"Come over here," he said, taking the decision from her hands.

"You okay?" Mel asked, as she ventured closer on cautious steps. She moved behind him encircling her arms about his waist and smiling when she felt the tension leave his body. "Better?" she asked.

"Much."

"Wanna talk?"

"Do you?"

Thankful for the darkness; and the fact that she stood behind him, Mel knew her surprise at his tone was effectively masked. "What do you mean?" she lightly probed.

Yohan didn't respond straightaway. He admired the darkened landscape a moment longer, before turning to sit on the window sill. He pulled her close, his hand rising to brush her jaw. "Do you even understand how well I know you? I guess it surprises me too, considering how much time has passed between us." His fingers traced her collarbone, moving down to cup her hip. "How well I know every inch of you." He went on, caressing the small of her back when such soothing, massaging strokes that her most achy parts responded.

"And how well I can read your reactions," he added, his deep set eyes finally coming to rest on her face.

"Exactly what are you getting at, Han?" Mel asked her words breathless with a nervous laughter.

Yohan cupped her bottom in both his hands, and then gripped her thighs. "I have the strongest feeling you're still keeping something from me."

Mel pressed her lips together, her slanted stare flickering past the windows. "Why would you think that?" she asked.

"We've been enjoying this," he noted, glancing around the living room, "being together after so long. I've been happy about it, have you?"

Frowning now, Mel brushed the back of her hand across his cheek. "Of course I have. Do you doubt that?"

"No," he assured her with a slow shake of his head, "but in spite of all that happiness-in your eyes and your face I see fear. Not always, just every now and then I glimpse it; sitting like a lone star against a black sky."

Mel forced a laugh over his assessment. "Han-"

"I don't like it," he said. "I don't like it one bit."

"Why are you doing this?" she whispered, bending a little to look directly into his dark eyes. "There's no reason for you to think this way-not now not when things are so nice."

Yohan rose to his full height and squeezed her hands to his chest. "Just so we understand each other Meli, my anger growing is the only thing you're accomplishing by keeping anything else from me."

Mel forced laughter past her throat. "You're really fishing!" she teased, determined to veer from a far too dangerous topic; at least until she had back up. "You're upsetting yourself unnecessarily," she said and linked her arms about his neck. "I don't want to waste time at odds with each other. We've been apart too long for that." Her head tilted as she followed the trail her nails grazed along his neck and chest. "Come back to bed," she urged.

Yohan's desire mixed with anger to produce an explosive match. A second later, his mouth came crashing down on hers. A rough sound rumbled deep in his throat amidst the feverish thrusts of his tongue. The kiss was intoxicating and seeking in its possessive intensity.

"Mmm," Mel's whimper held a helpless, needy quality. Her fingers tested the powerful length of his muscular arms, trembling a bit when they settled to the powerful, flexing biceps. A heavy, delicious tingle insinuated itself between her thighs. She could feel just the slightest trickle of moisture start to ooze in response to the arousal he could ignite with little effort.

Yohan's sleek brows were drawn close as he focused on kissing her. His hands curled around the hem of his T-shirt and he pulled it above her head. Mel gave a quick toss of her hair causing her coarse locks to bounce adoringly about her face. She felt on fire for him and gasped sharply when he pulled her high against his chest. Flesh to flesh the resulting sensation was a sizzling aphrodisiac.

Yohan turned, holding Melina against the wall and simultaneously plunging himself inside her. Mel bit her bottom lip and uttered a trembling moan. The pleasure on pain was overwhelmingly erotic as his rigid arousal lunged tirelessly inside her.

Mel curved her nails into his shoulders and allowed her airy, purely feminine cries of delight to fill the room. She wanted him to stop as much as continue, but didn't have long to debate the issue.

Yohan practically devoured her breasts in a savage display of suckling and nibbling. His hips moved in a slow deep rhythm; each time driving more deeply inside her. Then, a long shudder passed through him when his passion crested and he climaxed quickly.

They held onto one another for the longest time afterward, before Yohan carried her with him upstairs for more.

"Please Han," Mel whispered, when he tossed her to the bed and followed her down. "I can't … not now," she moaned.

Yohan grimaced and kissed her temple. "I'm sorry. I shouldn't have been so rough with you," he said, brushing his thumb across the swollen flesh guarding her womanhood. "Shh," he urged when she groaned.

"Han!" Mel gasped, reacting with a shiver to the delicious treat he began to ply her with. A soothing intimate massage dulled the raw ache she suffered and replaced it with a sweet sensation.

Mel had no control over her body as she ground lightly against his mouth. Yohan held her hips in a loose embrace, moaning each time her movements allowed his tongue deeper access.

Mel's fingers disappeared into the tangle of covers. Her movements grew quicker, frantic almost in her need for the ultimate satisfaction. Yohan smiled, feeling her contract around his tongue when she was in the throes of a potent orgasm. Sleep followed quickly, but not before Melina felt herself drawn into Yohan's secure embrace.

◆   ◆   ◆

Laughter and excitement ran high at Shepard's Steak and Spirits when eight of Seattle's most beautiful people walked through its doors one evening.

Quest, Michaela, Quaysar, Tykira, Fernando, Contessa, Yohan and Melina roused scores of stares and conversation when they arrived gorgeous, talkative and ready for a wonderful evening on the town. The group had reserved a large round table towards the rear of the dining room. Of course, that did nothing to lessen the attention focused their way.

The waiter received a twenty dollar tip just for saying good evening. He was promised there'd be more to come as long as he kept the drinks flowing. The dreadlocked college student uttered a prayer of gratitude when he set out to get the first round of beverages.

The tingle of a fork against a crystal glass sounded shortly after the drinks arrived. Everyone quieted and smiled as Quest stood.

"We're here tonight to celebrate and toast and congratulate my crazy brother and his beautiful wife," Quest began, his gray black stare narrowed as he joined in the laughter over his words. "They're about to do something so incredible and so right. We're proud of you and we love you both," he said, winking at the smiling couple. "To Quay and Ty!"

"Quay and Ty!" the group parroted, raising their glasses as well.

"Have you talked to her yet?" Contessa asked Mick, once appetizers arrived. The mingling of conversations at the table camouflaged her question.

"No, but I'll try again after dinner," Mick said, dabbing a napkin to her lips as she spoke.

Contessa tried to bite her lip on her next question, but failed. "Wouldn't it be better if you just waited until after the barbeque … after the baby comes?"

"No it wouldn't," Mick retorted, watching County as if she'd lost her mind. "This can't wait any longer. There're more answers out there and I'm damned well gonna find them."

"And what about Quest?" County challenged, nervously smoothing her hands across the white V-neck racer back dress she wore.

Mick glanced toward her husband who was laughing with Yohan and Fernando. "I gave my word that I'd see this through until the end," she said, forcing a resigned smile to her face. "I realize I've done a half assed job of that."

"What are you saying?"

Michaela focused on her best friend with a narrowed, determined glare. "I'm saying that if this is what I think it is, I want back on that book."

County clutched the sleeve of the black flaring blouse of Mick's pantsuit. "Are you crazy? Quest would-"

"You let *me* worry about him, alright?"

"What if she won't tell you anything?"

"She will."

Dinner began and it was the only time silence thrived at the big table. The group dined on New York Strips, T-Bones and Rib-eyes with sides of zesty rice pilaf dishes, fresh steamed and deliciously seasoned vegetables, with moist breads and creamed butter.

"The cooks here just keep getting better and better," Yohan commended, tossing his knife to the empty plate that had carried a massive Rib-eye.

"I couldn't eat another bite," Ty said with a sigh of delight.

"I think that goes for all of us," Quay said as a sly gleam sparkled in his dark eyes. "Except for Mick. She could probably eat a whole other T-Bone and Strip *and* Rib-eye."

Michaela simply raised her hand in a weary manner as her dinner companions roared with laughter. "I've run out of criticisms for all these bad jokes," she said.

"Bad jokes, but true statements," Quay continued to taunt his sister-in-law. "Come on admit it, you want the cooks to throw another side of beef on the fire."

"Not at all," was Mick's prim reply, "but I *am* wondering where that damn dessert cart is," she admitted, joining in when the laughter resounded again.

"Well, well, it's good to see everyone in such high spirits!"

The laughter and good vibes floating around the table stalled at the arrival of the unexpected and unwelcome guest.

"Sorry to interrupt," Stefan Lyons apologized.

"Then walk away," Fernando suggested.

Instead, Stefan tugged on the diamond cuff links adoring his sleeves. "I only wanted to make sure everyone is coming to the party."

"Man why don't you just tell us what the hell is up so we won't have to waste our time on that crap?" Quay requested.

Stefan's easy expression froze on his fair complexioned face, but he masked it quickly with a smile. "Sorry my man, but it's a surprise." His gaze traveled around the table. "Whether you all take it well or poorly is up to you. I hope you all received the location change for the event?"

"Speaking of which, why's it at Ramsey?" Quest asked, idly fiddling with the cuffs of his own shirt as he spoke. "Who gave the go ahead to do this?"

"Ah, forgive me Q, but telling you that would reveal too much of the surprise." Stef feigned regret, pressing a hand to his chest as his eyes moved to focus on Contessa. "I only ask that you all look your best and come ready to have a helluva time." His leering gaze moved from her face to closely appraise her bosom.

Fernando was now leaning back and viewing his *partner*-he'd been making plans to completely divest himself of Dark Squires. Fernando's translucent brown stare sharpened upon notice of Stefan's intense observation and County's unease because of it.

"Well the television and newspapers will be on hand to cover the event," Stef added, seeming to regain his composure as he looked away from County. "You'll definitely regret missing it, so I hope to see you all there," he said, and then strolled away as coolly as he'd approached.

"Son of a bitch," Yohan muttered, his fist clenched as he held it pressed to his cheek. "What are the odds of that fool comin' up in here on the same night that we're here?"

Quay raised his glass of gin in a mock toast. "You know us Ramseys, brotha we draw bad luck like flies to trash."

"Alright y'all come on," Melina urged, tapping her dessert fork to the edge of her glass. "This is supposed to be a celebration dinner!" she cheerfully reminded the now sullen group.

"Damn right," Quest agreed, a gorgeous smile brightening his dark face, "and I'm about to take my big, beautiful wife out on the dance floor!"

Michaela closed her yes and quietly accepted the dig while the rest laughed. She caught the edge of her husband's shirt and forced him to look directly into her eyes. "Never say that again," she warned in the sweetest tone.

Soon, all the couples had ventured to the dance floor.

Shepard's Steak and Spirits boasted its very own house band. The popular group specialized in everything from soft rock to neo-soul and reggae grooves. That evening's classical jazz pieces added a touch of elegance to the raw beauty of the establishment.

Melina smiled, content, happy and tingling all over in the shelter of her husband's embrace. Though the evening's celebration had been a welcome treat, Stefan Lyon's unexpected visit to the dinner table, had put a damper on everyone's moods.

Especially Yohan's, Mel observed. She could feel the tension pulse like a living thing in his arms as her hands kneaded the chords of muscle beneath his moss colored shirt. She knew the change in his demeanor had less to do with Stefan and more to do with the questions still remaining between them.

Mel closed her eyes and silently commanded the real world to remain at bay. She and Yohan barely swayed to the rhythms coloring the air. They twirled out to the rose and tulip lined patio when the warmth of the evening beckoned the restaurant's patrons to enjoy a bit of outdoor dancing. Suddenly, they stopped moving completely. Mel didn't think to question Yohan when he took her with him to a remote area in the depths of the foliage rich patio.

He sat on the patio's low railing and kept Melina standing before him. Her heart raced as their stance reminded her of a few nights earlier and the scene which followed her venturing downstairs to find him, Cupping his cheek with one hand, Mel used the other to brush the light furrows from his brow. "What is it?" she forced herself to ask.

He took a deep breath, his ebony stare intense. "Don't ever leave me again," he said. His deep maple smooth voice glided so softly.

It caused her heart to lurch. "Han," she could barely whisper. The bottomless pools of his eyes engulfed her in a swirl of sensation and she leaned closer. "Sweetie, I'm right here."

"But for how long?" he challenged. "How long before you run again Mel?"

"Honey, why are you bringing this up now? Tonight. Especially when everything's been-"

"Going so well. Yeah, I know." He snapped. "And why is that? Because I haven't been asking any questions, that's why."

"Oh no? You could've fooled me. All you've done is asked questions." Melina retorted, losing her temper as well. "Could we please just not do this here?"

Yohan's smirk was far from light hearted. "Don't worry, we won't. Not here," he said and stood from the railing. "Get your stuff. We're leaving."

CHAPTER TEN

Melina felt it best not to question Yohan's motives for taking her back to her room at The Montgomery instead of their home in Woodway. The trip to her suite was silent-no surprise there. Mel felt suffocated standing next to him as the elevator ascended the flights to her floor. He seemed to have swollen to twice his size in light of his boiling temper. The moment she pulled the card key from her purse, Yohan took it and opened the door to the suite.

Strolling ahead of him, she struggled to keep her cool, but fidgeted with the wooden O-ring clasp that secured the asymmetrical chocolate halter gown she'd worn that evening. Instead of pretending with small talk or politeness, she waited for him to begin. Her mind raced, conjuring quick answers to whatever questions he threw her way. Nothing, however, prepared her to hear him recite her Memphis address. Her breath stopped in the midst of inhaling.

"Yeah, I know your address. I've known for years," he said, watching her confusion clear.

Anger took its place as Melina's exotic dark stare grew suspicious. "You've got no right to snoop in on my private life," she blurted, regretting the statement the moment it was voiced.

Yohan turned his back, tossing the room key to the message desk as he spoke. "I had every right when you left in the middle of the night without so much as a word."

"I left word!" she cried, the situation now making it impossible for her to contain her emotions. "Don't blame me because your scheming father interfered-again!"

"This is about you, Mel," Yohan corrected, his voice still easy when he looked at her. "It's about you just up and leaving."

Mel shook her head, sending her heavy locks flying about her face. "How *un*surprising that you're blaming *me* instead of Marc. How many times, Han? How many times did I come to you only to have you refuse to listen to me! Why do you keep going back to this? You know why I had to go."

"And in eight years you couldn't tell me? It took you eight years to tell me this? Even then I had to drag it out of you."

"So are we gonna spend another eight years arguing over why it took me eight years to come to you, Han?" Mel challenged, propping one hand to her hip as she strolled the living area. "Because I'll tell you *that's* something I sure as hell don't plan to stick around for."

"Doesn't surprise me," Yohan muttered, massaging his neck as he paced the other side of the room. "It was probably your intention all along."

Her hand slid from her hip then and she took a moment to study him silently. Something wasn't right about this, she told herself. This argument about the past though not without merit, felt out of place. There was something else he wanted to know and it had nothing to do with Marc. "Exactly what is this all about Yohan? Whatever it is, it's been on your mind since we were in Alaska. I think it's time you tell me what it is."

"Crane Cannon," he replied simply, quiet as always. After a moment, he looked away but continued to explain. "His visits ... visits to your home that lasted into the wee hours of the morning."

Mel closed her eyes. "So exactly what do you want to know?"

"Who is he to you Mel?"

"Don't you already have an answer for that too?"

"Don't play with me," Yohan advised.

Mel swallowed a bit of her courage, seeing the uncharacteristic coldness flash in his gaze. "He's my boss and a dear friend," she confessed, folding her arms over her chest as she faced him. "He helped me when I first came to Memphis."

"I see ..." Yohan breathed, way past caring how his remarks came across. "So all those late nights, you were just repaying him for his kindness?"

Melina strolled past a brass dish filled with peppermints, but turned and snatched it from the table when she heard him. He ducked it easily when she threw it at his head.

"You've got some damn nerve Yohan Ramsey-who makes every woman melt when he walks by. I should be asking how many women *you've* paraded through my home in the last eight years!" she accused, almost grateful for a chance to scream and vent her frustration. "I wonder what I would've seen had I paid a visit on some late night or early morning."

"I can damn well guarantee it wouldn't have been someone leaving at four a.m.!" he bellowed, finally taking the SOFT mode from his voice.

Mel sent him a disbelieving glare. "So *you* say. But how am I to know that now?!"

"Dammit woman, have you taken a real good look at my gym?" he hissed, closing a bit of the distance between them. "Do you know how much time I actually spend down there and *why*?"

Her glare wavering, Mel acknowledged his words with a half nod. "It doesn't look like the … healthiest of places," she admitted, thinking of the forest of massacred punching bags and the scores of barbells and weights strewn everywhere. It was the dark, eerie nest of someone obsessed and angry. Forcing herself to calm, Mel buried her face in her hands and groaned.

"Yohan, I don't want to fight. Not now-not ever. We've been through so much," she said finally, not bothering to hide her tears when she turned to him. "Why can't we just let this go?" she begged.

Yohan's darkly gorgeous face still harbored coldness. "Because I don't believe Cannon's just your boss and when you're ready to stop lyin' to me, you know where I am."

"You're gonna storm out over this?!" Mel cried disbelief and exasperation coloring her voice. "Han, please don't go," she asked, as he strolled to the door and let it slam behind him in response.

◆   ◆   ◆

Contessa woke with a lazy smile and stretch the next morning when she found Fernando looming above her. "So you decided to wait on me this morning, huh?" she teased, her nails grazing the crisp whiskers of his light beard. Usually, she was awakened by the delicious treat of him plying her body with his intimate touch.

"What happened between you and Stef?" he asked, making no pretense at early morning niceties.

The ease left County's face, her eyes clouding with a distant look. She tried to leave the bed, but Fernando wouldn't move from above her.

"What?" she snapped, jerking on the covers tangled between her fingers.

Fernando's mesmerizing light eyes were intense as they studied her face.

Contessa refused to let him unnerve her any further. "What Ramsey?" she challenged, fixing him with her own intense gaze. "Are you upset because the man looked at me longer than you liked last night?" A naughty smile softened her lips. "I'm a gorgeous woman, you know?"

"Well my soon to be ex-partner wasn't the only one watching you last night," he informed her. "I was observing you too and now I want you to spill it because the next person I ask will be Stefan and I promise you I'm not apt to be nearly as sweet."

"And this is just why I kept quiet, dammit. I don't need you running off in some murderous rage," County blurted, running shaky fingers through her dark, cropped hair. "You already broke the man's nose. Next time, you're liable to break something more vital," she grumbled.

"So it's *that* intense, huh?"

"Ramsey-"

"Tell me."

"It's really not."

"*Now* Contessa."

"Fernando please."

He interrupted with a soft curse, then whipped back the covers and stalked nude from the bed.

County was silent until she saw him jerk into the navy blue trousers he'd worn the night before. "What are you doing?"

"Goin' to find Stef," he said, snatching a matching shirt from the floor, "beat it out of that son of a bitch," he added.

Knowing he meant every word, County bolted from the bed and grabbed the hem of his shirt as he jerked into it and stormed towards the door.

Fernando turned, taking her by the arms the instant he felt her touch him. Gently, he placed her back on the bed. "Talk or I go cave in that fool's nose again," he threatened.

"Alright!" she hissed, wrenching herself free of his hold. She concentrated on pulling the sheets tightly around her nude body.

Fernando knelt before her a knowing smile deepened the curve of his heavenly mouth. "I advise you to tell me the truth instead of the lie you're trying to put together."

County flashed him a scathing glare and brushed his hands from her knees. "If it matters, I think he was probably just trying to see how loyal I am to you."

Cupping her chin, Fernando tilted her head back and smiled. "What happened? That's *all* you need to tell me."

"The morning he came to my house to give you that invite to the meeting today he … said some things," she revealed in a tiny voice, her eyes widening when she saw him bristle. "Honestly Fernando, I don't think-"

"Did he touch you?"

"Fernando-"

"Did he put his hands on you, County?"

Contessa was fast losing her ability to remain unfettered. Memories of that day; and the way Stefan Lyons made her feel unsafe in her own home, came barreling forth vengefully. "He um … he pulled me to him and …"

Fernando nudged her chin with his thumb, but she wouldn't look at him directly.

"He reached beneath my shirt and …" she could go no further.

She didn't need to. Fernando studied her movements, noticing as she gestured toward her hips and thighs.

"Son of a bitch," he whispered and stood.

"Fernando!" County called, racing out after him when he stormed from the room. "Fernando wait!" she cried, blocking the door before he could walk out. "It's over. I handled it and it's done," she gasped, trying to hold the sheet around her and keep the door blocked at the same time.

"Not the way I'll handle it," Fernando promised, his expression soft as he watched her.

"Please let it go. Please," she urged, standing on her toes and linking her arms about his neck. "Please …" she soothed, showering his jaw with soft kisses.

Fernando tilted his head and kissed her deeply. County shivered from arousal and triumph, certain she'd succeeded in taking his mind off any and everything else. She thrust her tongue against his in wild abandon and relinquished her hold on the sheet when he lifted her high against him.

Fernando settled her back to the bed and tucked the heavy comforter around her. "Find something to do today. I don't want you anywhere near that meeting," he said, dropping a kiss to her shoulder.

County made no effort to argue further.

◆   ◆   ◆

"The perfect usher into a peaceful night's sleep. Yeah, right," Melina sighed as she scanned the boastings printed on the back of the box of herbal tea she held. The product had not lived up to its claims as she'd had one of her most peace*less* nights ever.

Of course, she had to admit nothing short of a full bottle of Bourbon would've put her to sleep after the blowup with Yohan the night before. Rarely had they ever argued except for the few times they had it out over Marc-another reason why she refrained from discussing the man with his son.

His son, Mel replayed the phrase in her mind. *How in the world did I wind up in the middle of all this?* She asked herself, fluffing out her hair as she paced the living area of her suite. Josephine was somewhere hiding out and Crane had left the job to her. Little did *they* know, she was far too much of a coward to go through with the deed. But why? The question stopped Mel in her tracks as she closely considered it. The fact that Marc wasn't Yohan's father certainly wasn't *her* fault. Why was she so against telling him? The possibility of Yohan racing off to kill Marc had worn thing long ago. While it was still a definite probability, it wasn't the reason she was so against telling him. The trouble was she hadn't a clue as to what *it* was.

The phone's ringing shocked her so, that the tea box tumbled from her hand to land with a low thud to the counter where the hotel provided coffee maker and condiments rested.

Mel closed her eyes, praying briefly that it was Yohan. Perhaps she could coax him out of his mood. "Yes?" she greeted, shoving a hand into the front pocket of her robe.

"Mel?"

"Crane," she sighed, massaging her forehead. "I haven't told him," she said, before he could ask.

"I'm sorry for this, Mel. So sorry," Crane whispered, hearing the strain in her voice. "I've put you in this difficult place and I'm so sorry."

"Difficult?" Mel snapped, her anger taking root. "*Difficult?* You have no idea what a difficult place is Crane Cannon. My husband thinks I'm having an affair. He's seen you visiting and leaving my house in the *wee* hours of the morn," she jibed humorlessly, punching a fist into one of the sofa cushions.

"He's been to Memphis? He-he's seen me?"

Melina felt her anger simmer and cool as quickly as it had heated. She truly realized then what a trial this situation had to be for Crane. He'd spent over thirty years unable to tell his only son who his real father was.

"Sweetheart, I *am* sorry," he was saying, sounding as though his emotions were lodged in his throat. "The last thing I want is for you to think I'm forcing you. It's just … whoever knows about Josephine and me wants this secret out."

Mel frowned. "Crane?" she inquired, not liking the sound of his voice.

"I'm beginning to think this is about more than ruining my chances to be elected. It may have nothing to do with the election at all. Whatever the reason, I'd much prefer Yohan being told by someone he trusts-loves."

Weariness took its toll and Melina flopped to the sofa, unable to argue Crane's logic. "I'll tell him-I'll find a way. I *will* tell him Crane."

He chuckled softly. "I know you will, love. I'll say goodbye now," he whispered and the connection ended.

Melina held the phone to her ear a few seconds longer, and then set it aside. She pressed her fingers to her eyes as they filled with water.

◆   ◆   ◆

"Oh my goodness! Look at you!" Johnelle Black laughed upon opening her door to Michaela around eleven a.m. that morning. "Are you sure there's only *one* baby in there?!"

Mick rolled her eyes, savoring the hug from Johnelle. "Bad jokes are definitely one of pregnancies nastiest side effects," she grumbled.

It was all in fun. Over the years, Michaela and Johnelle had become close friends. So much so, that Johnelle picked up her Georgia roots and completely relocated to Seattle, Washington. She often said that Mick was not simply her newest friend, she was her only friend.

"Sweetie, is it good for you to be out and about so late in the pregnancy?" Johnelle asked, keeping her arm about Mick as they journeyed toward the kitchen.

"Oh, it's fine," Mick assured the woman with a wave of her hand.

Johnelle gave a satisfied nod. "Let's get you a glass of juice," she decided and headed for the fridge.

"I came by because I wanted to tell you in person about Sera … about the book," Mick clarified when Johnelle looked up. "I've decided to write it."

"Oh Mick," Johnelle breathed, setting a glass of cran-apple juice to the white oak table before taking a seat, "that's so wonderful. I'm so glad that you'll see this through 'til the end." Her eyes clouded then. "Mick what about Quest? How will he take this?"

Again, Mick waved her hand. "He'll be fine. But I didn't just come to talk about the book, Johnelle." She said, fluffing out her elegant emerald green blouse. "I have some new information on the case and it's information I just can't believe."

"Well what, Mick? Please!" Johnelle urged, bouncing in her seat as she spoke. "Is it more evidence?" she guessed.

Michaela grimaced, propping her chin beneath her fists. "It's a story I was told."

Johnelle nodded. "A story."

"In essence, about a woman who discovered her husband was cheating." Mick began, knowing this had to be done delicately as well as accurately. "She followed him to the woman's house many times and continued to drive by the woman's house long after her husband had ended the affair. And one day she met the woman's husband and she was as unhappy as he was. Their friendship turned into a love affair. She got pregnant and aside from the fact that she was married to a very powerful man, the baby's father was white and in Savannah ... well, that would've been impossible."

"White?" Johnelle breathed, the tiniest lines of suspicion beginning to tug at her brow. "Mick what does this have to do with the book? With Sera?" She asked, sounding as though she already knew.

"The woman was Josephine Ramsey-the father of her child was Crane Cannon."

"How do you know that name?" Johnelle gasped.

"At first, I didn't know how. I couldn't think of where I'd heard it. Then, I remembered Sera's diary. She mentioned him in there." Mick shared, watching Johnelle hold her head in her hands. "Johnelle, how could you allow Sera to see a Ramsey much less be attracted to one when you knew they were blood?"

Johnelle looked up, her eyes were blank. "What are you saying?" she whispered.

"Johnelle, Crane is Yohan's Ramsey's father. You were having an affair with Marc Ramsey and got pregnant with his child-Sera." Mick slapped her hands to the table. "Josephine claims that's why he stopped seeing you. Because you'd become pregnant."

"It wasn't like that, it wasn't like that," Johnelle chanted, her voice trembling as badly as her body.

Mick's frown deepened. "Then what?" she snapped, bringing her hand down on the table again. "*What* Johnelle? How could you let this happen?"

Johnelle's eyes were red with tears. "Mick I swear to you I didn't know. I *didn't* know."

The whispered words stopped Mick cold. "What are you saying?" she asked, tilting her head to look directly into the woman's eyes.

"Marc can't be her father-he *can't* be," Johnelle moaned, rocking herself a little as she spoke. "Oh God Michaela, he can't be."

Mick was scared, but pulled her chair closer to Johnelle and began to rub her back. "Johnelle?" She whispered, knowing the woman's shock was just a bit too irregular.

"Oh my God," Johnelle spoke, suddenly her voice was clear. In her eyes, however, was a look of sheer terror and she seemed to tremble more violently.

Mick took her hands and shook her hard. "Johnelle?" she called, signing when the woman jerked out of her trance. "What is it? What aren't you telling me?"

Johnelle looked down at her lap, and then held her forehead in her hands. "Michaela … Sera wasn't my child."

CHAPTER ELEVEN

Mick sat still and remained quiet while Johnelle left the table and went to the bar in the living room that connected to the kitchen. Mick wasn't surprised to see her pull the familiar looking flask from somewhere behind several tall decanters. She waited, watching as Johnelle drank deeply from the silver container.

"I met Crane in Atlanta," she said after savoring the alcohol that warmed her insides. "We were both from there and back then … well white and black *love* was taboo," she smiled and gave a lazy shrug. "But we said 'to hell with what the world thought'. We decided to get married and foolishly believed relocating to Savannah would make things easier-at least no one knew us there." She strolled back toward the kitchen, still clutching the silver flask. "Crane was just getting his first gallery store open and he decided to just commute from Savannah to Atlanta where he usually spent the better part of the week. That was the second nail in our marriage coffin," she told Mick with a knowing smirk.

"Anyway, I was miserable and quickly discovered how bad I was at making the sudden change from miserable to ecstatic when my husband finally came home." Her expression lightened. "The one bright spot about being in Savannah was that my sister lived there."

Mick noticed Johnelle's expression dim as quickly as it had softened. "It wasn't such a bright spot, I assume?"

Johnelle's brows rose in confirmation. "She lived so bad, so shabby. Hmph, *shabby* is probably even too good of a word. More than once, I was tempted to call the housing authority or somebody who could force the landlord to get that place in order. But Grace told me not to make a fuss." Johnelle recalled, referring to her sister then. "She never quite had it all. Looks, but not much else, you know?" she asked, watching Mick nod in understanding. "And I probably could've walked away had it not been for the kids."

"Kids?" Michaela repeated.

Johnelle smiled. "Grace had a one year old and another on the way. A single mother raising two kids in that sort of environment … I snapped and finally decided to go blast the landlord, the owner-somebody." She began to smooth her hands across the sleeves of the lightweight yellow cotton top she wore. "*Somebody* turned out to be Marcus Ramsey. He owned the building and I had every intention of threatening him with the housing authority if he didn't fix up the place."

"Did he make any changes?" Mick asked, smiling at the scornful look Johnelle sent her way.

"His *changes* made it look like putting a fur coat on a pig and I remember having the distinct impression he was trying to impress me." Johnelle shook her head as though the idea made her ill. "I tried to get Grace to leave, but the woman wouldn't budge. She kept saying things were going to improve as soon as the baby came. *Anyway,*" she sighed, tossing the flask to the sink, "I kept pleading with Marcus about the apartment and *he* kept drawing me in. I never went to the housing authority or any other authority. Inside of two months, he had me in bed." Her lashes fluttered and she folded her arms across her waist. "With Crane gone half the time, it was easy to live the lie. Then, my sister had the baby and all hell broke loose. I went to visit Grace at the hospital and found her in tears." Johnelle said, her own voice shaking on a sob. "The father wanted her to give up the new baby and the fool was gonna do it!" she spat, throwing her hands up in the air. "I didn't take time to think, I told her to give Sera to me. I couldn't stand the idea of some stranger having my niece-my daughter." Her emotions got the better of her then and she broke into tears. "Oh Mick, I loved her like she was my own. You know that, don't you?"

"Shh …" Mick urged, walking over to bring Johnelle back to sit at the table. "Of course I do," she soothed, sitting close to Johnelle. "How did Crane handle it?" she asked after rubbing the woman's back for a time.

"Things were really good at first. Crane … he was a good father-he really loved Sera and he was even working more steady in Savannah." Her expression soured then. "Probably because of Josephine and; as we all know, not even a baby can freshen something that's already soured." She shrugged and brushed a tear from her cheek. "So we separated and eventually divorced. I gave Sera *my* last name and raised her on my own."

"And Marc?" Michaela asked.

"Cut things off the minute he realized I was a new mom-the jackass." Johnelle muttered.

"Did you ever meet Josephine Ramsey?"

Johnelle nodded. "Many years ago. In a park. Sera was a baby. I didn't know who she was until years later, she … she stopped by the house to offer condolences after Sera … died," she coughed, trying to smother a sob. "I was going through some of Sera's things-my mind was a mess. I ran out of the room crying while Josephine was still out there. When I came back, she was gone."

Mick folded her arms across her chest. "And what about your sister?"

"Hmph. Lived in that rat hole until Steffy went to college. She died a few years back-had a bad heart she never took care of."

A tiny frown sharpened on Mick's dark face. "Steffy-a girl?"

"Boy. Short for Stefan." Johnelle grimaced. "The only reason my sister could keep him instead of Sera, I guess. The father craved sons. Obviously he didn't crave taking care of them. Although he *did* send Stef to college."

Mick leaned forward. "And you never knew him?"

"The father? No, all I knew of the man was his last name. Lyons-the name she gave to Steffy. It wasn't until some years ago when she was dying that I found out there was no Lyons. She gave Steffy the name because it sounded powerful." Johnelle began to fidget with her fingers. "I don't think my sister knew who fathered either of those children."

Mick debated on sharing what she suspected. Finally, she decided the time for hiding information had passed. "No Johnelle, I think your sister knew exactly who their father was."

◆   ◆   ◆

Mel was walking on the very edge of her nerves when she arrived at Ramsey Group that morning. She and Tykira had planned to meet for brunch before the gathering at Ramsey Acquisitions that afternoon. Jasmine had already instructed her to go on up to the top floor where Ty was. The moment her feet touched the carpet in the penthouse office, Mel saw her friend across the room.

"Hey girl. Sorry for the confusion." Ty whispered, rushing over to hug her friend. "We had some paperwork to finish on the twins, so I thought it'd be best to meet here especially since Quay had to meet with Yohan anyway."

Mel blinked, her stomach churning at the mention of her husband's name. "Yohan's here?" she asked.

Ty was pulling the strap of her purse across her arm. "Mmm hmm, I figured you might already be here."

"Oh Ty …" Mel groaned. Before she could explain, there was Yohan laughing and talking with Quay as they strolled down the hallway.

"Hey, hey!" Quay called, when he spotted Melina and came over to envelope her in a hug.

The swelling tension in the room, eased a bit thanks to Quaysar. It resumed when Quay pulled his wife aside to talk privately. Melina and Yohan were silent, trying not to look at each other and failing miserably.

"Han please, stop this," Mel pleaded, moving close and clasping her hands against the front of the pea green capped sleeved top she wore. "Don't do this, don't shut me out."

"Shut *you* out?" Yohan retaliated, his deep voice a rough whisper.

Mel swallowed her unease and moved closer. "Can't you get past this? Just let it go? Please Han?"

Her soft words and closeness were his undoing. With Quay and Tykira on the other side of the room, a modicum of privacy presented itself. A second later, Yohan had pulled Mel into a crushing embrace and kiss. Onlookers were irrelevant then as desire, anger and loved swirled in an intoxicatingly passionate mix. Melina rubbed her fingers through Yohan's wavy close cut hair and melted into his massive frame. Her soft whimpers of need were barely audible yet added a throbbing intensity to the already heated encounter. She tingled from head to toe, but Yohan pulled away just as her hopes began to soar over their make-up. Her heart fell at the narrowed lingering glare he sent her way before he left her alone.

Refusing to submit herself to any more of the emotional scene, Mel turned and punched the down key on the elevator. "Ty I'll meet you in the lobby!" she called and hurried into the car the moment it arrived.

"Dammit Mel, why are you dragging this out? You're letting something that has nothing to do with you, ruin a reconciliation with your husband." Tykira preached as she and Mel brunched around eleven thirty a.m.

"I understand what you're saying Ty. I've said it to myself," Mel sighed, massaging her shoulders as she spoke. "It's just not that easy," she said.

Ty shrugged. "I don't see why not. I lost so much time with Quay because he didn't just tell me what was going on. Even though his initial intentions to protect me were honorable, they paled next to all the time that passed and all the hurt that built."

"I appreciate your advice Ty, I do," she added when Tykira sent her a doubtful look, "but can you honestly say that you could stand before Quay and tell him something like this?"

"Yes! To save my marriage, yes Mel. Damn right I could."

Mel only smiled and focused on her hands clasped atop the polished maple table. Ty leaned close and covered them with her own.

"Honey do you really need Quest or anybody else to be there?" she asked her probing stare as brown as the scoop-necked dress she wore. "This is Yohan and you know him better than anyone. Having you there is probably *all* he needs." Ty leaned back in her chair and studied Mel with suspicious eyes. "You're not this big of a coward, girl. It takes guts to walk away from your husband to save your cousin. There's more to this-a deeper reason for you not wanting to tell Yohan and I don't even think *you* realize it. When you do, this aggravation will end. I know it will."

Mel reached across the table, pulling Ty's hand into hers. She gave a quick kiss to the back of it and prayed her friend was right.

◆   ◆   ◆

Media, Ramsey execs and members of the Ramsey family were all on hand for the announcement coming from the office of Ramsey Group Acquisitions led by Marcus Ramsey. More interesting than what the announcement was, was *who* would be giving it.

"What's up man?" Quest greeted his brother who'd recently arrived in the conference hall.

Quay responded with a grin and hug. "Same ole, same ole," he said.

Quest's gray eyes narrowed. "Where's Ty?"

"Brunch with Mel? And Mick?" Quay asked, noticing his sister-in-law was no where in sight.

Quest cast an agitated glance toward his wristwatch. "Haven't heard from her since this morning when she dashed out the house. Not even answering her cell," he grumbled.

Quay gave a slow nod. Clearly, the man was trying to keep a lid on his emotions, but Quay knew how obsessed his brother was with his wife's safety. He understood because he felt the same about Ty. Clapping a hand to Quest's shoulder, he gave him a reassuring shake. "She's fine man. Probably just had a lot of runnin' around to do before this thing got started." He cast a tired glance toward the front of the room. "When's Stef makin' his big announcement, anyway?"

"Who knows?" Quest muttered, his now onyx gaze traveling the circus of reporters, execs and other Ramsey personnel. "Damn waste of time's what this is. But I'd pay a bundle to know why Stefan Lyon's is makin' an announcement on behalf of Marc Ramsey," he said, folding his arms across the front of the cobalt blue shirt he wore beneath a navy blazer.

"Whatever it is, I hope he says it fast."

The feminine voice behind them caught the twins by surprise. They turned, laughing when they saw Contessa. They took turns hugging her, but it didn't take them long to realize she was upset about something.

"Have you guys seen Fernando around?" she asked.

"No." Quay said after a quick glance at his brother.

"Why?" Quest asked.

"It-nothing. It's probably nothing," County sighed, smoothing her hands across the long cotton sleeves of her sky blue wrap dress.

"Nothing?" Quay parroted. His dark eyes fixed on County as he pushed both hands into his mocha trousers.

"Doesn't sound like nothing, does it Quay?" Quest inquired, his stare also fixed upon County.

She clasped her hands to stop their shaking. "I really don't want to go into it," she said.

"Mmm, too bad you don't have a choice," Quay said.

County realized she'd already said too much. Double teamed by the twins, she submitted. "Short version is Stefan's been making … passes. Fernando found out. He's not happy."

"Son of a bitch," Quest breathed, exchanging a foreboding look with his brother.

"So we need to be on the look out in case Fern comes up in here and tries to wail on this fool's ass?" Quay guessed.

County managed a smile. "That's the jist of it," she confirmed, her eyes scanning the crowd. "In an atmosphere like this, it wouldn't look good for the family," she noted.

Quest massaged the back of his neck and grunted. "What *does* look good for this family these days?"

Just then, a petite Caucasian woman approached the podium at the front of the room. A hush fell over the area as the group waited-watching with hungry eyes.

"Ladies and gentlemen, thank you so much for coming out today and thank you for your patience as we tend to a few last minute details. We'll be introducing our speaker in five minutes."

"Have you seen Michaela?" Quest turned to ask County, when the woman left the podium and conversation rose in the room once more.

Contessa shook her head. "I haven't talked with her today."

Quest rolled his eyes and uttered a sharp curse. He tried his cell again.

"I'm on my way, Sweetie," Mick promised, seeing Quest's name on the faceplate of her cell phone. Closing her eyes, she pressed a fifth wet towel to her forehead. She'd arrived at Ramsey Acquisitions fifteen minutes ago and had spent the majority of the time in that restroom.

She couldn't remove the vision of Johnelle's face from her mind. The woman seemed to crumple when Mick confirmed that Marcus Ramsey was both Sera's and Stefan's father in addition to being the man she'd once had an affair with.

Of course, Mick believed it was the realization that Sera had been having an affair with her own uncle; and that her own father was aware of it that truly threw Johnelle over the edge. Leaving was the last thing Mick wanted to do-given the woman's state of mind. Still, she knew Quest would be worried if she didn't show-not to mention livid that her running around had anything to do with Sera Black. If she spoke to him over the phone, her voice would be a dead giveaway that things weren't *peachy keen*.

"Besides, he's counting on me to be there," Mick said, fluffing her curls absently before a flicker of realization dawned in her eyes. *He's counting on us to be there*, she repeated quietly. Her thoughts were centered on Stefan Lyons.

The man had been playing to their curiosity about why *he* was delivering announcements for Marc. He was going to tell them who he really was at the meeting. With all the media in attendance, it would be another explosive and damaging day for the Ramseys.

"I can't let that happen," she said, grabbing her purse and running from the washroom.

"Damn," Quest practically growled after ending the call to his mother. Catrina hadn't talked to Mick all day either.

Quay and County tried to reassure him, but even they were beginning to feel edgy. Just then, another wave of silence filled the room when the petite woman reappeared at the podium.

"Ladies and gentlemen, thank you again for your patience. My name is Bethany Welch. I'm Ramsey Acquisitions Director of Marketing and PR. Today is a very exciting day for us here at Ramsey Acq. We have a special and very important announcement from Mr. Stefan Lyons. He and his partner Fernando Ramsey are the very successful team who head Dark Squires Communications. Mr. Lyons also …"

Michaela arrived amidst Bethany Welch's introduction. She was about to tug on the sleeve of her husband's suit coat, but he seemed to sense her behind him and turned before she could touch him.

"Where the hell have you been?" Quest hissed, his hands smoothing along the back of her emerald green blouse. "Why haven't you been answering my calls?" he demanded to know, cupping her face as though trying to prove to himself that she was really there.

"Quest I'm sorry," Mick gasped, almost out of breath. She took his hands from her face and squeezed them urgently. "Let's go on and leave and I'll explain on the way," she said, speaking also to Quay and County who were looking on as well. "I promise I'll tell you guys everything if we can just get out of here now."

Quay pulled his sister-in-law close and kissed the top of her head. "Don't worry, babe. We're outta here as soon as this fool makes his big speech."

Mick was shaking her head. "We need to get out of here before he does that."

"Honey, why?" County asked.

"Dammit would you three just listen to me. Hell, just take my word for it!" Mick snapped, stomping her foot and growing frustrated by their reluctance to go.

Quest stood watching his wife strangely, but agreed that he should go with her. Before he could say anything to that affect, a thunderous rumble rose near the front of the room. A crash followed as several television cameras tumbled to the floor. Someone screamed. County gasped, slapping the twins' shoulders when she discovered the cause of the ruckus.

Fernando was at the center of the melee, having caught Stefan on his way to the podium. Thankfully, the remaining cameras stood too far away to pickup the vicious words Fernando hissed to his business partner. Unfortunately, the cameras did an excellent job of capturing the bloody fight in which Stef suffered the most.

Quest and Quay wasted no time heading into the scuffle. It took their combined efforts to pull their cousin off of Stefan. It was a loud and ugly scene. Contessa stood rooted to her spot, eyes wide as her hands covered her mouth. Fernando looked like a stranger. She had never witnessed him so enraged. Stefan could have never gotten to his feet had it not been for the assistance of a few Ramsey execs who finally felt brave enough to come up to the stage area.

Mick went to comfort County, but her good-deed was short lived. A tearing pain jagged into her side and curved deep into her belly. A breathless cry flew past her lips and her fingers cut into County's shoulder. The long moan she uttered next was soft, but Contessa heard it clearly.

"I'm okay Mick," County assured her friend when Michaela's hand slipped from her shoulder. Her expression tightened again when she saw the drawn, miserable look on Mick's face. "What?" she inquired, glancing toward Mick's stomach. "Mick? Mick?!"

An answer was not forthcoming as Mick slumped against County and clutched her belly. The pain pierced with renewed intensity and it was all she could do to remain standing.

"Mick?!" County was frantic, tears streamed her cheeks.

Suddenly, Mick caught her friend's hand and clutched it in a death grip as she leaned closer. "Get Quest," she whispered.

The simple order, sent County's heart to lurching but she wasted no time. "Quest!" she screamed. "Quest!"

The noise was at a deafening pitch inside the conference room, yet County managed to increase the volume in her voice each time she cried out. By then, Quest and Quay were issuing calming words to Fernando-who still raged, but who at least was now sitting a ways off from the stage.

Quest's brow cleared as he tuned in to a faint frantic scream from the distance. It sounded like his name and quickly he turned in the direction of where he'd left Mick with County. His eyes were at first narrowed in confusion and then unease when he saw his wife leaning close to her friend. *Too* close and he cursed himself for not leaving when Mick wanted him to.

Several eyes and several cameras followed Quest when he leapt off the stage and raced across the room. Quay followed as well as Fernando, who'd forgotten all about murdering Stefan Lyons.

"I don't know what's wrong! Oh God!" County cried, watching as Quest lifted Mick gently against his chest.

"Michaela?" Quest whispered, uttering a prayer as he pressed his face into her hair. "Shh, shh … I'm gonna get you out of here. Just hang on to me," he urged, kissing his wife's forehead a dozen times as he headed for the rear exit.

Michaela closed her eyes, turning her face away from the cameras as her hand lay weakly against Quest's chest. Quay ordered the eager reporters away, while Fernando kept County close. They each followed Quest and Mick from the noisy room.

CHAPTER TWELVE

Melina and Ty received the news about Mick the moment they arrived at Ramsey Acquisitions some fifteen minutes after the majority of the commotion had subsided. They wasted no time getting to the hospital. Mel spotted Quay first with much of the family in one of the waiting rooms. She called out to him and, with Ty, they rushed to his side.

"She's fine, she's fine," he soothed, pulling them both into a tight hug.

"What happened?" Mel cried, stepping back to fix him with a searching gaze.

Quay's mood was surprisingly light. "We found out the girl *ran* from the restroom to the conference room and caught one helluva stitch in her side."

Melina and Tykira expelled sighs of relief in unison.

"So the baby's alright?" Ty asked.

Quay rubbed her back and nodded. "They're both fine. What Mick described sounded like a contraction before we got all the facts. But since she's due in another few of weeks, Dr. Steins wants to keep her overnight just to make sure nothing else is goin' on."

"But the baby's going to be alright?" Ty wanted to be sure.

"Our niece is fine," Quay promised his wife, kissing her temple as he spoke. "Her heartbeat's strong. Doc did another ultrasound. She's fine."

Quay was hugging both his wife and Mel when Yohan arrived. Quay nodded to his cousin and, without a word, relinquished Mel to her husband.

Feeling the familiar secure embrace surrounding her, Mel looked up. Seeing Yohan, her expression softened and her shoulders slumped as she put her weight on him and drew strength from his power. Quest came out into the hall a few minutes later to announce that all the tests checked out properly. He and Mick would be spending the night at the hospital.

"Can we talk?"

Mel smiled, hearing Yohan's voice rumble through his chest and into her ear. "Yeah," she said, nodding resolvedly and knowing the time had come so long ago.

They said their goodbyes to the rest of the family and set off. They hadn't been walking long, when Mel began to frown at the path they were taking. Clearly they were moving away from the exits and deeper into the hospital.

"We'll talk here. I don't want you to change your mind," he murmured.

"Good idea," Mel breathed, smoothing both hands across the beige linen pants she wore.

They walked in silence, until they arrived at the chapel. The room was peaceful and empty. Lit candles flickered wildly at the unexpected rush of air when Yohan opened the door. The light slowed and once more grew steady as its rays cast the room in gold.

Silence reigned a bit longer and Melina couldn't argue the location. She certainly needed God on her side. Yohan spoke no words and simply took a seat on one of the pews close to the altar. He watched Mel pace for what seemed to be an eternity. Still, he remained patient. His heart beat thunderously in his ears as he studied the expression on her dark China doll-like face. Whatever she had to tell him wouldn't be pretty and he couldn't be sure if he possessed enough nerve to hear it.

"It's not my place to tell you this, Han," she began, suddenly regretting the capped sleeves of the top she wore. Her entire body shook with cold. "Since Josephine's gone who knows where … it's now my responsibility."

Yohan leaned forward, bracing his elbows on his knees. "What's my mother got to do with this?"

"There was more to what we were talking about the day you walked in on us."

Yohan's jaw tightened noticeably, his deep set stare narrowed and focused on the chapel floor. "What is it?"

The darkness of his voice chilled Mel more than the temperature ever did. The shiver hit her deep and she turned toward the altar, her eyes closing for a brief prayer.

"Mel!"

"Marcus isn't your father!" she blurted, while whirling around to face him. The chill vanished and she blinked as if she couldn't believe she'd finally said it. She waited, trying to judge Yohan's reaction but there didn't appear to be one. In fact, he didn't seem surprised at all.

"Han?" she whispered, stepping closer slowly. "Sweetie?"

"Who?"

Mel shook her head once, confusion clouding her gaze. "Who? What? Honey?"

"Who is he? You must know his name."

"I-I yes. Yes, Han."

He simply stared, waiting for the rest.

"Crane Cannon. The man I work for," she confessed, watching Yohan close his eyes and cover his face with his hands.

"Baby," she whispered, kneeling before him and pressing her forehead to his hands. More words escaped her she knew nothing could surpass the shock he'd just had. When Yohan moved his hands away from his face, she kissed his cheek.

"So Mr. Carnes had the right information after all."

"What do you mean?" Mel asked, having pulled back to watch him.

Yohan massaged the back of his neck. "When I saw you with Crane Cannon, I had him checked out. At the time, Mr. Carnes was my father's attorney so I figured I could trust him to keep quiet about whatever he found out. Mr. Carnes was a good man and I always wondered how Marc could have someone with ethics privy to all his dirt."

Yohan shrugged. "Anyway, Mr. Carnes checked him out as best he could-no family, ex-wife in Georgia but he couldn't find a thing on her. Said he'd keep digging if I wanted him to, but I didn't."

Mel pushed a coarse lock behind her ear. "So how did you find out?"

Yohan massaged his forearm where he'd rolled the sleeve of his maple shirt. "About a month later, Mr. Carnes came back to me-said he had more info, assured me he hadn't been digging he just sort of ... *happened* upon it."

"Happened upon it?" Mel parroted with a quick laugh.

Yohan managed a smile. "Said he heard from one of Marc's business associates that Marc Ramsey's wife had two of his sons and he thought there were three. Crane Cannon's name was mentioned along with my mother's ... I never had the nerve to ask more." Yohan seemed to shiver then. "I think a part of me always knew I was the one."

Mel was sitting on her knees, looking up at Yohan as if she were a child listening to a fascinating story. "Did Mr. Carnes tell you for sure?"

"No, he told me just enough. No more. I always figured he had the whole story, but felt it best I know as little as possible."

"And he didn't tell you who the business associate was?"

Yohan shook his head.

"But how? How could someone else know?"

"After that day, Mr. Carnes never said another word about it. I cast it off as a rumor-made it easier not to think on it. I did a good job too, until I started to think of killing Marcus." His mouth curved into a menacing smile. "I thought of killing him every time I thought of you with Cannon."

Mel looked down at her lap. "Crane is running for Senator. He told me someone is out to ruin his chances and threatens to leak the information."

"Do you think it's me?"

"Is it?"

"Would you believe me if I said no?"

"Yes," she answered without hesitation, standing on her knees before him. "But Han that still leaves someone out there with a score to settle." She sighed, her expression troubled. "I never even asked Crane if his wife knew. Hmph, I never knew he *had* a wife until I talked to Josephine."

Yohan smoothed one hand across the olive green trousers he wore. "So my mother did know?" he inquired tentatively.

Mel nodded, though his question caused her heart to lurch again. Still, she'd hidden too much from Yohan to keep silent any longer. He deserved to know it all. "She would never threaten Crane with it. She didn't want anyone to know."

"Did she say why …" Yohan cleared his throat of the unexpected emotion that caused his voice to waver. "Why she slept with this man?"

"Because Marc was cheating-had been for years. There were other children," she added quietly, swallowing her distaste at the mere mention of Marc's name. She turned away then.

Yohan stood, following Mel across the chapel. When she made no move to face him, he caught her arm and took the decision off her hands.

"Crane's wife was one of the women Marc slept with," she said, upon looking up into his face. Instantly, she recalled what Josephine said about telling her child that he was the product of revenge. Melina realized that having to tell the man she loved why he was on this earth, hurt just as much.

Yohan's hands fell away from Mel's arms and he put space between them; covering his face in his palms. Mel waited a while, and then noticed him shuddering. She went to him, offering no words of comfort or encouragement; simply holding on to him as he absorbed the truth.

◆   ◆   ◆

"How many times do you have to hear the word 'no' before you accept it?"

Michaela slammed her hands to the bed and fixed Quest with her darkest scowl. "I can't believe you're overreacting this way when it's *me* who's pregnant."

"*You* can't believe it? How do you think I feel standin' here listening to you?" Quest snapped, his striking gray eyes darkened by aggravation. "Do you recall that we almost lost our baby last week?"

"Oh please," Mick groaned, rolling her eyes. "It was nothing as sinister as that. It was a stitch in my side. The baby wasn't in danger."

"It could've gone either way, you know that." Quest warned, massaging the dull ache surrounding the fraternity brand on his arm.

Mick leaned back against the pillows lining the towering oak headboard. "I know you were scared. So was I," she admitted, smiling when Quest looked over at her. She shrugged. "It's just that we've all been through so much and I guess I just figured this Fourth of July thing might be what everyone needs to relax and let go of all that mess. With Marc gone and Houston in jail, we won't have to worry over anyone popping in to cause trouble," she spoke in a refreshing tone as her amber stare sparkled with promise. "Don't you think we could use this after everything?" she asked, extending her hand while she spoke.

Quest seemed to hear her, for the drawn look on his dark, handsome face softened noticeably. He made a mental recall of everything Michaela had told him about Johnelle and Marc ... and Sera. Moving away from the dresser he leaned against, he came to the bed and sat next to his wife.

Mick giggled when he tugged on one of the heavy curls framing her face. A slow kiss followed and was rounded out by a hug.

Quest pressed his forehead to Mick's his thumbs brushing her plump cheeks. "You know, if our little girl can wrap me around her finger as easily as you can, I'm gonna be in big trouble."

◆   ◆   ◆

Melina sat staring blankly out of her office window from the gallery. She fidgeted with the tassels dangling from the fringe hemline of the coral colored asymmetrical top she sported. Her thoughts were focused on Yohan as they had been since she'd left him at the house a few days earlier.

She'd never seen such a lost look on anyone's face. Seeing it on Yohan's struck something within her. So many explosive blows he'd had to deal with and they'd all come from her lips. Where she'd found strength to reveal it all, she doubted she'd ever know. Now, she was left wondering when he'd snap-when the true depth of what she'd told him would make him snap.

She hadn't wanted to leave him alone, but Yohan wouldn't let her stay. She put little validity in his claim that he was fine and that he wasn't going to do anything stupid. She was on edge whenever the phone rang, fearing it was someone with news that he'd found Marc and killed him.

When one day passed and then another; however, she thought of something she'd never entertained. Perhaps Yohan wasn't going to fly off the deep end. Maybe he just needed her to go. Maybe he just didn't want to be around *her.* She'd brought him so much pain. From the day they married it had been a challenge. First, it was her barely concealed hatred of Marc-for good reason, but still she knew it agitated Yohan to see two people he loved so distrustful of one another.

Then, she'd left him and it almost killed him. She knew that, because leaving had done almost the same thing to her. In all that time, she'd never given up on them, knowing it could never be, yet hoping just the same. It was a pathetic existence-a shell of a life but she'd endured it with good reason.

Yohan, however, had no reasons, no explanations. He'd suffered without knowing why and then Melina returned and tried to carry on the lie-the hurt.

Now, though, it was all out in the open. He had his reasons, his explanations, but he was hurt just the same and it was all her doing.

Closing her eyes, Mel accepted the obvious. She would always remind him of this. The dramatic turn of events-the ugliness … How could they move beyond the past when her mere presence would always be there to remind him of it?

The knocking on the office door began softly, and then increased in volume when the sound went unanswered.

"Come in," Mel called, having finally tuned in to the world beyond her thoughts. Seeing Johari Frazier stick her head inside the room and perform their sorority call drew much needed laughter into the air. Mel forgot her depression and whirled her chair around to the door. Her cousin stood there happy and smiling, which did more to raise Melina's spirits than anything she could have conjured. She left the desk and went to pull her cousin into a stifling bear hug.

"What's this?" Johari laughed, when Mel seemed reluctant to let go.

Mel dismissed the desire to confide in her cousin, wanting nothing to overshadow the homecoming. "Just so glad to have you back," she whispered, turning her face into Johari's glossy sandy red hair. "So tell me about South America, is it as grizzly and beautiful as it seems on TV?"

"Is it?!" Jo cried shaking her head as visions of her recent trip came to mind. For the next twenty minutes or so, they spoke of her adventure. Johari provided a detailed account of all she'd seen while photographing the South American rainforests and following a team of environmental journalists on their treks through the lush jungles.

"Well it did you a world of good," Melina noted, a sly grin causing her slanting stare to twinkle devilishly. "Finally got some color on that white skin," she teased, thumping her fingers along her cousin's arm.

"*Ha-Ha*," Jo replied in a dry tone, tugging on a portion of the high ponytail Mel had drawn her thick hair into. "Just because you're melanin-rich don't mean you have to rub it in. Anyway ..." she sighed, rubbing her hands together as she took a seat before the desk. "How's it feel to be back after eight years?"

"What?"

Johari's doe-like silver stare widened in a telling manner. "That bad, huh? Or ... maybe that good?"

"Please take your head out of the gutter." Mel advised sweetly.

"Come off it Mel, you don't expect me to believe you ain't at least *seen* the man since you've been in town?"

Mel leaned back in her chair. "Oh I've-I've seen him."

Jo's lips curved into a sultry smile. "Details please."

"You don't know what you're asking. "Mel warned, twirling a lock around her finger. "It's a long, *long* story."

"And I've just had a long, *long* exhausting flight," Jo countered, tugging off her black hiking boots, "my only plans are to relax on that sofa in the corner and listen as you tell your tale of woe."

Mel appreciated her cousin's light hearted mood, but knew Jo's heart would be anything but light once she'd finished her story. Since she had no desire to keep any more secrets, Mel got comfortable and began to share.

Sure enough, there was a definite air of dread in the office, once Mel concluded her story. Johari had abandoned her relaxing place on the plush sofa and now stood before the tall windows. She stared blankly at the bustle of people on the streets below.

News that her sister; presumed dead close to twenty years, may very well be alive removed the light probing smile that usually added more of a glow to her flawless café au lait complexion.

"Are the police involved?" she asked, her husky voice sounding more hushed.

Mel shook her head. "No," she said.

"No? Why?" Jo snapped, turning to face her cousin. "Have the Ramseys covered it up?"

"No Jo."

"Then why isn't somebody out there trying to find her?" Jo raged, her chest heaving as the sobs demanded release.

"Jo-"

"Why don't they make that son of a bitch tell them where he has her?"

"Jo, Jo …" Mel urged, pulling the woman into a tight hug as her cries gained volume.

"Stop," Jo ordered, pulling back from Mel and brushing tears from her cheeks. "It's because of Yohan, isn't it? You're dragging your feet getting the police involved because-"

"You know that's not true," Mel snapped.

"Why not? Marc's the only father he's ever known. Maybe-"

"Jo, you shut your mouth!" Mel hissed, her index finger rose in warning.

Like a pendulum, Johari's emotions tipped to the other end of the spectrum. Her tears resurfaced and fell from her cheeks to sprinkle the front of the chic black halter tee she wore.

"I'm sorry, sorry Mel I-you know I didn't mean it."

Melina shook her head, pressing a kiss to Jo's forehead. "I know sweetie. It's alright. Listen to me," she ordered, looking directly into Johari's crystalline gaze. "Marc's gone. No one's seen him in months."

Jo seemed to go limp and would've slipped right to the floor had Mel not held her tight.

"Listen to me, they'll find him, you hear? They *will* find him."

Jo's smile screamed clear disbelief.

"The Ramseys have all turned against Marc. This time, he's gonna pay."

Jo smoothed the back of her hand across Mel's cheek. "To pay, he has to be found. To be found, he has to slip up. My sister's been gone close to twenty years cousin. I'd say he's pretty good at covering his tracks, wouldn't you?"

Melina had no reply.

CHAPTER THIRTEEN

In spite of the upsets and drama over the last weeks, the July fourth gathering at Quest and Michaela's home was a happy success. Mick congratulated herself on having a firm grasp on the family's needs. Everyone seemed refreshed by the energetic, light atmosphere. No one wanted to be reminded of anything negative and they didn't seem to be.

There was food galore, the pool and Jacuzzi were ready to be enjoyed and the tennis and basketball courts were waiting. Quest even had tons of new DVDs that would be shown in the home's private theater later that evening. Everyone appeared to be coupled off which added a romantic charm to the event. There was plenty of room to house the guests comfortably for an overnight stay.

Mick rolled her eyes and aimed a spatula toward Contessa who'd been fussing ever since Mick's release from the hospital. County, like Quest, didn't think Mick should be doing anything even remotely energetic. Mick, of course, refused to listen.

"Why don't you go relax in the study? It's close enough that you can come runnin' if I go into labor," Mick teased.

"You've been trying to get me out of here all afternoon," Contessa noted, folding her arms across the peach halter dress she wore.

Mick clasped her hands together. "Should I take that to mean you're finally getting the hint?"

County didn't have a chance to issue a comeback. Fernando had returned to the kitchen and pulled her close.

"Can I steal you away?" he asked.

"Yes!" Mick offered.

Fernando's rumbling laughter filled the kitchen. County rolled her eyes, but noticed the tense look on Fernando's face.

"What's wrong?" she asked.

Fernando shook his head, absently fingering the straps that criss-crossed her back. "It won't take long," he promised.

Shooting Mick a tired glare, County pushed her hand into the back pocket of Fernando's sagging jeans and they left the kitchen.

"I was headed to the study for some quiet time," she told him.

Noticing the drawn tone to her voice, Fernando smoothed his hand across her arm. "Are you having a good time?"

"Mmm hmm, I'll just be happy when the baby's born," County admitted, pursing her lips then. "Mick's too wild to carry a baby properly," she criticized.

Fernando stroked his beard. "Well ... she seems to be doin' a good job so far," he championed, laughing again when County responded with a disapproving snort.

"At least she's got Quest to keep her halfway in check," County was saying when they entered the study and took seats on the sofa.

Fernando sat silently for a while, watching County as she grazed her nails along her bare arms. "Yeah," he sighed and nodded slowly. "It's good for a woman to have a husband ... if she wants one."

"Yeah, she-" County stopped and turned to look at Fernando more closely. "What does *that* mean?" she inquired almost uneasily.

Frowning as though he were focusing, Fernando moved his hands across his thighs. "Do you want one?" he asked in a purely adorable manner. "A husband?"

Contessa held her breath, her mind going completely blank for a second. "I-I suppose um ... if the right man were to ask."

He nodded once, and then eased his hand into the breast pocket on the front of the short sleeved pine shirt that hung outside his jeans. County pressed her lips together and watched him open a small, maroon velvet box. Inside, there was a gorgeous round diamond set on a silver band.

"Would you please wear this until you decide whether I'm the right man?" he asked, pulling her hand into his.

"Fernando-"

"I'm asking you to be my wife Contessa," he interrupted, his translucent brown stare focused on his ring adorning her hand. "I pray you'll say yes."

County knew exactly what she wanted to say. Sadly, she just couldn't get the words to form on her tongue.

Fernando smiled and leaned close to brush his mouth across her cheek. "You relax and I'll see you later."

Contessa watched him heading out the study. Her eyes were wide and she couldn't believe he was just leaving. She couldn't even open her mouth to tell him to wait, or yes, or *I'll marry you.* When he'd left, she studied the ring again wondering when he'd gotten it-when he'd decided that he wanted her to marry him. She was so deep in thought that it took her some time to register that something was very wrong with the chuckling and clapping that rose unexpectedly in the room.

Relaxing in a chair hidden in the shadows of the massive study was Stefan Lyons.

"Damn bravo. Bravo Fernando. My man's finally takin' the leap," Stef commended, standing from the arm chair. "You know, I always figured *I'd* get hitched before Fern." He shrugged, looking as though there were nothing out of the ordinary about him being there.

County's fingers curled into one of the throw pillows nearby. Clutching the pillow was the only thing that prevented her from screaming.

"My man Fern," Stef still raved as a telling smile curved his mouth. "But I guess being a Ramsey's always given him the jump on things."

"Well you're a Ramsey too," County finally found her voice, smirking at the surprise on Stef's face. "Yeah, we know," she confirmed. "Too bad your sick daddy didn't own up to it when it could've made a difference."

Stefan's expression hardened into a cold mask. 'I'm glad Fern finally found a freak he wanted to lock down."

"What the hell do you want?" County hissed.

Stef's smile looked even more menacing in light of the busted lip he sported since the tussle with Fernando. The grin sent a frightening wave through County and she wasn't sure she wanted an answer to her question.

A shrill sound shattered the silence. It was Stef's cell which he answered before the ring tone could pierce the air again.

"Pop," he greeted Marcus Ramsey.

County leaned forward on the sofa, trying to pick up as much of the conversation as she could. Unfortunately, Stef's end of the discussion was mainly a series of *mmm hmms* and *uh-uh's*. When he turned to look at her, she felt that sick feeling overtake her again.

"I know you got a dime waitin' on me over there, but she can't be better than what I'm lookin' at right now." Stef boasted, yet the easy look on his handsome face tightened. Clearly, Marc was issuing a scolding response.

"It *will* be quick Pop." Stef assured, his gaze narrowing towards Contessa again, "but I've been wanting some of this for a long time. I'll be in and out-literally."

County didn't need to hear more and intended to make a dash for the door. Stefan was there, blocking her way before she could leave the sofa.

"Gotta go Pop," he said, clicking off the phone and pushing it into his jeans. "You'll like it, don't worry," he promised.

County began to punch his chest and was about to call out when his hand covered her mouth. She bit into his palm and he retaliated with a vicious backhand slap. Dazed and feeling murderous at once, County lost her verbal skills again.

Stefan's sinister expression oozed a confidence. She'd not cry out again, he was sure. Unmindful of her gasp of pain, his hand tightened harshly about her arm and he jerked her close.

"That damn jackass Fernando always walkin' around like a god. Him and his punk-ass brothers," he breathed against County's dark close-cropped hair. "I hate 'em, always have, but had to play nice. Those days are over," he swore, his other hand closing over her breast. "Marc needs me now and since his *sons* turned their backs … well I'm damn well gonna benefit and that's gonna start with me enjoying one of my half-brother's goodies," he decided and lowered his face to the scoop neck of her halter.

Terrified, Contessa's breathing was heavy, much to Stefan's delight. Her chest heaved against his mouth.

"You know how I like it," he commended, settling himself against her. "After I'm done with you I'll have a taste of Yohan's toy and then her cousin … too bad you won't live to talk about how good it was."

At last, County found her voice and screamed with all her force. In the same moment, Stef was literally ripped off her. She heard him breathe the word '*you*', but didn't look up to see who had come to her rescue. She escaped through a side door, screaming as she ran.

"I can't believe you just left without finding out if she'd say yes," Melina noted. She'd joined Michaela in the kitchen to talk when Fernando had returned from the study.

Fernando took another swig of his Heineken. "She may not say yes," he warned.

"Why wouldn't she?" Mick challenged, trying to maintain a serious expression instead of smiling at the little-boy uncertainty on Fernando's face.

Mel sat close, rubbing her hand across his knee. "She wants to marry you very much, trust me. You should've stayed in the study until you got an answer."

Fernando set aside his beer. "I felt like I was gonna faint in there," he groaned, holding his head down and rubbing his fingers through the silkiness of his brown hair. "I think I needed to get out of there more than she needed me to leave."

Mick and Mel exchanged dreamy looks and fawned even more over Fernando. His uncharacteristic show of unease endeared him to them both. Mick was pressing a kiss to his cheek and Mel was hugging his neck when Quest, Quay and Tykira arrived with Yohan.

"Hey, hey what's goin' on in here?" Quest demanded playfully.

"Yeah, break this mess up," Quay ordered.

"Oh hush," Mick urged with a wave. "Fernando just proposed to County."

"Oh!" Ty gasped and went to fawn over Fernando as well.

Amidst all the love and laughter, Melina and Yohan's gazes held. Clearly, they missed one another and Mel couldn't hide the longing in her exotic slanting stare. She turned away, missing Yohan's hazel gaze soften as a smile began to tug at his mouth.

A heavy boom resounded over all other commotion when County burst into the kitchen crying Fernando's name. Everyone turned, in slow motion it seemed. Their expressions went from happy, to confused to stormy when the group took in Contessa's disheveled appearance and the trickle of blood oozing from her lip.

"What happened?" Fernando growled, already on his feet and catching her as her legs gave way.

County's fingers curled into Fernando's shirt and she took several moments to catch her breath. "Stef-the study-he-he tried to-"

She didn't have a chance to say more. The guys went charging out of the kitchen, headed for Quest's study. When they burst into the room, it was in shambles. There was a body lying on the floor. Fernando grabbed the man by the back of his shirt and turned him over.

"What the hell?" Fernando breathed, his eyes widening in disbelief.

The group watched, stunned as Wake Robinson regained consciousness. The women came into the study just as Fernando was tugging Wake to his feet by the collar of his shirt.

"What the hell are you doin' here?" Fernando demanded.

"And alive," Quay added, his fist clenching reflexively.

"Wait!" County blurted, when it appeared the guys were about to render Wake unconscious again. She rushed in, pulling Fernando's hands away from the man's shirt. "If I'm not mistaken, you just saved my life," she said, watching as Wake smiled.

"I had to fake it," Wake said of his death.

Stefan was long gone having knocked Wake unconscious shortly after their fight began.

I figured it was the best way to get the goods on Marc," Wake said, his dark brown eyes narrowed in frustration. "Problem was, he left Seattle before I could put my plan into affect. So I've been on Stef's butt the entire time hoping he'd lead me to Marcus."

"So you knew about Stef being Marc's son?" Yohan asked, watching Wake nod.

Wake leaned forward, resting his elbows on his jean clad thighs. "Sorry I didn't tell you guys before," he said, looking at Quay.

"Don't sweat that mess, man," said Moses who'd arrived shortly after the ruckus had settled. "This is small potatoes next to all the other crap our father is into."

Wake smashed his fist against his palm. "I just hate that I didn't get what I was after-concrete evidence against that man."

"Like Mo said, don't sweat it," Yohan advised with a slow smirk, "if you hadn't been here County could've been raped and killed and-"

"Mel," Contessa whispered, drawing everyone's attention.

"What?" Yohan probed.

County appeared as though she'd just remembered something awful and the full realization of Stefan's threats hit her.

Fernando made her face him, his thumbs brushing her cheeks. "What is it, love?" he urged.

"Once he was done with me ... he-he said he'd have a taste of Yohan's toy and then her cousin.

"Johari!" Mel gasped, leaning against the doorjamb, her eyes wide.

Mick and Ty rushed to her, while Moses turned away in deep concentration.

"Did he say anything else?" Fernando asked County.

She was shaking her head. "He … he was talking to Marc. I did hear him say his name," she whispered, trying to ward off shivers as the memories resurfaced.

"I heard him say something about a dime waitin' on him *over there*," Wake recalled, folding his arms over the front of the black Nike T-shirt he wore. "He didn't say where *over there* was," he added.

"Oh my God," County groaned, closing her eyes. "I'm so stupid."

"What is it?" Fernando asked, rubbing her back with wide reassuring strokes.

"I'd forgotten, I'd forgotten that girl." Her eyes met Fernando's then. "The girl I met on the ship-on the Wind Rage."

Fernando stilled. "What about her?"

"That night we-we went to dinner. Cufi pulled you away to talk about something …" her eyes drifted across the room. "There was a girl. I doubt if she was even eighteen. She was all excited because Cufi promised to help her acting career, said he was taking her to the house-this great place he had in Nice."

"Moses?" Melina called, reaching out for her brother-in-law. "What if Stefan wasn't talking about Jo?" She asked, once they were holding hands. "What if he meant Zara?"

Moses' black eyes narrowed with a sinister intensity. A second later, he was on his cell and telling one of his men to round up the rest of the guys-he wanted everyone on this.

"We'll find her," Moses promised, once the call was done and he was hugging Mel. "We'll find her," he stressed, kissing her cheek before joining his brothers and cousins in a huddle around Wake.

◆   ◆   ◆

"Runnin' off half cocked and without me. We agreed that I'd go with you, but nooo you had to run off and have everyone scared to death you'd done somethin' crazy." Rita Hotchkiss spoke without taking a breath as she chastised her boss.

Josephine relaxed on the lounge near the bay windows in her bedroom. In spite of Rita's admonishments, a content smile graced Josephine's face. The smile remained in tact even when Rita let loose a piercing scream. Sighing, she snuggled in more securely on the sofa. "It's for my own protection," she explained, knowing what the woman had uncovered in the suitcase.

"That's what dogs and security men are for," Rita countered, looking down at the gun she'd discovered amidst Josephine's clothing.

Josephine grimaced. "Those *security* men work for Marcus."

"So you buy this? Woman what in the world do you know about using a gun?"

"Enough," Josephine replied without hesitation, folding her arms across the front of the white silk lounging robe. "Became licensed while I was away. I can shoot any gun there is."

"Or any*one* there is," Rita warned, propping a hand on her hip.

Josephine smirked. "There's only one person I want to share my skills with."

Rita slammed the case shut. "He ain't worth it," she said, taking a seat on the bed.

"Oh yes he is. He is *very* worthy of being shot to death with my gun."

Shaking her head, Rita left the bed and went to close the room door. Then she stomped over to the lounge and whipped the cloth from Josephine's eyes. "Think about what you're sayin' dammit," she ordered, giving Josephine a harsh shake. "Hell, he may deserve that, but it's *not* worth you going to jail for the rest of your life because of it."

Josephine propped herself up, her expression suddenly appearing tired and defeated. "Rita you know everything-more than my own family. You know the horror I've been through with that son of a bitch."

"Then *leave* him Josie. Leave him." Rita urged her glare stormy. "Don't waste any more of your life by killing him."

"Him being dead is the only way I'll have a life," Josephine decided, her tone brooking no further disagreement. Turning to her side, she closed her eyes.

Rita stood, shaking her head morosely. She cast another wary look upon the suitcase that carried the gun.

◆   ◆   ◆

"There can't be any mistake?"

"I don't think so."

Fernando and Moses watched their younger brother with stunned looks darkening their handsome faces. Yohan had just told them the story of his true paternity. The trio stood in silence, but their thoughts were the same. They were thoughts of hatred for all Marc Ramsey had taken them through.

Fernando stepped closer, his eyes crinkling adorably as he smiled. "We share the parent who counts," he said and clapped a hand to Yohan's shoulder. "Josephine is our mother and even if she weren't, nothing can change the fact that you're my brother and I love you."

"*We* love you," Moses corrected, stepping close as the three brothers shared a tight hug.

"Man there's nothing I could say to-to tell you how sorry I am … for everything," Wake said to Quay and smiled at Tykira who stood at her husband's side. "If I'd been man enough to step up back then, Quay wouldn't have felt he had to push you away and lose all those years."

Ty shook her head. "We won't talk about this anymore. We all have futures to look forward to."

"Which includes parenthood," Wake said, watching the couple exchange uneasy looks.

Ty pressed her lips together and took a step closer to Wake. "We certainly understand that you'd want to be there for your sons."

"I'll be there Tykira, but it'll be as their *uncle* Wake."

"Man? What are you sayin'?" Quay asked, stepping close as well.

Wake smiled. "Come on kid, you know I always wanted a life like yours. Not because of the money or clothes like my mom and everybody else thought. It was because of Damon and Catrina," he admitted, referring to Quay's parents. "They raised you and Quest together. Catrina was always ready to listen to your chatter and girl problems-never too tired from working two jobs to support you on her own. Damon was there to show y'all what it meant to be a man. I wanted that."

Quay raised his hand, but words escaped him.

"Wake? What happened to their mother if you don't mind my asking," Ty inquired.

Wake bowed his head. "We met in college, dated off and on and then more steady once we graduated. We lived together … things were rough with neither of us having jobs in our major so we decided to call it quits. Then a few years ago, she came back strung out on … cocaine, crack take your pick. She needed a friend, I couldn't turn her away. After a while it looked like she was gonna get better, we got close again. Then one day, she was gone-no word, nothing. She was pregnant, thank God she wasn't back on the stuff but it'd done so much damage to her body … she died in labor. They found me from the information she put down when they checked her in. Ma and I did our best, but we both knew they needed more and now with Ma sick …"

Ty stepped closer. "You can still be a real father to them Wake. They can still have a very good life."

"I damn well want my boys to have that life," Wake continued, "I see Damon and Catrina in you both and knowin' my guys will be loved and educated in matters of the mind and heart makes me proud to give you my children to raise."

Ty was crying then, while Quay stood frowning to keep his own tears at bay. Soon, another three way hug was commencing in the study.

◆   ◆   ◆

Mel finally managed to assure Mick that she was fine and didn't need to partake in an overnight stay at the house. If anything, she needed to get away from the hubbub and get some quiet time alone. She was rushing toward her rented Acura, her head bowed as she searched for the key ring in her purse. She didn't notice Yohan already leaning against the car.

"It'll be fine if you leave it here."

Melina shrieked, clutching her purse to her stomach. She blinked-dumbfounded to find him standing there and speaking so calmly. "Um I'm-I'm fine, you don't have to-I just need to get home."

"Home is exactly where I want to take you," he said, his deep set dark eyes raking her with seductive intent.

Mel clutched her bag a bit more securely against the strapless lemon tube dress she wore. "I can't," she whispered.

Yohan nodded as if he'd expected her reaction. "Until we find Stef, I'm keeping you in my sight."

"Isn't that a bit much, Han? I mean, I really don't think-"

"Listen to me Mel, you can either come with me or I can take you."

She wanted to moan over the implications his words suggested.

Yohan was already closing the distance between them. "Either way, you're not going anywhere without me," he promised.

CHAPTER FOURTEEN

Mel was walking into her hotel suite, when she thought of a perfect reason not to stay with Yohan who was following close behind her.

"Johari," she blurted, turning to fix her husband with her most pleading look. "I can't just leave her alone now-not with everything we found out today. Unless you're planning to move us both in with you?" she challenged, propping a hand to her hip.

Yohan responded with a slow smile. He dipped his head, massaging his jaw to shield the expression that proved he knew what she was up to.

"Maybe you should check your messages," he suggested.

Melina blinked, catching the chord in his voice. After studying him for a moment, she went to the phone and wasn't surprised to find the message light flashing.

"*Hey Mel, it's Jo,*" Mel heard her cousin's voice come through the line, "*Yohan called and told me everything. He says he wants to keep you with him and that's a good idea-don't fight him on it. Anyway, I'm going to Mama and Daddy in London. I-I don't want to tell them about Zara over the phone and we should ... we should be together now anyway. So ... I'll talk to you soon and you be safe. Love you. Bye.*"

Mel fidgeted with the scarf holding back her lengthy coarse locks. She deflated a bit with the knowledge that Johari wasn't a concern, yet she was comforted knowing her cousin was safe.

"I'll wait while you pack," Yohan said once she set down the phone.

Mel bowed her head and debated.

"Please don't argue with me anymore," he asked as if reading her mind.

Melina began to pack; making progress at first. Then, a dazed feeling overtook her and she sat on the bed to think over all that had occurred since she'd returned to Seattle. Never, had she expected to learn the things she had.

At last, she could relate to Yohan's anger-for it was the feeling she held toward Marcus Ramsey now: hate and anger. The rich desire to avenge the hurt he caused to she and her family, flowed like warm syrup through her veins. She'd never harbored such consuming dislike for anyone and it was as frightening as it was exhilarating.

Still, what unnerved her most was knowing that these feelings were yet another obstacle in the way of getting her husband back. Her *intense dislike* of Marc was the cause of the problems with Yohan at the onset of their marriage. How could they manage-how could they start fresh when her *intense dislike* was now a *deep seeded hatred* for the man?

She wouldn't rest until he paid. Until Marcus Ramsey was behind bars, her thoughts would be consumed by him. Behind bars? Ha! The man had eluded charges for well over a decade even after all he'd done. He was powerful and he was evil and no one was going to take him down.

Melina jumped when knocking sounded on the open door to the bedroom. Yohan stood there, leaning half in half outside the room.

"You need any help?" he asked.

The soft, simple question sent a wave of emotion rushing through her chest. Yohan frowned, never expecting such a reaction and came to the bed. He wiped her cheek, watching tears pool in her slanting stare.

"Shh …" he urged, pulling her close to rock her slow while she cried. "Baby it'll be alright," he whispered. "Shh … it'll be fine."

Mel swallowed her fingers curled into his beige T-shirt and searched his face with a desperate look. "Are you sure? Can you promise me? If you promise me, I'll believe you. I'd believe anything good right now."

Yohan pressed his forehead to hers. "Shh …" he urged again, brushing his thumbs against the tears moistening her cheeks. When her shuddery sobs quieted, he kissed her temple. "Come on, let's get you home." He said.

◆   ◆   ◆

Contessa pulled Fernando's hand from her bruised lip and kissed his palm. "I'm fine," she told him.

Fernando didn't appear convinced and growled another foul curse into the air. "Bastard hit you," he noted in a rough tone.

"Baby, it's fine," she tried to sooth him and kissed his hand again. "The cops are on this, so are Moses' men-they'll find the son of a bitch."

Fernando toyed with her cropped dark hair and grimaced. "If Wake hadn't been here-"

"Shh … but he was, he was …"

"I can't lose you. I waited too long to find you," he said, sounding as though he were reminding himself.

County nuzzled her nose against the side of his face. "I know how you feel," she said, watching him take her hand and brush his thumb against the ring she wore.

"Does it fit alright?" he asked.

Smiling, County nodded and started to stroke the ring as well. "It's fine and it's beautiful. I can't wait to see my wedding ring."

Fernando's hand stilled and slowly he focused his translucent brown eyes on her face. "What?" he blurted.

Contessa frowned playfully. "Well you *are* planning to buy me one, aren't you Ramsey?"

He cupped her face, planting a quick hard kiss to her cheek. "Are you saying-"

"I'm saying yes. Yes Fernando. Yes, I'll be your wife," she said, laughing when he closed his eyes as though he were uttering a prayer before he pulled her into a tight hug.

◆   ◆   ◆

"Can you hand me the okra while you're in there?"

Yohan pulled the frozen green vegetables form the freezer. There was a reverent smile on his dark face as he passed the bag to Melina. "Damn have I missed this," he said. His black gaze was riveted on the huge pot that was steadily filling with the ingredients for Mel's jambalaya.

Melina's giggles filled the kitchen. "Is that why you quickly and *loudly* suggested this when we went to the market this afternoon?"

It was the day after the disastrous July fourth gathering and there was a rather surreal quality to the atmosphere.

Melina and Yohan woke that morning doing things as though the last eight years had simply been some awful dream. They made breakfast and ate with the morning paper spread on the table. They conversed and bickered lightly over the latest current events. They even managed to chuckle over the fact that the Ramseys had remained out of the black and white print. *The day is young* Melina had teased. They worked from home and after lunch, Yohan suggested they cook in and together they headed out for groceries. Deep down, Melina reeled with happiness. She imaged this was her life and a tiny seed of hope sparked inside her.

Melina caught the bag when he tossed it over. "I don't know why you're missing this when you're just as good a cook as I am. Maybe better," she commended, smoothing her damp hand across the seat of the brown boy-shorts before turning to tear into the okra.

"'Preciate that, but you're wrong," Yohan argued, closing the freezer side door of the fridge. "You do somethin' special to it. I can never get it to taste the way you do."

"Mmm hmm," she drawled in clear disbelief. "Do you ever even try, Han?"

"Tried once," he said after a brief silence. "One night when I was … missing you so damned bad and wanting to come down to Memphis and not leave until you agreed to come back with me or until I lost my mind and carried you back here kicking and screaming."

Melina's hands stilled over the bag as she listened to his soft confession. "Why didn't you?" she heard herself inquire in a whisper, her hands trembling on the bag causing it to crinkle in the silence that followed her question.

Yohan pulled his hands from the back pockets of his sagging black denim shorts and braced them on the kitchen island. "Why didn't I … what?"

Mel cleared her throat and forced herself to respond. "Why didn't you come to Memphis and not leave until I came back?"

Yohan stepped closer until he was standing right behind her. "Would you have come back with me?"

"I may not have let you leave," she admitted, unconsciously holding her breath.

After an eternity-it seemed-Yohan reached out to trail his finger between her shoulder blades bared by the tan backless halter top she sported. Melina leaned back her head, a helpless sound rising from her throat. Yohan pulled her back secure against her, burying his beautiful dark face in her lush tresses. His hands moved up to cup her breasts, his fingers beginning to manipulate her nipples into rigid peaks.

Instinctively, Mel moved her bottom against the iron power that steadily stiffened beneath his denims. She arched her neck when his lips traveled her nape, then began to nip at the satiny sensitive spot beneath her earlobe. Eventually, his hands found their way beneath her top and she shuddered at the feel of his thumbs grazing and circling her pleasure hardened nipples.

Gasping his name, Mel turned and kissed him desperately. She winced when his powerful arms flexed about her and she thrust her tongue deeper into his mouth. A low sound rumbled from Yohan's chest and a second later he was dragging her to the floor. His hands were everywhere-kneading her breasts, massaging the small of her back and lifting her into the solid length of his arousal.

"Han, make love to me please … please … I need you so much …"

Melina's lashes fluttered open when she realized Yohan had stopped touching her. Confusion clouded her face as she watched him move away and leave the kitchen.

Mel fixed her clothes and finished preparing the jambalaya before she ventured off to find Yohan. She wasn't surprised to hear the savage clang of the machinery from the weight room. Taking a deep breath, she descended the stairway into the dark, foreboding dwelling. She hadn't seen him working out in years but she'd fantasized a million times about what he looked like; chiseled dark as midnight and glistening with sweat. She'd dreamed of seeing him that way ever since that first day at the house when she'd come into the gym and they made love there.

Her mouth fell open at the sight of him working out and none of her memories came close to the lusty vision before her eyes. Moving closer, she could hear another sound mingling with the clang of the equipment. Savage, tortured grunts filled the air as he lifted the excessive weights with his arms and legs.

Then, the weights fell with one final clang and he stopped lifting. He turned partially as though sensing her presence.

"What?" he called, but his voice held no trace of harshness.

Mel gave a start anyway, but ventured forward. "Did I do something? Say something wrong? Han?" she said when he didn't answer.

"You haven't done anything Mel."

"Then what happened?"

Yohan smoothed one hand across his silky dark hair and shrugged. "I don't know," he sounded honest.

Mel bowed her head and smiled. "Then why don't I tell you?" she offered, stepping closer to the weight bench he occupied.

Remaining silent, Yohan simply watched her moving through the dim room.

"I've told you all there is to tell, Han. Now I need to tell you why I waited so long to share everything. I know the sight of me must remind you of all the terrible things you've found out about Marc-about yourself, since I came back," she said, sounding as though she were relieving herself of some heavy burden. "I've been nothing but a source of pain to you and even something as enjoyable as making love probably only reminds you of all the years I've been gone-gone with no explanation to you about why I had to leave."

By now, Yohan was reclining against the bench. His dark, deep-set stare held an incredulous intensity. He couldn't believe what he was hearing. *My God, does she actually think I feel this way about her?* He marveled.

Melina was baring her soul without a care. She spoke of how she missed him, how she'd longed for him-always wanting to come back, but so terrified, such a coward …

"I know you could never be happy being reminded of all that. I know that and still I came to stay with you," she said her expression solemn and pleading at once. "I could've easily gone to my parents or stayed with Quest and Mick." She shrugged, fluffing her thick hair while she paced. "I guess deep down, I prayed you'd touch me, kiss me. Making love was more than I hoped for. When we were in the kitchen, I almost screamed I was so happy your hands were on me. I wished you'd never stop; that you would-would rip something off me and do what I wanted you to. If having you again wasn't in the picture, I wouldn't care because I'd have that moment and that would be enough."

Yohan's intentions to correct her belief that she'd brought him nothing but pain, drained away. He could only focus on her strolling just within his grasp and lost in her despairing thoughts. She spoke with such unconscious seduction on her lips, that every part of him felt heavy with desire.

Melina bowed her head, coming to the end of her rambling. "I'm sorry," she whispered, turning to make her way out of the gym when her hip brushed a massive shoulder.

Yohan's hand snaked about her thigh and brought her to him, taking no heed of the gasp she uttered.

"Han-" Mel whispered, but couldn't continue the statement. Her lashes were fluttering close, her lips forming a perfect O as his mouth worked her into a frenzy. He tongued her through the stretchy material of the shorts she wore.

Melina's happy cry floated into the air when she heard the material of the shorts rip. She was bared then to his eyes-his touch. Yohan curved both hands about her thighs and pulled her forward as he lay back on the bench press. Mel wound her arms across the weight bar and virtually screamed her pleasure as he lowered her up and down the length of his tongue while it thrust and rotated inside her. When he was done, he held her draped across his body. His sneaker shod feet were planted firmly on either side of the bench.

His kiss was wet and deep, forcing lusty moans of pleasure from Mel as she suckled his lips and tongue as if she were trying to drink him in.

Yohan sat up then, taking her with him. He stripped away the halter that had teased him all afternoon along with the tight shorts she'd bounced around in.

Beautifully naked, Mel straddled his powerful body clothed in the nylon sweats that slung low on his hips. She ground against him kissing madly-eagerly until Yohan broke the kiss and filled his mouth with her breasts. Melina was weak with passion and cheered Yohan's strength as he held her to him with one hand braced at the center of her back. The other tugged at the drawstring of his pants and he freed himself.

Mel went to touch him, but he repositioned her and effortlessly set her down upon his erect desire. She climaxed almost instantly but wanted all he had to give. Yohan took his time, carrying her from the weight bench and into the living area across the gym.

Dropping her to the sofa, he covered her with his magnificent form. He feasted on the firm peaks of her bosom-holding her thighs apart as he did so. Mel reveled in the feel of his muscular torso beneath her fingers. Her eyes snapped open when she felt him move to lie upon the sofa. He straddled her across his lap once again. This time, however, he kept her back toward him as she rode his length. Melina could barely perform the act, yet it mattered little. Yohan played her like a puppet; keeping his hands around her slender hips as he manipulated her movements. He made her ride him hard and fast at times, slow and torturous at others.

Mel begged him, but had no idea what she plead for. Her mind was filled with only the way he directed her movements. At last, he settled behind her and took her body with swift, deep lunges that drew deep, satisfied groans from his throat. He allowed her to melt onto the sofa only when the last of his passion had spent itself.

◆   ◆   ◆

The following morning, television sets all over Seattle were tuned to one of the city's morning shows. The top news: Houston Ramsey tells all. Brief snippets from the interview to air in a special broadcast that evening; revealed that a spokesperson for Houston would release comments regarding the man's startling confession. It was a confession that would implicate many-including members of the Ramsey family.

"Damn," Quest muttered, his gray eyes now onyx with aggravation, "wonder when the phone'll start ringing off the hook?" he mused. "Maybe Marc'll come out of hiding now. Unless he plans to send Stef back out for another hit," he continued in a teasing voice. His expression sobered when he looked over at Mick who had joined him in the study when he told her what was on TV.

Michaela reclined on the sofa. She stared fixedly at something across the room.

"What?" Quest called, tilting his head as he watched her.

"Dr. Steins warned me not to panic if the contractions started," she calmly explained after a moment had passed.

Quest, however, shot up out of his desk chair.

"He told me to time them," she relayed calmly, while her husband stood across the room looking the complete opposite of calm. "He told me not to do anything until they were five minutes apart-ten minutes could easily be contractions of false labor."

Quest swallowed. "How far apart are they?" he asked.

Still calm, Mick smiled. "They've been five minutes apart for about a half hour."

Another curse rang out in the study. Quest had fallen back into his chair.

"I really need you to be standing right about now," Mick requested, still maddeningly calm.

"Right, right …" Quest breathed his handsome face a picture of anxiety and uncertainty.

"My bag is packed and in the foyer closet. You'll need your keys and they're right in that gold tray on the corner of your desk."

"Right," Quest whispered, dutifully pushing the key ring into his jeans and then going to get the bag from the closet.

Mick smiled, folding her arms across the front of her housedress. She nodded as though she'd expected to hear the front door slam soon after. Little over a minute passed before Quest rushed back inside looking apologetic and embarrassed. Michaela patted his cheek when he lifted her off the sofa.

"At least you remembered me *before* you drove off."

"Now is not the time for you to cut me down with your jokes, Mick," he argued in a soft hurt tone.

"I'm sorry sweetness," she cooed, pressing a kiss to his jaw and then resting her head against his chest while struggling to hide her smile.

◆   ◆   ◆

Following their enthusiastic lovemaking over every square inch of Yohan's gym, Mel found herself back in the guest bedroom suite that morning being ravished all over again. She had no complaints of course. With a soft smile, she realized Yohan must have tuned in to her need to remain out of the master bedroom. The sounds of her breathless cries of pleasure mingled with Yohan's baritone moans of satisfaction. The queen bed was a mass of tangled covers and pillows were strewn across the room. She knew walking would be quite a feat afterwards, but there were far more *pressing* matters occupying her at the moment. Her slender fingers curled into the crisp, silver gray linens as she arched up to meet Yohan's powerful thrusts. A surge of triumph flooded through her, when his deep moans lost some of their fervor and took on a more helpless, tortured sound.

"Mmm," Yohan grunted, slowing his thrusts to grab her bottom and increase the depth of his penetration if that was possible.

Mel felt him stiffen a bit more inside her and seconds later his seed erupted. They lay there: still connected-still breathless. It gradually became difficult for her to breathe, but she didn't want to move. The TV had been auto-programmed and it clicked on just as she was about to reposition herself. The announcement of the evening's expose on Houston Ramsey, pulled their attention to the screen. By the end of the broadcast both Yohan and Melina were sitting up in bed.

"Oh please let Moses get there in time," Mel prayed, folding her hands atop her raised knees.

Yohan pulled her close. "He will," he promised hugging her close.

The embrace only reminded Mel of the conversation that previous evening. *Conversation* however was probably not the best description. It was more of a confession from her. Sadly, she'd not heard his reaction. *Things* had quickly traveled down another road. She'd asked for one moment-telling him that would be enough and he'd given it to her. Now, in the bright light of the morning, she realized she didn't want to hear his reaction to what'd she'd told him. She'd already guessed, hadn't she? How could he feel any other way?

Yohan felt her bracing against him, but ignored it. His kiss and touch affected Melina as always but she couldn't give in. Not now when she was once again facing the bleak reality of the future.

Surprising herself Mel found the will to push away and leave the bed.

"I'll be leaving right after the gallery opening," she announced, sounding as if she'd just reached the decision. When Yohan made no comment, she nodded as though the matter was truly settled, and went into the adjoining bathroom.

Yohan lay back in bed, stroking his abs with the sheet twisted provocatively around his privates. He smiled, happier that he could remember being in a long time. His smile widened as he pictured the look on her face when he told her he wasn't about to let her walk out of his life again.

CHAPTER FIFTEEN

Nice, France

"Alright, first team in with me. Second team hold back. Wait for our signal. Don't worry you'll know when we give it."

Moses finished relaying orders to his men and shut off the walkie-talkie. He motioned to the group surrounding him. Like clockwork, they hunched, guns in hand and headed toward the fortress-like structure in their midst. The place was still and silent with the exception of the birds, insects and the brush of leaves against the wind. Of course, the soothing ambience gave a false sense of security.

Moses and his men had to focus more heavily on their mission than the beauty all around. Raising one leather-gloved hand, Moses ordered the men to halt. Then, he motioned again and a group of five went hurrying in the opposite direction-towards the side of the building.

Moses closed his eyes and said a quick prayer that he'd find his father. More importantly, he prayed Jahzara Frazier would be there and alive. And ... well? He wasn't so sure of, but he'd not leave until he had her or until he was sure that she wasn't there.

He'd told himself that he was doing this for Mel. She needed to be rid of the hell she'd lived with not knowing her cousin's fate. In truth, he was doing this for Johari. Everything he'd done had been for Johari. Why? Because he owed her?

True. Because he'd hurt her? True. Because he stilled loved her? Most definitely. He'd never stopped, but a relationship was as impossible now as it'd been all those years ago. Especially when he'd always feared Johari would share her sister's misfortune.

Had he always suspected Marc played a hand in Zara's disappearance? Perhaps a part of him did and he just refused to believe it. But he was here now and whether for Johari, himself or Melina, he was about to discover the truth. Catching the eye of his team leader, Moses gave the signal to proceed.

Jahzara Frazier bowed her head and let her thick, black locks slap his chest-the way he liked. Then, she straightened and began to ride him with renewed energy.

Marcus Ramsey closed his eyes and smiled, savoring the pleasure he received. "You've come such a long way," he commended, closing his hands over her breasts.

"You taught me well," Zara purred.

"Hell you already knew quite a bit, messin' around with my flaky nephew Quay."

Something flickered in Zara's eyes, but she shielded it. "Why are you speaking of that?" she asked.

Marc shook his head, looking as though the comment had shocked him as well. Then shrugging, he squeezed her thighs. "I just enjoy what we have," he said.

Zara smiled, leaning forward again to brush her nose along his cheek. "I enjoy it too."

The couple lost themselves in a lusty kiss and they were in the throes of pleasure when a thundering commotion reached their ears.

"What the hell?" he hissed, sitting up and almost toppling Zara off his lap.

Marc looked towards the door and his body went cold. There in the archway stood Moses.

◆   ◆   ◆

"She looks just like you. Only tinier," Quest said his deep voice awe-filled as he lay next to his wife on the hospital bed and toyed with the thick, glossy, blue black curls atop his little girl's head.

"God Mick, thank you," he breathed, leaning close to kiss the top of the baby's head as she dozed in her mother's arms.

"Thank *you*," Mick returned, brushing her lips across his jaw.

A sweet kiss followed, until tiny cooing broke them apart. The couple looked down to see their daughter-who appeared to be laughing up at them.

Quest shook his head. "Hmph, not even a day old and we're already amusing her."

"It's just a reaction. I don't think she can show emotion yet." Michaela kissed her little girl's forehead and lingered there as she inhaled her daughter's unique baby scent. Quest noticed when Mick closed her eyes and tears streamed beneath her lashes.

"Hey," he called, knowing what had affected her. "We're gonna do fine. *You're* gonna do fine," he assured her.

"Promise me that," Mick whispered, fixing him with her intense amber gaze.

"I don't need to promise. It's a fact," he said, helping himself to the taste of her mouth.

"Mmm," Mick moaned contentedly-once the kiss ended. "You know, folks are gonna be stopping by soon and we don't even have a name for this woman yet."

Quest felt his heart lurch when the baby curled one tiny, plump hand around his pinkie. "Any ideas?" he breathed, too captivated to think just then.

Mick shook her head, just as mesmerized as her husband was. "Not a one. You?"

"How about 'the most beautiful girl in the world'?"

Mick giggled. "I love it, but I don't know if it'll go over too well. Maybe we should have a back up?"

The parents mulled over the decision for a while. Finally, after little debate, they settled on Quincee Mahalia Ramsey.

◆   ◆   ◆

Mel checked her high ponytail and then smoothed one hand across the front of the pale pink cotton blouse she wore with khaki flare legged trousers. Satisfied that everything was in place, she hurried in past the double doors of Jansen's Southern Fried Café.

Making her way through the casual, crowded establishment, Mel found the host and told him who she was there to meet.

"Follow me ma'am," the man instructed with a nod. He took a menu, before leading the way into the dining room.

Mel's breath caught in her throat when she saw Crane stand to greet her. It seemed a lifetime since she'd seen him and Mel thought of all that had happened since then. They shared a tight hug before Mel took her place at the table.

"I don't know where to begin," Mel was saying quickly, as she dropped her bag to the table. "So much has-"

"Love?" Crane called, silencing her with a wave of his hand. "You know what I want to hear?"

Mel nodded, bowing her head as she inhaled deeply. "He knows. Yohan knows everything."

This time it was Crane who bowed his head in thankful prayer. "How'd he take it?" he asked eventually.

Mel smiled. "He-he was blown away. There wasn't much he could say," she shared, not sure if she should tell him he'd already suspected. "Honey why don't you talk to Yohan yourself?" she advised.

"It's the best play I know … I think I should see Josephine first, though. How is she?"

Mel was reluctant to speak on that meeting, but swallowed her unease. "I had to tell Yohan on my own. Josephine couldn't handle it. She ran-hid out at some clinic. She's fine-she's back now."

"She ran?" Crane repeated, clear concerned marred his handsome bronzed face.

"She's fine I promise, but she's not at her best," Mel cautioned with an apologetic smile. "She's had to deal with a lot over the years. Sweetie, do you have any idea who else could've known about Yohan?" she asked when Crane was silent.

He shook his head. "I have no idea. Who ever it is hasn't made any other moves."

Mel sat back in the cushioned armchair. "That tells me two things. Either they're bluffing or they already know I told Yohan."

"But how could that be?" Crane asked, leaning forward.

"Why didn't you tell me about Johnelle?"

"John-how-how do you know?" Crane shuddered, looking as if a wrecking ball had slammed his chest.

"It was one of the things I talked about with Josephine."

"But what does Josephine have to do with Johnelle?"

On cue, Mel felt her phone vibrate and pulled it from the hip holder clipped to her trousers. "Yes?" she greeted.

"Melina? Melina it's Josephine. I'm back."

"How was your trip?" Mel asked, fixing Crane with an unwavering stare.

"I should never have gone. How's Yohan?"

"He's fine. He knows everything. He's devastated, but he's not in a murderous rage. But you need to talk to your son Josephine," she advised, her voice suddenly stern. "You need to *really* talk to him."

"I know, I know," Josephine sighed, clear regret coloring her words. "I waited so long and Melina I'm so very sorry for leaving you in the position of having to handle this. I've been such a coward," she admitted, clearing her throat when a sob began to take root there. "I've just always been so alone in everything. I know it's not an excuse, but this was the one thing I knew I couldn't handle on my own."

Mel smiled, not about to rake the woman over the coals for having feelings of cowardice. She herself had suffered with them for what seemed a millennia. "Maybe you won't have to handle this on your own," she told her mother-in-law before passing the phone to Crane.

Across the dining room of Jansen's, Yohan sat waiting for his lunch partners to arrive for the scheduled business meeting. He saw Crane Cannon and took a moment to evaluate all he'd discovered over the last several weeks. Marcus wasn't his father. The man he'd felt guilty for hating wasn't worthy of his guilt. He wasn't even entitled to call him son.

Yohan was curious about this new man-this Crane Cannon. Who was he really? Why did he stay away especially, when he had to know about Sera's death? Did he love Josephine? Or was she just a quick toss? The thought made him cringe. Thankfully, his cell rang before his tension took hold. It was Moses.

Forgetting about everything else, Yohan focused on his brother who told him Marc fled, the house was real and that he'd found Zara.

"Well how did Pop-"

"Hold it Yo, just hold on. I know you've got questions and you'll get your answers, I promise. Right now, I need to get Z settled. I'm taking her to a hospital in Paris."

Yohan nodded. "Alright," he said, dragging one hand across his face. "What can I do?" he asked.

"I need something."

"Name it."

"Johari's number."

Yohan was silent for a time, figuring the best way to handle the request. "Is that a good idea, Mo? Maybe me or Mel should-"

"*I* need to do this," Moses interrupted, "I've hurt her, badly. I know there's nothing I can do that could *truly* make up for it, but I need her to hear this from *me.*"

"You think it'll make a difference?" Yohan asked.

"No."

"You want her back, though?"

"I never wanted to let her go."

Yohan grinned. Moses Ramsey was the least known for his softer side. In fact, he wasn't known to have a soft side at all. Yet Johari Frazier was the one person who could get him to reveal it using no effort. No one ever asked why it fizzled between them when it seemed they were soul mates. Yohan was happy to see his brother wanting to step past his wall and only prayed Johari would be receptive.

"You got a pen?" Yohan asked, preparing to give Moses the number.

◆   ◆   ◆

After lunch with Crane, Mel dropped by to look in on Michaela and the baby. She found she wasn't the only one who had the idea. Both Tykira and Contessa were already there. Once everyone was done laughing over the story of Quest's behavior when Mick went into labor, the conversation turned toward the expose on Houston.

"I can be ready to start the book in a few weeks."

"Mick," Ty gasped, clearly against it.

Contessa simply rolled her eyes and shook her head over Mick's statement.

"Honey you should really think on this. Marc's still out there and now we've got Stef and God knows who else to contend with," Ty cautioned.

"Not to mention Quest," Mel interjected, drawing Mick's eye. "I mean are you really ready to do this girl? Knowing how he feels about it? Are you comfortable keeping it from him?" she asked.

"I want to bring down Marc along with his brother," Mick answered without hesitation. "I hear the phone lines at Ramsey are tied up with calls about the broadcast on Houston the night before."

"So?" County snapped.

"*So,* a book would undoubtedly settle those questions because until Marc's brought to justice the Ramseys-*all* the Ramseys will look bad. I'm exactly the person to write this book," Mick decided folding her arms across her chest in a defiant manner.

Mel sat closest to Mick on the edge of the bed. "You know, it *is* possible that Moses will bring him in."

"And you don't believe that anymore than I do," Mick challenged.

Mel's slanting ebony stare faltered. "No, I don't, but I still pray he can find Zara."

Ty walked over to comfort her friend when her emotions swelled. Michaela and County comforted Mel with their silence.

A knock sounded on the door and Yohan walked in to a round of hellos. Melina graced him with a smile he found hard to look away from, but managed to do so and grinned toward Mick.

"That Quincee's a dime," he complimented playfully. "I didn't know a woman with no teeth could be so beautiful."

Hearty laughter filled the room for quite some time. Once it silenced, Mick fixed Yohan with a somber gaze. "Have you heard from Moses?" she asked.

Yohan sobered. "I have," he confirmed, smiling uneasily as the ladies listened intently. "County, your lead on the house paid off. The authorities were called in. No doubt it'll be the top news story for weeks."

"Months," County acknowledged, shooting Mick a quick glance.

"Is Marc in jail?" Ty asked.

Yohan's uneasy smile turned into a grimace. "In all the confusion, he got away."

This time, Mick tilted her head towards County and watched her with a challenging glare.

"What about Zara?" Mel asked, standing off the bed and wringing her hands.

Yohan walked over to pull his wife close. "Mo found her. She's safe, alive and healthy. Physically at least. They aren't sure how much of an emotional toll the last twenty years have had on her," he explained.

Melina's lashes fluttered, her dark skin appeared ashen and she looked faint. "Has it been that long?" she breathed, clutching the lapels of his saddle colored suit coat.

Yohan could see she was on the verge of tears and soothed her with hushed words of encouragement. The tears arrived anyway and he hugged her tightly. Again, silence filled the room.

◆   ◆   ◆

Josephine willed her hands to stop shaking when she opened the door to Crane Cannon. Though the years had matured both their features, Josephine could see the man she'd loved in the dark depths of his eyes. They drew close in an instant-apologizing and trying to explain their actions in unison.

"Why don't we go inside?" Crane asked, after they'd dissolved into laughter.

Josephine nodded, fiddling with the gold chains adorning her neck. "We'll be alone," she assured and stepped from the door.

"If it hadn't been for Melina ..." Crane noted his dark gaze intense as it devoured Josephine.

Josephine shook her head. "She's an incredible woman."

"I've always loved her like she was my own."

"Hmph, so have I."

"She told me about Johnelle, but I can't recall ever telling you about her. Did you meet her when Sera died?" Crane asked.

Josephine felt chilled, but she wasn't about to succumb to another moment of cowardice. "At first, my interest in you was about revenge," she confessed and waved him into the spacious living room. "Revenge against Marc. My husband and your wife were having an affair long before I ever met you. I followed him to your home, saw them together many times when you were away."

Crane drew a hand through his dark hair, but didn't appear overly surprised. "I let go of my suspicions once Sera came."

"I believe Sera was the reason Marc stayed away. Oh Crane, why didn't you come back when she died?" Josephine sobbed.

Crane was just as distraught. "I wanted to, but a part of me died with Sera. I raised her like she was my own and I was ashamed for leaving," he raised his hands helplessly. "I wasn't there to protect her when she needed me most. What sort of father did that make me Josie?" he asked his dark eyes red with tears.

"Shh ..." Josephine urged, closing the distance between them. "Don't do this. Don't chastise yourself so harshly. Especially when her real father watched her be raped and murdered and did nothing."

Crane frowned, his confusion evident.

"Marc was her father."

"What?" Crane murmured, seeming to wilt. "He-he knew?"

"Yes."

"And he let his brother-"

"Yes."

Crane folded his hand over his mouth, looking as if he might be sick. When he closed his mouth and began to shudder, Josephine drew him close and began to rock him.

"It's over Crane, it's over and everything's out in the open. I helped see to that."

"What do you mean?"

"I visited Johnelle when Sera died. When Johnelle left the room I happened upon a diary that belonged to Sera. I held onto it until I found someone I was certain wouldn't be swayed by Ramsey money or promises-my nephew's wife Michaela." She nodded, a confident smile brightening her lovely honey toned face. "That bastard Marc will soon be joining his brother in a cell and from there, the gas chamber."

Crane and Josephine hugged, attempting to ward off their grief and pain with closeness. They never saw Marcus-who watched them from the doorway.

◆   ◆   ◆

"Do you realize what Quest will do when he finds out about this?"

"He won't find out."

"Mick-"

"I'll write under a pen name," Mick argued, fixing her friend with a stubborn glare. "Come on County," she urged, having started in heavily on Contessa the moment Ty, Mel and Yohan left the room.

County, however, was clearly not wanting to *come on*. She eyed her friend curiously, crossing her trouser clad legs as she reclined in the bedside armchair. "What's goin' on here Mick? I mean, why are you really so obsessed with this? And don't you dare say because of Sera and her mother and how much their relationship touched your heart," she drawled, placing a hand across her chest. "There's more. Spill it."

Michaela sent County a scathing look, and then rolled her eyes toward the floral arrangement painting on the far wall. "I hate Marc. I hate him so much I sometimes feel the bile in the back of my throat when I hear his name," she admitted, her voice taking on a strange hollow tone. "The son of a bitch almost robbed me of a relationship with Quest.

I overheard him with Quest that day at the cabin … telling him to forget the Ramseys if he chose to be with me. I wanted to give up on us because it was so important to me that he not lose touch with his family. If Quest hadn't fought for us, Quincee would've never been."

"Oh Mick," County breathed, moving off the chair to hug her friend. "Sweetie, don't you see? Marc didn't win. You and Quest are happy. You've got a real live baby doll to raise. Your life is wonderful. Let someone else worry about bringing down that jackass. You've done enough."

Mick said nothing more and she didn't have to. County knew she was wasting her time trying to change her mind and muttered a vicious curse. "This better be a damn good pen name," she grumbled, snatching her cell phone off the window sill. "Spivey?" she said once the connection was made. "It's County-yes yes I'll be back soon. Look, I've got news. The Ramsey book? We have our author."

◆   ◆   ◆

Arm in arm, Melina and Yohan strolled the distance from the maternity ward to the elevator bay. While waiting for the car to arrive, Mel leaned against the wall. Head bowed, she appeared as though all the fight had left her. She dragged herself into the elevator when it arrived and slumped against the mahogany paneling.

Yohan stepped over, one hand pushed into his trouser pocket. "You okay?" he asked her.

Mel could only shake her head at first. "Zara, Sera … how many others were there, Yohan?"

"Don't do this," he urged, pulling her close to hide his handsome face in the fragrant cloud of her hair. His concern mounted when she just lay lifeless in his arms. Pulling away, he gave her a small shake. "Don't let Marc defeat you too."

The words sparked life in Mel and she nodded. She stood on her toes, intending to thank him with a quick peck to his jaw. Yohan had other ideas and dipped his head to capture her mouth in a more thorough kiss.

A tiny whimper escaped her throat and Mel could feel herself falling deep into the spell of the kiss. She felt his powerful hands caressing and kneading her back through the material of the pink grapefruit tube jumpsuit she sported. When his thumbs grazed her nipples she forced herself to pull away. The elevator doors slide open before Yohan could reach for her.

"Meet me at the house," he said, guiding her to the parking deck elevators.

"I um really need to get a move on. The gallery show is tonight, remember?"

"You can spare me a few minutes, can't you?"

"Han, I really-"

"Please Mel," he said, stopping to turn her toward him.

Mel closed her eyes. "Yohan … I just can't-I'm not up for any more emotional moments now."

Yohan's dark eyes narrowed with playful intensity. "Please, Meli," he whispered, moving closer to kiss the pulse point below her ear. "Please," his voice was a soft rumbling.

Mel arched into the brush of his mouth across her earlobe. "Only for a few minutes," she agreed, her lashes fluttering madly amidst the soothing pressure of his lips.

"I'll see you there," he said, smiling down and watching as she made her way to the elevator that would carry her to the level she'd parked on.

CHAPTER SIXTEEN

Melina hesitated, not wanting to leave her car when she arrived home. Home? She'd so wanted it to be home again. But her relationship-her marriage to Yohan was a tie best ended. She swallowed and left the Acura she'd parked haphazardly next to Yohan's Expedition. Using her key, she entered and found the house almost totally dark.

"Han? Yohan? It's Mel."

Clearing her throat to ward off the onset of a bout of nervousness, Mel ventured deeper into the house. She found Yohan waiting for her in the den just off from the foyer. Awkwardly slow, she stepped into the room and waited. After a few seconds, Yohan pushed himself from his perch on the arm of the sofa and stood. Mel frowned when he took her by the hand and led her from the den.

"Han?" Mel queried, as the ascended the hardwood staircase. She wasn't very surprised when no response met her greeting.

Yohan led her past the hall of guest bedrooms and Mel began to resist his hold; realizing they were heading towards the master bedroom suite.

"No-Yohan no. Please, I-" she quieted when his steps halted.

At the room door, Yohan let go of Mel's hand. "You can either walk in or I'll carry you in," he promised.

"Why are you doing this?" she asked, her hands extended. He stepped toward her and she waved her hands. "Okay," she whispered and preceded him into the room she'd not set foot in eight years.

Chills slammed her body when she crossed the threshold. Silently, she praised the fact that he'd redecorated. Clearly, this was a man's room now-from the burgundy, blue and navy color scheme to the bulky, hand-crafted pine furniture. Although ruggedly beautiful, Melina didn't know whether the changes set her more or less on edge.

The door closed and she whirled around to face him. She twisted her hands nervously.

"Yohan-"

"Do you really think I'd stand by and do nothing while you leave me again?"

"Yohan ... I didn't, didn't we settle this?"

"Hell no we didn't," Yohan breathed, his features drawn tight with frustration. "How could you think I'm only reminded of everything bad when I look at you?"

Mel shook her head. "Everything that's happened-everything I told you-"

"I'm still waiting to hear how that brought you to this stupid conclusion."

"Dammit Yohan!" Melina hissed, losing her temper at something she felt he should've easily understood. "I stood down there in that gym and went through this with you. You sat right there and didn't say a thing to dispute me-or weren't you listening?"

"I was listening," Yohan admitted with a grimace. "I should've told you. You were talking like a fool then, but other things were on my mind," he said, walking towards her as he spoke.

Mel was completely clueless, even when he'd closed the space separating them and brought his hands to the buttons at the front of the halter blouse.

"Do you love me?"

Her chills resurfaced again, this time in response to the raspy intensity of his deep voice when he spoke the question. "Yes I do. You know I do," she told him, Yohan's ebony gaze was focused on undoing her shirt. "Then wherever you go, I'll be there. I'll be right there Meli," he promised, bringing his gaze to her face. "You won't get rid of me. Have me arrested for stalking and I won't care. I've existed in a prison for the last eight years. I can't *exist* anymore. I want to live."

"Han-"

"I need you," he said, while pulling her into his massive, unyielding frame.

A moan escaped her lips when she felt the true potency of his words pressing against her abdomen. Her head fell to his chest.

"I don't want to leave," she sobbed.

"Then stay ... stay," he urged softly, sliding his mouth from her temple to the satiny curve of her jaw. He continued to pronounce the word, keeping her attention dually focused on the allure of his words and the pleasure stirring as he finished unbuttoning her blouse.

Mel raised her head, her slanting dark gaze fixed on her husband's incredible face. His fantastic features were blurred as tears continued to pool her eyes. For the first time, they weren't tears of sadness, fear or doubt they were tears of happiness. They were tears that spoke volumes; saying the future had arrived and it was good-she had Yohan by her side.

His thumbs were brushing her nipples, turning them firm with desire. The sounds of labored breathing and intermitted cries of satisfaction filled their bedroom. Mel raked her nails across the rippling chords in his muscular forearms, before the need to feel more intervened.

As Yohan had done to her earlier, she now unbuttoned his shirt-aching to see and feel the sleek dark expanse of his chest. She pulled her lower lip between her teeth when he was bared to her sight. The tell-tale tingling within her womanhood grew more insistent-the image of him aroused her so. Knowing that he loved her-wanted her always, fueled her arousal to a fiery pitch.

Yohan tossed away her shirt long ago. Now, he was working on the fastening of her pants. When they were undone, he tugged them just a bit past her hips and insinuated his hand inside the lacy white panties. Mel threw back her head and moaned again, arching herself just a bit-desperate to feel every inch of his middle finger as it delved and rotated inside her. Her fingers grew weak against his chest as a wave of moisture signaled her delight. Yohan captured her earlobe between his perfect teeth and bit down softly, smiling when she uttered a playful shriek.

Melina was thrusting against the lunges of his middle and index fingers. She was desperate to feel every ounce of sensation available to her. Eventually she pulled her trousers further past her hips allowing him more room to explore. Yohan disappointed her then, removing his fingers from their erotic locale. Her bra fell to the carpet, meeting the pool made by her trousers, panties and sandals. Easily, he lifted Melina from the pool of clothing, trailing kisses along her neck and collarbone, across her chest and the undersides of her breasts.

Mel curved her nails in to the sinewy expanse of ebony skin stretched across his shoulders. She felt herself being carried and gasped when crisp linens touched her back. Her eyes opened and, for a time, she gazed in awe at the bed.

"You didn't change it," she noted, upon realizing it was the bed they'd bought the day they moved into their home.

Yohan's darkly gorgeous face was buried in the fragrant crook of his wife's neck. "Keeping it was the only way I could sleep in here."

His muffled reply rang clear in her ears. Her heart soared and she literally moaned at the pleasure his words provided. "I love you," she gasped.

Yohan cupped her thighs in his powerful grip and settled himself between their satiny length. He plunged down, his cry mingling with hers; as the true depth of their lovemaking, encompassed them. "I love you," he returned, repeating the phrase each time he thrust forward.

Melina draped her shapely legs across his hips, holding tightly to the pillows as she met his thrusts eagerly. At last, she smoothed her palms across his buttocks and forced him deeper inside her.

They climaxed in unison, trying to absorb one another. They were overwrought with desire and love as it swirled in a mixture of reciprocated emotion.

Much later, Mel had returned to the guest bedroom. She saw that a beautiful white pantsuit had been taken from the closet and she smiled envisioning the alluring contrast the suit would cast against her dark skin. The fitted jacket with its white, snap-front closure allowed for no blouse or other undergarment to be worn with it. The coordinating flare legged pants molded to her hips and bottom adoringly.

While she wouldn't have chosen quite so provocative attire for the gallery opening, she'd be delighted to wear it. Clearly, her husband had made the selection.

Yohan walked into the room as Mel was choosing a pair of white slide-ins that would add several inches to her height. The moment she set the heels to the floor, she was pulled back against him.

"Can't wait to see you in this," he muttered against the nape of her neck.

Mel nestled herself deep within his embrace. "Don't you think it's a bit much or … less?" she rephrased, eyeing the daring cut of the suit coat.

"Mmm mmm," Yohan disagreed, undoing the tie around her robe. "I want easy access tonight."

"It's a gallery opening. We can't get too crazy," she warned playfully.

"Speak for yourself."

"Oh no," she resisted, when he cupped her breasts, "we need to get ready," she said and turned to slide her arms about his shoulders. "And *you* should call Josephine," she suggested, feeling him tense against her.

Yohan offered no arguments however. His wife was right. A conversation with his mother was long overdue.

Mel stood on her toes and kissed his cheek. "I'm going to the shower. Call your mama," she ordered.

Yohan watched her head into the adjoining bathroom. He closed his eyes, taking time to say a prayer-thanking God for the unexpected yet overwhelming reunion with his wife. He promised to treasure their second chance with every ounce of strength he possessed.

A moment later, Yohan took a seat on the edge of the bed. Absently, he studied Melina's jewelry on the nightstand before his dark eyes strayed to the phone. Bracing himself, he took the receiver and dialed his mother's private line.

"Josephine Ramsey," she greeted after a second ring.

Yohan cleared his throat. "Hey Ma."

"Baby," was the only word Josephine could manage.

The word made him smile and melted some of the edginess that chilled him. "I know everything and I have questions."

"Yes," she breathed. "Yes, I know. Can you … come over?"

"I have this gallery opening with Mel-"

"So I'll see you there?" Josephine suggested in an eager tone.

Yohan nodded. "Sounds good."

"Yohan I-" she hesitated momentarily. "I love you."

"I love you too," he said, smiling when he heard her relieved sigh.

Josephine held the phone to her chest when the call ended. Then, she turned to Crane who stood across the living room.

"Would you like to meet your son?" she asked.

◆   ◆   ◆

London, England

"This is Johari Frazier."

"Hey Twig."

Jo knew the thin cell phone she held was just moments away from sliding out of her grasp. She tightened her grip and decided to focus on standing since her legs felt just as weak.

"Moses?" she whispered, her voice barely audible in the vastness of her parent's sitting room. The silence on the other end of the line, gave her time to assess the fact that she was speaking to a man she hadn't talked to in over a decade-a man she thought she'd never speak to again.

"What do you want?" she asked, forcing her voice to reveal itself and grateful for the firm quality in her tone.

"We need to talk," Moses responded, his strong, sure baritone voice sounding firm as well.

Jo's exceptionally long lashes fluttered and she settled a hand to her swirling tummy. "I'm in London," she told him.

"I know. I'm standing right outside your door."

Whirling around, Jo stared in the direction of the foyer. She half expected to find him walking right across the threshold. Finally, on determined steps, she moved towards the front door. Only a second or two passed before she was pulling it open. This time, the cell phone she carried *did* slip from her hand. It shattered upon contact with the polished checkered floor.

Moses pushed himself from the doorjamb. He absorbed the missed sight of her and clenched his fist in order to prevent himself from reaching for her.

Johari was just as affected. Still, she recovered far more quickly than he when she stepped close and greeted him with a vicious slap.

◆   ◆   ◆

The gallery show was a virtual success. Mel refused to accept any accolades or compliments regarding the event. She instructed the guests to lavish their comments upon her staff; who had really done the bulk of the work while her personal life had demanded the lion share of her time.

Representing the Ramseys were Quay and Ty, Fernando and County along with Yohan who'd escorted Melina. Within moments of their arrival, the gallery was alive with happy conversation concerning the safe delivery of the first Ramsey grandchild. It was a welcomed, refreshing change from the incessant ramblings regarding Houston Ramsey's scandalous tell-all interview.

"Han?" Mel called, nodding when he looked in her direction.

Yohan turned to find Josephine approaching from the entryway.

"This is a wonderful event Melina," Josephine complimented her daughter-in-law before looking at Yohan. "Hello Honey," she whispered, uncertainty filling her voice and eyes.

Yohan offered no words and simply pulled his mother close. Josephine's laughter mixed with her tears and she savored the crushing embrace.

Arm in arm, Yohan and Josephine let Mel lead the way into her office where they could talk privately.

"Oh, Yohan thank you. Thank you so much for not hating me. I-I never set out to hurt you or betray Marc in our marriage. You must understand that."

Yohan cupped his mother's lovely face, urging her to silence. "You're sadly mistaken if you think I give one damn about Marc-let alone his feelings after everything he's done."

Josephine smoothed her hand across his where it lay against her cheek. "I should've gone to the police so long ago when I first suspected him of something illegal," she shook her head, closing her eyes as she lamented. "I was so afraid-afraid of what he'd do. I was so afraid I'd lose you and Fernando," she said, looking up at him with red eyes.

"And Moses too?" Yohan corrected in a pointed manner.

Josephine blinked. "Of-of course," she stammered, an uneasy laugh rising. "I-I wanted to hurt Marc as he'd hurt me," she confessed, sobering a bit as her expression tightened. "But I never wanted you to know. I never wanted you to think you'd been born out of hate and revenge."

Yohan stepped closer, pulling her hands into his. "Did you love Crane Cannon? Did he love you?"

"He was the calm in the midst of a storm for me; and yes-when our relationship became intimate, yes I loved him," she massaged the side of her neck and smiled. "I can't speak to *his* feelings, but I believe he felt the same."

"And you never told Pop? Marc?"

Josephine's hazel stare darkened with fury. "*That* was for revenge," she confessed. "It overjoyed me-seeing him make a fool of himself over you. It was so easy to fool him. Marc loved you so," she mused, her eyes filled with love then as her eyes caressed Yohan's flawless skin and fiercely magnificent features. "You were so strong and dark. Of course, you took that after *my* father's side of the family. Then later ... when it became clear how smart you were-*overly* smart-oh boy ... it made you shine in his eyes." The pride in her own eyes dimmed slightly. "He made such a fool of me all those years ... I wanted to do the same to him. Oh Love, can you ever forgive me?"

Yohan pressed a hard kiss to her cheek. "I love you-nothing can change that."

Josephine began to cry again. Tears of relief and love soaked the lapel of Yohan's tux as they hugged. After a while, the tears began to subside and she stepped back a bit. "There's someone you should meet," she said, drying her cheeks.

Yohan watched his mother go to the office door and pull it open. Crane Cannon stood in the hall. Obvious uncertainly clouded his face as he stepped part the doorway. Yohan appeared just as uncertain as he too moved forward. For a time, they stood close as though observing one another. Then, they shook hands.

Josephine remained behind once Yohan and Crane left the office together. They were talking-just a general conversation, but the words flowed easy between them. For that, she was more than grateful and couldn't help but wonder how it may've been to raise Yohan with Crane. It might've made all the difference in so many things ...

A thud rose behind her, but Josephine took no heed as she turned in the direction of the sound.

"What do you want?" she asked her voice hushed and monotone.

Marc's gaze was focused and probing as he studied his wife. "You don't seem surprised to see me here."

"Should I be?" Josephine challenged, crossing her arms over her chest. "You're always lurking, but, then again, such is to be expected from a devious son of a bitch like yourself."

"Devious?!" Marc spat, his features further darkened in the wake of his fury. "You dare call *me* devious when you've tricked me all these years."

"Tricked is a damn sight better than deceived, humiliated, dirtied. *That's* how *I've* felt since the day I married your sick ass!" Josephine lashed out, her eyes blazing with living hate. "I have despised and wanted to vomit you out of my system-out of my life for years-decades. But I bided my time," she shared, her voice softening then. "Oh yes, Marcus I bided my time and let all the bastard children, the affairs, all the nasty little things I had to witness and endure through the course of our nightmare of marriage just pass me by. I had to act like they didn't faze me. I had to wait until my time came and now it's finally here." A wave of triumph surged through her at the surprise she saw in Marc's eyes. Never had she spoken of her true feelings with such passion-such power. "I have no remorse about anything I've done to you," she added with a cunning smirk.

Overwrought with a completely foreign feeling of helplessness, Marcus expelled a furious roar and charged for his wife. Josephine had no time to scream as his hands closed around her neck. His hold tightened and he simultaneously shook her.

"No remorse-eh? I'll give you things to be remorseful about Josephine. I'll give you things you've never dreamed about," he threatened softly, his dark eyes sparkling with vicious intent.

Josephine clutched and scratched at his hands, hoping to loosen their grip. Her actions had no affect, until she found a way to put them to better use. Marc let out a hiss, closing his eyes when her nails clawed both sides of his face. He released her and backed away as Josephine raced to grab her purse off the desk. Reaching inside, she withdrew the gun and fired.

"Lunch, dinner, I'm pretty flexible and it helps to be the boss," Crane said, laughing a bit.

Yohan nodded, a smile softening his features as well. "I hear ya. Let's try dinner, a week from tonight sound good?"

Crane shrugged and extended his hands. "Sounds good."

A second later, the gunshot reached their ears. Crane and Yohan stood rooted to their spot outside the office for only a moment before they dashed inside. They found Josephine standing over Marc. She was rigid-not even breathing. She held the gun on Marcus, her finger caressing the trigger-preparing to pull it again.

Yohan reacted instantly when he saw his mother aim the gun at Marc's head. He caught her wrist and the shot went into the air. The sound seemed to bring Josephine out of her trance. At once, she began to tremble.

"Shh ..." Yohan soothed, handing the gun to Crane while he hugged his mother. "Shh ... it's alright, it's alright," he promised while she cried.

Melina was next to burst into the office. "Someone thought they heard-!" she stopped when the full scene was in focus. Her hands covered her mouth in horror, but her eyes were filled with wonder. Trancelike, she moved toward the credenza and reached for the phone. Her intention was to dial 911-though no one suggested she do so. In fact, her fingers paused over the keypad as she even debated on making the call. With a quick shake of her head, she pressed the digits.

◆   ◆   ◆

The bullet round to Marcus's side would heal. The shot went right through and there had been no organ damage. The man would make a full recovery. The news was bittersweet for the Ramseys; who couldn't decide if the diagnosis was to be celebrated or mourned. They took some solace in the fact that Houston's confession had been taken seriously. Upon his release from the hospital, armed guards would be present to carry Marcus Ramsey away in handcuffs.

❖   ❖   ❖

Yohan found Melina in a deserted waiting area just down from the small snack room in the hall where Marc's room was located. He sat next to her, smiling when she grabbed his hand and held it close to her chest.

"I wanted him to die, Han. I almost didn't dial 911," she confessed.

"Well, no one told you to," Yohan teased, trying to sober when she sent him a withering look. "Congratulations Melina Wei Dan. You're human."

"Mel's lashes brushed her cheeks when her eyes closed. Clearly she wasn't consoled by the summation. "I've always disliked the man-hated him even. But I never wanted him dead," her expression hardened and she drew both hands through her coarse shoulder length hair. "I feel completely different now. I feel like we'd all be so much better off if he were ..."

"Hey?" Yohan called, nudging her knee with his. "I feel the same way. Hell, so does everyone else in the family. But baby after this hospital, his next stop is jail."

Mel shook her head. "I don't believe it."

"Believe it."

"How?" she challenged, turning to face her husband. "How? When he's got all the advantages-including someone willing to kill for him," She bristled as the thought settled. "They still haven't found Stefan," she noted, spotting the muscle clench in his jaw.

"Look at me," he said when he'd taken her chin and waited several seconds for her eyes to meet his. "I'm right here and I'm not going anywhere. You're safe and you don't need to be worrying about that fool."

Mel pulled his hand from her chin, but kept hold of it. "I don't want our lives to be about you protecting me," she said.

"Believe me Mel, protecting you isn't the utmost thing on my mind," he countered, the glint in his dark eyes leaving no doubt about what he was referring to.

Mel couldn't help but smile.

"Protecting is part of loving," he went on to say. "I love you and I swear that I never stopped."

Leaning closer, Mel stroked the side of his cheek. The caress of her eyes across his face was as soft as her touch. Eventually, her kiss replaced the brush of her hand. Yohan tilted his head, capturing her mouth in a throaty kiss.

Mel gasped his name, kissing him back with the same feverish intensity. At that moment, she wished they were anywhere but a hospital waiting room. A tiny whimper slipped past her lips when she felt something cold against her finger. Looking down, she saw that Yohan had slipped on her wedding ring.

"I saw it on the nightstand when I called Ma from the guestroom," he explained, once he leaned back to judge her expression. "I didn't think you still had it," he admitted, glancing at the ring again.

"I never stopped thinking of myself as your wife," she swore, nuzzling her nose along the strong column of his neck. "I love you, Yohan," she vowed, smiling when he pressed his mouth to her palm and held it there as if he were praying.

"Say you'll marry me again," he commanded in a gentle voice.

Melina's laughter tumbled forth. "I'll marry you Yohan Ramsey. I'll marry you."

"And the next time you have something even remotely important to tell me?"

"I'll tell you right away. Even if I have to tie you down to get you to listen."

Yohan nodded, his black eyes narrowing as though he liked the sound of her words. "You know, you can tie me down even if you *don't* have anything remotely important to tell me," he suggested slyly, one hand venturing beneath the daring suit coat she wore.

Melina's laughter was full and honest. It floated down the silent corridor, until it was quieted by Yohan's kiss-a kiss she surrendered to body and soul. They held onto each other, savoring the love they had recaptured amidst a sea of unrest.

Dear Readers,

The Ramsey series has seen many twists and turns. Still, there is much more to be revealed in this scandalous family. I truly hope you've enjoyed Book IV "A Lover's Regret." Yohan and Melina's story has set the stage for even more explosive revelations and shocking outcomes.

Next up, is Moses Ramsey's story "A Lover's Worth."

As always, please let me know your opinions of the work.

Email me: altonyawashington@yahoo.com

Visit my website: www.lovealtonya.com

For inside scoops on the Ramseys, join my Yahoo web group LoveAl-Tonya.

Be Blessed

Love,

AlTonya

978-0-595-48656-4
0-595-48656-8

CPSIA information can be obtained
at www.ICGtesting.com
Printed in the USA
LVHW111618300720
661977LV00003B/518